PRAISE FOR ELDERSONG

How appropriate that the Shaker song "'Tis a Gift to Be Simple" and Kate Wolf's "Give Yourself to Love" waft through the pages of Rain Zohav's novel , *ElderSong*. The rich quest for simplicity and love lasts a lifetime for anyone up for the trip. Enjoy Brooke Kumara's remarkable journey as you travel your own.

— Marietta McCarty, NYT bestselling author, *Little Big Minds: Sharing Philosophy with Kids*, and *Leaving 1203: Emptying a Home- Filling the Heart*

ElderSong is a sweeping portrait of a woman facing the realities of this strange experience of life: at times frightening, at times marvelous, and at times mundane. Written in memoir-like style…the (story is) set in a wide range of geographic locations…The author has woven together… philosophical reflections, generational continuity, political action, and a genuine love of life. Despite the difficulties experienced, the story doesn't fall victim to cynicism. Rather, it looks at life directly with honesty toward both hard times as well as the good. It is a refreshing look at life from the perspective of a progressive, modern woman…(and) filled with insight regarding relationships with male partners. This is a book that will appeal to all persons interested in contemporary values of the social justice movement era."

— J.L.Dildine, author, *The Cry of Cicadas*

ElderSong

ISBN Paperback: 978-1-877850-04-2
ISBN E-book: 978-1-877850-06-6
Cover and interior design by Nuno Moreira, NM DESIGN

Activism
Communal living
Growing older
Parenting
Relationships
Publisher: Life in the Liberated Zone

ELDERSONG

RAIN ZOHAV

Dedicated to the memory of Tamar Raine.

I'm sorry that you did not live to see the completion of this book.

TABLE OF CONTENTS

PROLOGUE:

AUTUMN
REMEMBERS SPRING

"To every thing there is a season, and a time to every purpose under the heaven"
—Ecclesiastes 3:1

"Why is it that coming-of-age stories are a dime a dozen, but I can't think of even one story about becoming an elder?" Brooke grumbled to her best friend Rachel.

They were sitting in Brook's sunny kitchen at the foot of the Blue Ridge Mountains of Asheville, North Carolina.

"Maybe you should write one," said Rachel.

"Hmm. Maybe I will. Now that I'm retired, I have the time."

"I would read it," Rachel said emphatically. "I'm one of your biggest fans."

Brooke smiled. "Thanks. I'm sure you would. We have been friends for thirty years. I'm one of your biggest fans also.

"And I have had quite an interesting life that I could draw on for inspiration. I think I've learned a few things along the way that I could pass on to the younger generation. Things about communal living, relationships, parenting, and nonviolent activism," mused Brooke, wrinkling up her forehead thoughtfully.

"I think it's a great idea," said Rachel, getting up and looking out the window with a restless kind of energy. She was a small wiry woman, not known for sitting still for very long. She noticed the sun was lower in the sky.

"Well, thanks for the iced tea and conversation. I have to put in some new plants in the garden, now that it's not so hot outside. Let me know about your new writing project," she said, smiling.

"Okay. See you soon, Rachel."

As soon as Rachel left, the phone rang.

"Hi, Marissa. What's up?"

"Oh, Mama, I just wanted you to know I met a new guy. He's so cute! I really like him."

"Yeah? Where did you meet him? School?"

"No," Marissa said, laughing. "He's a waiter at my favorite restaurant."

"Not again! How well did that work out last time? What's with you and waiters?"

More laughter. "He's just so charming I can't resist. Just wanted to let you know so you wouldn't freak out if you saw us together."

Brooke sighed. *I wish she would make better choices around men. Her last boyfriend punched a hole in her dorm room wall.*

"Okay. Thanks for letting me know," Brooke responded, trying to sound neutral, but failing.

Later that evening Brooke relayed this conversation to John, her significant other. "I hate being so judgmental. It can't be useful. If I think about what I was doing at her age, it wasn't so different."

Later that night it all came back to her. After graduating high school in June 1970, an aunt had given her enough money for a month in Europe. She started in Paris. Her last day, she visited the Louvre, and then was "museumed out." Walking along the streets of Paris was entertaining, but a bit lonely.

Steel-colored clouds began to gather and a summer storm quickly blew wind and rain upon her. She ducked into a little café. With its bright blue-and-white-striped awning and display of pastries in the window, it was a welcome respite.

She ordered a café au lait and a croissant. The coffee and roll arrived with a flourish from the young waiter, along with a pat of fresh butter and a little bowl of strawberry jam.

As she savored the pastry and coffee she couldn't keep her eyes off the waiter. He seemed to truly enjoy his work, smiling and chatting with each customer. She especially liked the attention he gave to the children, throwing them up into the air to their mutual delight and laughter.

When he directed this care and attention right at her, she quickly looked down, blushing. But again, she looked up and met his eyes and this time she didn't hide, she stayed. And smiled. He smiled back and winked. Blushing again, she looked down at her plate and fiddled with her spoon, wondering if this would lead to anything.

He had dark curly hair and sun-browned skin that mirrored her own Mediterranean looks. *I wish I knew some French,* she thought as she lifted her backpack onto her shoulders.

While she stood, thinking about where she could go next, she was startled to find herself being kissed on the mouth while the waiter declared, "You are so beautiful. Wait for me. Soon I finish. You come with me?" Blushing even more and thinking to herself, *I guess American tourists have a reputation for being easy to pick up,* she nonetheless sat back down and waited.

After all, what's the point of having a European adventure if you can't let a cute young man pick you up, she thought as she waited.

After a few minutes, the waiter took off his apron, smiled right at her, and led her out of the little café. As they walked down the narrow sidewalk, he took her hand. *I wonder where he will take me. Am I making a huge mistake? He seems nice enough. And I'm on birth control. And no one, except my father, has ever called me beautiful before this.*

Soon, they entered a dingy-looking grayish-brown brick apartment building. The sour-faced woman at the desk glowered at them. She looked like she had just sucked on a lemon. Brooke ignored her. The handsome young waiter led her up a flight of stairs and into a small apartment. *This must be where he lives.*

She walked in and saw a single bed neatly made with a thin plaid blanket against the wall. A small table and plain wooden chair sat in the middle of the room, a woven placemat in the center, with a small vase of daisies in the center. In one corner stood a four-drawer dresser and next to it a bookcase. *Nothing to be afraid of,* Brooke reassured herself.

He kissed her again and gestured to the bed. Heart pounding, she followed. Brooke knew no French and he spoke very little English, but they managed to exchange names, laughing and looking into each other's eyes.

What was his name? Brooke thought now. *Ah, well, that is one of the disadvantages of getting old. One forgets the names of past lovers.*

Whatever his name, he was a gentle and skilled lover, caressing Brooke and taking things slowly. *I'm so glad I live in this time where women are allowed to have sexual desires and access to birth control,* she thought as she dozed off, leaning on his chest.

Around dusk, her Frenchman let her know she had to leave. He was not allowed to have women overnight in his apartment. He escorted her out of the building, past the scowling concierge, and back to the bus stop that would take her to her bed-and-breakfast. Smiling to herself, she nodded to her landlady, walked back outside to the café around the corner, and ordered a simple omelet and salad for supper.

The next day would take her to Italy and then Greece. What a lovely trip that was. She enjoyed watching the beautiful countryside from the window of the train to Italy. She recognized the look of brown hills terraced with grape arbors and olive trees from pictures her Italian grandmother had shown her of the Old Country. The stone buildings in small villages along the way, with only a few older people about, brought her back to stories of Grandma Christina's childhood before she came to America.

She was advised to be sure to visit Florence, and it did not disappoint. It was filled with nooks and crannies where fountains and stone statues lay in wait for her wandering steps. The Old World's love of beauty was such a contrast to the large plastic statue of John Bunyan that towered over a freeway exit near her home in Los Angeles.

But also the sweet memories of other men in other countries who found her beautiful. It's too bad that she had to leave the U.S. to discover that. Growing up in a beach town outside of L.A., where long straight blond hair, big breasts, thin hips, and long slender legs were the standard for beauty, was hard for Brooke. As a petite young woman with small breasts, wide hips, and an ample backside, she did not fit in. She often felt invisible there. Before this trip, she'd never been asked out on a date, gone to parties in high school, or even been kissed. Her few female friends also led this kind of unappreciated life. Her decision to start birth control was grounded in a hope that things would change when she was in a different part of the world.

Of course, I was so clueless in high school that I probably didn't notice if any boy did like me. When I went back and looked at my high school yearbooks and read the comments, I realized that probably that boy in my history class who did my homework for three weeks when I had modern dance rehearsals might not have just been "a nice boy." He might *have liked me.*

Coming out of her reverie, Brooke thought, *I really must apologize to Marissa. Might as well do it while I'm thinking about it. Hmm. There's a piece of elder wisdom right there. Do a thing when you think about it.*

So she promptly picked up her phone and called.

"Hi, Mama," answered Marissa.

"Hi. I'm just calling to apologize for being so judgy about your new boyfriend. I remembered myself at your age." Brooke proceeded to tell Marissa about her Parisian waiter.

"Wait! You mean you went home with him right then? I can't believe it. That was so stupid. And you are telling *me* what to do?"

"Yeah. That's why I called to apologize. I don't have a leg to stand on," admitted Brooke, laughing.

Marissa laughed too. "Well, next time think twice before you judge me."

There—it's good to be honest with our children and also good when they can scold us, thought Brooke. *I will make a note of that to put in my book.*

Drifting off to sleep later that night Brooke thought, *Of course, there's no need to tell Marissa everything.* She didn't need to know about the other men on that European adventure. Not the older man who had deliberately bumped into her on the street, and then seduced her in a remote area of a city park, nor the one who took her dancing and then home for a few days. It was a different time then. "A window of opportunity after birth control and the sexual revolution, and before AIDS," as her friend Becky once put it.

Yes, a different time, she thought as Joni Mitchell's song "California" drifted through her mind as she fell asleep.

SPRING: BUDDING, BLOOMING

"Spring will come and so will happiness. Hold On. Life will get warmer."
—Anita Krizan

MARCH

"If you knew me before my 20s, you never actually knew me. You knew season 1 me. We were severely underfunded and the writing team was going through a lot."
—Audre Porne

CHAPTER ONE

The next morning Brooke sat down to start her book in earnest. She pulled her wheelchair up to the sturdy pine kitchen table that had seen so many homework pages, science fair projects, and protest posters over the years. A perfect place to get started!

The sun was streaming through the bay windows, dancing along the glass containers of mint, basil, and other herbs, lighting up the already cheerful yellow kitchen. The spider plant hanging from the handmade macramé holder was doing well. Brooke looked around and thought, *I love this space.*

She looked at the walls and appreciated the shades of yellow she had chosen and hand blended: lemon yellow paint for the small wall by the window over the sink and butter yellow for the neighboring wall. And despite what Marissa thought at the time, she never tired of the orange trim. *I'm so lucky to have a room this bright to maneuver in my wheelchair.*

She pulled out her laptop and hummed the tune to Kate Wolf's song, "The Trumpet Vine."

With her laptop opened, she wondered where to begin. She had gathered some mementoes to jog her memory, old letters, political fliers, photos.

I'll draw on my own life, but tweak a few details to protect the guilty. A little bit of background for the main character's family would be helpful. Let's see— she'll be kind of like me with one Catholic parent and one Jewish one, which will explain her Mediterranean looks and how she ended up as a Unitarian.

I think I'll tell the story of how my family navigated my two grandmothers at Christmas. She began to type.

My maternal grandmother was the Catholic grandmother, who would have been devastated if we didn't have a Christmas tree. In fact, she believed that my father had converted to Catholicism in order to marry my mother. He didn't, but he did take a class and go through the motions of a conversion, none of which he actually believed.

We had a tiny plastic Christmas tree, decorated with red and gold balls and placed right by the bay window in our small house. But we always had to keep a lookout in case my Jewish grandmother, who didn't know my father converted to marry my mother, was sighted walking up to the house.

When it did happen that Grandma Frida, dressed in her floral house dress, approached the front door, my friends and I would quickly grab the Christmas tree and hide it in the basement. It would stay there until Grandma Christina, dressed in all black, wearing sensible shoes, was about to arrive. At which point we'd run down to the basement and put it back at the bay window like it had been there all along.

Brooke laughed out loud to herself remembering this silly charade. But, in retrospect, maybe not so silly—it kept the peace, didn't harm anyone, and showed a certain respect for both elders. Another wisdom worth noting in her book, *In-laws can have a voice but not a veto in the marriage.*

After both grandmas died, my parents decided they would join the Unitarian Universalists.

My mother told us that once she took human biology in high school and learned the true "facts of life," she couldn't accept the story of the virgin birth. And once she started questioning that, she started questioning everything. She still believed that Jesus had good teachings and that there is a creative force in the universe, but she became a very lapsed Catholic.

My father grew up in a typical Jewish socialist household. His parents had even voted for Eugene Debs, the five-time Socialist Party of America candidate for the U.S. presidency. My dad valued the Workmen's Circle summer camp, the communal picnics and sing-alongs he had attended as a boy, and he wanted us to have similar fellowship.

My mother also wanted us to have an experience of a liberal values-based community, a place that would respect both my parents' traditions and cultures. That's how my family joined a Unitarian congregation. I felt at home in the Sunday school and community services. I liked the values of egalitarianism and respect that mirrored the values of my family, and were so missing in my public schools. There, authoritarianism was the rule. And most of my classmates were Republicans.

I also loved that we celebrated so many different traditions, especially the pagan ones, such a summer solstice and May Day. For May Day we would have a Maypole, with each student holding a different colored ribbon. And then, in a choreographed dance, we would go over and under each other, weaving an intricate multicolored pattern around the pole.

It was my egalitarian values and desire to live communally that sent me to New Zealand for what I thought would be a gap year. I found out about an intentional community founded by conscientious objectors to World War II. They grew their own food and raised lots of sheep. When I learned that New Zealand had more sheep than people, I thought, *This is the perfect place for me!*

* * *

The plane hadn't even made it out of the smog-filled sky of Los Angeles before I could already feel a sense of freedom and lightness. I was leaving adolescence, the trauma of high school, and a sense of futility behind. Although several of my friends had talked about living communally, no one was making any moves to actually do so. I couldn't motivate them to move out of their parents' houses. It was incredibly frustrating.

I was flying toward a life based on my own goals and values for the first time. I would get a chance to experience things I had only read about. The man sitting next to me offered to buy me a glass of wine, which I gratefully accepted. He must have known this was a celebratory occasion!

Flying into New Zealand on September 1, 1970, was a sight and a date I will never forget. A phrase came to mind from one of the Anne of Green Gables books. It looked like "the soul of an unwritten poem."

Even though I grew up in Southern California, which is beautiful, the coast of New Zealand surpassed it. The huge snowcapped mountains coming down to a sparkling blue sea, the verdant green meadows—it's one of the most beautiful sights in the world. As we descended, I spotted hundreds of small white clouds. As we got closer, I realized those clouds were the sheep!

Melinda, a member of the Olive Branch Community, met me at the airport after I had cleared customs. She looked to be middle aged, with light brown hair, a sturdy body, and weathered skin.

"Welcome to New Zealand. How was your flight? Are you hungry? I packed a couple of sandwiches. Cheese or vegemite?"

All of her questions came out at once. And since I'd never heard of vegemite before, I went with the cheese sandwich.

The drive to Olive Branch was punctuated by breathtaking views of the ocean on one side and mountains on the other. It was spring in New Zealand and a lush green covered the rolling hills and the fields. Fruit trees were blooming, scenting the air with a sweet fragrance.

"Did you have a good flight?" Melinda asked.

"Yes, thank you. Long, but uneventful," I answered. But then I was overcome by the view. "Oh, it's so beautiful here!" I exclaimed.

Melinda smiled and let me enjoy the ride uninterrupted the rest of the way.

My first view of Olive Branch Community was love at first sight. Simple wooden cottages, a community dining room adorned with bougainvillea vines, the shade of eucalyptus trees—it all looked inviting and homey. The olive tree in the central courtyard, planted by the founders in the 1940s to symbolize their commitment to peace, had grown into a good-sized tree in its protected location.

Seeing both the sea and the mountains I felt a sense of possibility in me I'd never felt before. The bright green pastures dotted with yellow, blue, and lavender wildflowers danced in the spring sunshine. Was I in a fairy tale?

The community members were welcoming in the typically understated New Zealand manner. "Hey, welcome. I'm Jake." A lanky young man about my age, long hair tied back in a ponytail, reached out and shook my hand. He held it just a second longer than necessary and covertly seemed to be sizing me up. I blushed and mumbled, "Nice to meet you."

Jake and Melinda showed me around, pointing out the communal buildings, all of which were built with natural wood to keep to their Quaker sensibilities.

The small family cottages were similar in their simplicity, with flower gardens in front of each home and an enticing path that led into the national forest. I couldn't help but wonder, had I visited this all in my dreams before? It felt like a home I'd seen but never known.

I was assigned to work in the vegetable garden most of the year. The first few weeks were brutal. I had never done much physical labor and the palms of my hands easily blistered and bled, turning over soil and hacking at weeds. But I developed a mantra and repeated it until it came true. *I'm going to be strong, I'm going to be strong.* And soon enough my hands developed calluses and I did become stronger.

Looking back on this now, I think it's good for women to take on difficult physical tasks. It builds confidence that can transfer to other areas of life. But it also can be taken too far, as I learned a bit later.

CHAPTER TWO

One morning a few weeks after I arrived, I was woken up by banging on the door.

"Brooke, wake up!"

Groggy and still slightly asleep, I responded, "Mmmm?"

"It's pouring out. A major flood is predicted. We have to get the sheep and lambs to higher ground!"

As soon as I heard the news I sprung into action. Heart pounding, I threw on some clothes, rain boots, and a poncho and ran out the door. Everywhere I looked, people were running. Some had sandbags, wheelbarrows, and shovels, and others, like me, were hurrying to the sheep in the back pasture.

With the experienced shepherds in the front and us newbies in the back, we managed to get most of the sheep and baby lambs to higher ground. It's a weird fact of sheep herding that the sheep are generally herded from in front. One lamb, however, panicked and ran downhill toward the river, which was churning. We could hear it bleating above the sound of the rain. When I looked down at it I saw its eyes wild with terror.

Jake ran after it, but its front legs buckled under and it slipped on the muddy banks of the river, sliding into the choppy, muddy, debris-laden water. For a moment the lamb kept its head above the water, but then we saw it go under. We watched the lamb's head bob up and down until it was swept away by the raging waters. Jake couldn't reach it.

I had never encountered the fragility of life in such a visceral fashion before. When Jake returned he was heartbroken. We were both crying. And still it was a confusing mix of emotions—as a storm can be. At first forceful, then a serene calm. We'd saved most of the lambs and sheep, but watching that one helpless lamb perish felt like I'd sunk myself.

As we trudged back to the dining hall we met Sheila.

"The henhouse is safe," she reported grimly, her mouth turning downward. Robert joined us as well.

"All the houses are secured. Thank goodness they were built on higher ground." He shook his head and I could see from his eyes he knew how bad it could have been. We all slowly gathered back together in the dining hall, each person reporting the known damage.

Before Mindy opened her mouth, I knew it didn't look good for the vegetable garden. With her shoulders slumped and her head in her hands she said, "The vegetable garden is flooded. The root vegetables will probably survive, but all the lettuce is gone."

"Main road is washed out," Joe reported.

"Lots of lost homes in Nelson," said Carly.

"Brook Stream has burst its banks and the Maitai River overflowed in Nelson," added Louise.

Hours later we learned that the storm killed two people in Nelson, the nearest large town. Breakfast was grim that morning. We sat huddled around the radio listening to updates and local reports. None of us had the heart to go back out into the rain after we secured what we could. But eventually, Bruce, one of the elder members, heaved himself up and said with the confidence of a true leader, "There's still work to be done, folks. Let's get back to it." Some of us went to help in the kitchen as there was nothing more to be done in our outside areas of work.

The rain finally stopped four days later, and boy, did we have our hands full! Our own small river overflowed its banks, completely destroying the path that went alongside it. The roofing crew was busy patching all the leaks that sprung up from the flood. Lettuce needed to be replanted, sandbags removed, and mud cleared away from all the buildings and pathways. Piles of laundry were waiting.

It was heartening to watch the community pull together and get everything done. All of us going above and beyond our normal hours. This was why I came here. I wanted to experience a community that worked together beyond baking a cake for a funeral or knitting booties for a new baby.

CHAPTER THREE

In the short chilly winter, when there was less to do in the vegetable garden, I worked part-time in the wool-dying shed. We cultivated plants and also gathered wild native plants like madder root to use for natural dyes. The wool we created was beautiful. The colors were softer and more muted than the commercial chemical dyes that people are so fond of now. I found the work both soothing and satisfying. The pace was slow, as the wool boiled in the dyes. It was a nice respite from working in the vegetable garden.

* * *

Marissa came into Brooke's room around 10:00 p.m. Christmas Eve the year after her son was born.

"Hi, Mama. Will you help me label the Christmas presents I got for Seth?"

Sigh. She inherited this tradition of overdoing Christmas presents and staying up late on Christmas Eve from her father's side. But Brooke agreed to help, albeit grumpily.

"You know he's so young he would be happy with far less," Brooke couldn't help saying.

"I know, but this is how I grew up," Marissa said cheerfully.

She wrapped and wrapped, and Brooke labeled and labeled until everything was done. Brooke couldn't help remembering

Christmas in New Zealand.

* * *

Christmas at Olive Branch was a simple affair. People drew names from a hat and made homemade gifts as a Secret Santa. I tended to make wreaths for people from the Pohutukawa tree with its beautiful bright crimson red flowers. I would decorate my own small tree with seashells and spirals of colored tissue paper. Over the years I also collected beautiful gifts like a seashell mobile, a pine cone mobile, and one year, my friend Susan knitted me a beautiful sweater using our own Olive Branch wool.

On Christmas Day, we'd all go for a picnic at the beach. People would pack food for their own families and also food to share. I always made Italian Christmas cookies and packed goat cheese and cucumber sandwiches.

Other folks would undertake Scottish eggs, bacon and egg pie, and sausage rolls. These were not things I would eat as a vegetarian, but they were considered treats by the omnivores. Luckily there were always lots of fresh fruits and vegetables from our garden and delicious baked goods. My favorites were the whole wheat walnut and date loaf and an awesome kiwi, ginger, and honey cake, besides of course my own cookies.

Even though it was a lovely day, I still got lonely during the holidays. My family and I exchanged packages from New Zealand and America at some point leading up to the holidays. Receiving these packages, I'd sometimes find myself missing my family and crying. *It's funny how sometimes loving actions can move me to tears.*

CHAPTER FOUR

Dear Brooke,

When are you coming home? We miss you! It's been over a year. Have you thought about college?

Everything is pretty much the same here. My roses are blooming very nicely this year.

Your father's work is going well. His students love him. And I'm learning a new kind of needlework.

Love you,

Mom

Dear Mom and Dad,

I've decided to stay in New Zealand. I'm very happy here. I go for walks in the forest or by the ocean almost every day when it's nice, which it is most of the year.

I like getting up each morning knowing that I live in a community where no one goes hungry and all the people from youngest to oldest are taken care of. Almost everyone does their part and contributes to the best of their ability.

I have applied for and received a resident visa.

You should come visit me!

Love, Brooke

One day another American showed up at our community. I noticed the bounce in his step right away. When he sat down on a bench outside the dining hall, pulled out his guitar, and began singing Woody Guthrie's "Worried Man Blues," I was immediately charmed. We began spending time together. I loved listening to Frank play and sing. I learned some new songs too, like Tom Paxton's "I Can't Help but Wonder Where I'm Bound."

He had a love of puns and corny jokes, which I found funny. One day he was looking at a few of the books I had brought with me, like *Zen Mind: Beginner's Mind*, and said, "I have a joke for you. What did the Buddhist say to the hot dog vendor?"

"What?"

"Make me One with everything."

It took me a moment because I got distracted thinking a Zen monk wouldn't eat meat, but then I got it and laughed.

Another day, he came by and said: "Knock, knock."

I played along. "Who's there?"

"Kee."

"Kee who?"

"Not kee *who*: kee-wee!" and handed me one of the brown oval fruits.

* * *

Brooke was in the kitchen, beginning to prepare dinner, when the phone rang.

"Hello? Oh, hi, Sean. Wow, it's been so long since we talked! How are you?" As soon as Brooke heard her son's voice her body relaxed and settled down.

Sean's voice sounded like his usual good-natured, calm self. "I'm fine. Sorry I haven't called. I keep meaning to but forgetting."

"Me too. I'm glad you called." Brooke couldn't keep a smile from her face.

"Yeah. I'm good. I got a new job working at a café as their food manager," he said.

"That sounds good. Is the pay decent?"

"It's okay. Enough to pay rent and I get free lunch."

"Cool. All's well around here. I got some help planting some fall bulbs for the spring." *Sean used to help me with this when he was younger,* Brooke thought nostalgically. *He even once wrote a whole essay on how to plant a garden. It's funny how I don't always know I miss a person until they are right there on the phone with me—and then it all comes back.*

"Nice. Well, I've got to go. I'll try to call you more often."

"Yes. Me too. I'll try to call you also."

I've never been good at keeping in touch with family. My parents would get so mad at me in those New Zealand days for only writing one thin aerogram less than once a month. It's not that I didn't care. I just like to be present to where I am. It used to annoy me when my grandma would go on about how much she missed me when I went away for two weeks to summer camp. I think I made a decision that I wouldn't be like that.

* * *

I could stay on the farm for months at a time, but Frank would get restless. He had grown up in NYC and the quiet country life could get a bit boring by comparison. He would come by my room with a suggestion to go into the nearby town of Motueka.

"Wanna go into town and get some 'fush' and chips," he'd ask, trying for an authentic New Zealand accent. "How about some ice cream?"

I was game for the adventure. We would hike out to the main road and hitchhike into town. Motueka had one main street with a milk bar where we could get ice cream, milkshakes, candies, or small pastries. This was my favorite, but Frank also liked the pie cart that sold fish and chips along with savory handheld meat pies. The pie cart was similar to what we would call a food truck in the United States, and the milk bar was something like an American soda fountain. There was also an actual fish-and-chips shop called Talley's that had really good fish and chips.

We could go to Motueka after work, but the larger town of Nelson was a longer trip. We rarely went there, and when we did it was on a day off.

But my preference was always to go to the beautiful golden sandy beach after work. The beach was often blooming with the purple-flowered ice plants. Or if I didn't go to the beach I'd follow along the sun-dappled hiking trails into the Abel Tasman National Forest. The colors of nature drew me in. Eventually Frank began accompanying me on these excursions into nature.

Nowadays, it's trendy to speak about forest bathing, as if some of us haven't been bathing in nature for decades. Just remembering it now, I can feel the colors, the sunlight, the vibrant leaves, the winding path as my body dropped deeper into a place of peace.

Getting "off the farm" was necessary sometimes, as the community was small and tended toward gossip. When community members saw Frank and me hanging out so much, they were sure we'd be the next couple to get married. And although I hated to give the gossips more to talk about, I did find Frank very attractive. I tend to gravitate toward tall men with cute noses. And I don't mind if they are a bit heavy or a bit skinny. Frank was a bit heavy and Jake was skinny and I was attracted to them both. But at this point, Jake seemed out of reach. It's always much more about kindness and shared values for me than looks. Although apparently I do have a "type." Eventually Frank and I became a serious couple.

CHAPTER FIVE

After Frank and I were together for about a year, my parents came to visit. They immediately liked Frank, even though he made fun of me and my slovenly ways by telling them their daughter had invented "floor hooks."

My mother furrowed her brow and asked, "What are floor hooks?"

"You throw your clothes on the floor and they are instantly hung up," Frank said with a mischievous grin.

My father laughed uproariously at this.

I was comforted by their approval of him. They went off to tour the other island and when they came back, my mother sat me down for a serious conversation.

"Look. You guys seem serious. We can't afford to come back in a year or six months for a wedding. Would you consider getting married before we go back to the States?"

I paused. "We'll think about it."

I didn't quite know what to do. On the one hand, I liked Frank a lot. On the other hand, I wasn't ready to cut off the possibility of having other intimate relationships in my life in addition to Frank.

"Okay, but don't take too long. We are only here for another two weeks."

Later that night I broached the subject with Frank. He slyly asked me, "So, would you like to make some babies with me?" The man knew how to get to me. I'm a born earth mother and although truthfully I wasn't ready to be married, I *was* ready to have children. The thing I disliked about the idea of marriage was the exclusivity. I've never liked the idea of someone "owning" me. So I negotiated an open marriage. This meant that we were free to sleep with other people. Although we were honest with each other, this arrangement remained a secret to the community. It would have shocked the older generation.

We agreed to get married and wired Frank's parents to come join us.

"Are you excited?" I asked Frank on the day of our wedding.

"I'm happy, a little nervous, but I wouldn't say excited," he replied.

"Well, I'm happy too and excited," I answered.

I had found a lovely dress in the common storeroom. It was a simple linen-colored dress with antique lace trim. Frank found a peasant tunic to wear. On a sunny day we gathered the community and both sets of parents in the main courtyard, right under the olive tree. There we had a small ceremony.

Melinda read the vows we had written ourselves: "I promise to love and trust you. I promise to listen to you. I promise to support you in your goals."

We then exchanged rings and declared, "With this ring I thee wed."

Our best friend, Susan, read a poem she wrote specifically for the occasion:

These two friends
hands clasped together
eyes looking toward the future
have surprised us all with their gracious love.
We welcome their multiplied energy
into our lives
our hearts
our community
and the world.

She then turned to our parents and the community. "Do you promise to support this couple in their good times and their struggles?"

"We do!" they joyfully replied.

We didn't wait for anyone to give us permission to kiss, we jumped right in. After a few moments I heard my mom shout out from behind me, "Enough already!" While the crowd laughed at my mother's prodding, I felt annoyed in my joyful moment. *Mothers should take a back seat at their children's wedding.* This annoyance didn't last for long, though, because the community started to sing "Tis a Gift to Be Simple" and people threw flowers fresh from our gardens at us.

And just like that, we were married. It was a moment of pure joy. Later Frank told me I looked like I had won the lottery.

The community held a nice dinner party for us, with homegrown music, flowers, and food. The tables were set up outside in the lawn in front of the community dining room. We had vegetables that I had helped plant and harvest, homemade pickles, lamb stew, and for the vegetarians a lovely cheese soufflé. Our moms helped with the baking. My mom made her famous devil's food cake with buttercream frosting and Frank's mom made angel food cake with chocolate icing. And of course there was the New Zealand delicacy of pavlova—a meringue concoction covered with whipped cream, strawberries, and kiwi fruit. People stayed up late chatting, reminiscing, and joking with us.

"Do you know I wore that same dress when I got married to Tom here in 1953?" asked Sandra, one of the founding members of the community. "And we also stood in front of the olive tree to say our vows. But it was just a sapling then."

"Hey, congratulations! When can we expect the newest member of our community?" joked David, one of the high school students.

Frank and I stayed up pretty late with our friend Susan. When we finally went to bed, we fell right to sleep.

I thought I was all grown up at age twenty-one. Boy, was I wrong about that! But that is something you cannot tell a young person. They have to discover some things for themselves.

* * *

"Hello, Mama?" Marissa tentatively poked her head into the kitchen.

"Hi, Marissa. Come on in. What's up?"

"Sit down. I have something to tell you."

Uh-oh. Sigh. This doesn't sound good.

"I am sitting down."

"Well, I'm pregnant."

"Oh, Marissa, how did this happen? Didn't he wear a condom?"

"He did."

"Are you sure?"

"Yeah, I checked."

"What are you going to do? You just started school. It's really hard to have a baby and do school at the same time. Trust me on this. I know. That was one of the reasons it took *me* so long."

"I know! I'm not sure what to do. I have to think about it."

Brooke told herself to take a deep breath, which she did. Then she said firmly, "No matter what you decide, I will support you."

She meant it. She watched Marissa struggle with her decision. Some of her friends were advocating an abortion. A couple of her friends from high school had babies already and talked about how much joy they brought them, but Brooke stayed silent. This needed to be Marissa's decision.

APRIL

"Spring work is going on with joyful enthusiasm."
— John Muir

CHAPTER SIX

In my own time, when I was pregnant with Sean in New Zealand, I had blithely said, "Children come in their own time."

Frank and I got pregnant very quickly due to the miraculous fact that my body can ovulate more than once a month. Over the years I've noticed that all it takes is for sperm to be in the near vicinity of my body and, like magic, I'm ovulating!

I've warned my daughters about this. "If you are anything like me, you need to be very careful if you don't want to get pregnant."

Good Lord! Even now, as I approach seventy I will sometimes get a distinct twinge on my left side if I so much as cuddle with my partner, John. But the warning had not protected Marissa from this unplanned pregnancy. None of us knew how she had gotten pregnant, but I suspected her boyfriend.

I watched as she tried to make her decision. When Marissa leaned toward abortion, she got very depressed. When she leaned toward keeping the baby, she got very happy.

One day, she went to talk with her dad, who promised to help.

And then next thing, she burst into my bedroom, full of joy and declared, "I'm keeping the baby!"

John, who was staying the night, turned and nestled into me. He looked up and said, "You're going to be a grandmother." Through all of her decision-making I hadn't even considered my role in this, but when John said that I leaned back into the vision and thought, *I'm going to enjoy being a grandmother!*

"I love seeing how happy this decision makes you! You know I'll be here every step of the way if you want help. I'm so glad you told me. Can we talk in the morning? We were just about to go to sleep."

Marissa saw how sleepy we looked and said, "Sure, Ma. Let's talk in the morning. Good night. I love you."

"Love you too," I replied. I felt a mix of emotions. Sorry that Marissa was in this position, along with a sense of determination to be helpful. And I wanted to make sure she didn't feel criticized or judged.

I snuggled up next to John. "Thank you for being positive about this." Drifting off to sleep, I remembered my first pregnancy and baby.

* * *

At the Olive Branch Community, it bothered me that some of the elders—in their forties (*I know, but back then they felt like old folks*)— seemed to know I was pregnant before I did. Now, having given birth to three children I can also notice the shadow-like mask on a pregnant woman's face. But I still remember saying very dismissively "I'm not pregnant!" to Melinda, only to find out a few days later that I most certainly was.

Mindy, the head of the garden crew, was not too happy about my pregnancy. She shook her head and said, "Great! More work for me!"

That was quite a blow. It was already hard enough to work with her and I was afraid that now it would be even harder.

She turned out to be right, though. During the pregnancy I ended up on bed rest for the first few months and then was restricted to light work, like setting seedlings.

*   *   *

Early one morning about a month after Marissa made her decision to keep the baby, I was deep asleep, dreaming I was swimming in a beautiful lagoon. The telephone rang. I turned over, still very sleepy, thinking, *I'll just ignore it. I need a bit more sleep.* But the phone didn't stop ringing. I thought, *This must be important.*

"Hello?" I answered somewhat groggily, running my hands through my hair.

All I heard were tears on the other line. Then I noticed the sound of Marissa's voice.

"Marissa? Is that you? What's wrong?"

"Mama, I think I need to move back home!" The rest came out like it was all one sentence. "My boyfriend, Joe, just left, he said he's not ready to be a dad, I'm throwing up all the time, everything makes me feel nauseous and I can't concentrate on school at all!"

"Oh, honey. I'm so sorry to hear all this. Of course you can move back. Your old room is empty right now and I'll get Sean to help me take it off the Airbnb site tonight. Just make sure you drop your classes before the deadline."

"It's already too late. I thought I could do this. I really did!"

"Okay. Come home and we'll see if there is anything we can do. I love you, sweetie."

"Thanks, Mom."

Marissa moved into her old room. I helped her get through one semester of school by editing her papers and coaching her on quizzes. Then we began making preparations for the baby.

CHAPTER SEVEN

One day Marissa said to me, "I'm thinking about naming the baby Seth. What do you think?"

"I like it," I said. And I did, but I probably would have said that to any suggestion she gave.

For me, names, their meanings, histories, and connections can be important. Since I had chosen my own name and those of my children, I had put much thought into what a name can convey. I remembered the intricate process of choosing names for my children, and the new last name that Frank and I had settled on.

I had not appreciated my in-laws making suggestions when I was pregnant. "How about naming the baby after Uncle Tony?" from Frank's dad.

"You know, Great-aunt Celia never had anyone named after her," from my mom.

Instead, once Frank and I knew we were pregnant that first time around, we began to look at names that resonated for us. Sitting on the lawn outside of our small cottage, we went through a lot of names from a baby book. However, Frank and our mutual friend Susan made fun of each name in turn.

"You can't name the boy John. I mean who wants to be mistaken for a bathroom?" quipped Frank.

"Have you seen John? John or *the john*?" replied Susan, laughing.

Frank continued, "John is outside playing, but yes—I have seen *the* john and it needs cleaning." And they would both laugh. I would shake my head in dismay.

And then, just to make things even more frustrating, Frank would seriously suggest names that are in vogue now, but seemed outlandish at the time. He was thinking about Old Testament prophets such as Jeremiah, or family names like Conner. It got to be so difficult that for a while we gave up thinking about names.

At first, we didn't know the gender of our child. I did have a dream about a little chubby girl with blond curls. And later, a friend announced, after a night of copious drinking, that we were having a girl. But even back then I was skeptical of my own intuition. Eventually, through a clearer sonogram we learned we were going to have a boy. Then the search for a name became more serious.

I had always liked the name Yohanan. But I thought a Hebrew name would be hard for folks in New Zealand to pronounce. Upon further research, we discovered that Sean is the Irish equivalent. Both mean "God is gracious," which is how we were feeling about this pregnancy. And since part of Frank's heritage was Irish we settled on that.

Frank came from a different type of intermarried family than my own. He was Irish Catholic on his mother's side and Italian Catholic on his father's side. Neither side had to convert and both parents were lapsed in their beliefs and practices. But even so, the grandmothers still competed for who would host family holiday dinners and what kind of cuisine would prevail. Frank said this resulted in amazing feasts that included roast turkey, stuffing, mashed potatoes, and lasagna for Thanksgiving. Which may explain why he was a bit chubby when he arrived in New Zealand.

In the late 1960s and early '70s women began refusing to give up their last names for their husbands. It was a part of Second Wave

Feminism and it reached as far as New Zealand. Frank supported me in not wanting to take his last name, which was Giannini. He even offered to take my last name! But I wasn't fond of my own last name either, which was Ziemniak—Polish for "potato."

When Jews were forced to take surnames in Europe rather than follow their traditional custom of identifying people as "son or daughter of parents' first names," they had to pay for their new surname. The prettiest names like Rosenbaum, which means "rose bush," cost more money. My ancestors' class background was literally written in their name. It could have been worse. I met a woman once whose last name meant "cockroach."

We didn't think to consult our parents. And even now I still believe people should be able to choose their own names. Also being young, we thought we would live in New Zealand forever. We had no idea how life can come along like a storm and throw all your plans overboard in a single instant, like deck chairs on a cruise ship.

I wanted a name that was rooted in New Zealand, the land that brought us together. Frank brought his usual sense of humor to the task. "How about Madder Root—you love red! Or Titirangi—also red. That's a nice native New Zealand plant."

"Could you *please* be a bit serious? It has to be something that English speakers won't immediately laugh at. Admittedly, that does eliminate a lot of Māori native plant names that have repeating syllables like *whakataka*, *harakeke*, and *makamaka*."

"Okay. Let me delve a little deeper. Maybe we can find a name both grounded in New Zealand Māori culture and one that has some connections to ours. I'll do some research," he graciously offered.

It turned out that on Frank's Irish side of the family there were some folks with the last name of Calder, which means "big potato."

Maybe they were relatively rich? We don't know, but we settled on the last name of Kumara—which is the Māori word for a kind of sweet potato they brought and cultivated here over a thousand years ago. Everyone eats *kumara* in New Zealand. Either roasted, boiled, or made into fries, which they call chips.

Today, this would be considered gross cultural appropriation, but I'm not about to change my name. It just goes to show that each generation learns and progresses.

When we finally decided on a new last name, Frank and I were thrilled. Frank tried it on. "Brooke Kumara!"

"Let's call our parents and let them know," I said.

Frank paused. "Hmm… you go first. Your family will expect you to give up your name, so it won't be such a shock for them. I'm kind of dreading telling my dad. He's very proud of his heritage."

"I think my father will think it's cool. He's always been supportive of my choices. He didn't blink an eye when I declared in tenth grade that I would no longer be Becky, but would now go by the name of Brooke."

CHAPTER EIGHT

As expected, my father took our name change in stride.

"You took our name and made it sweeter!" he said.

We could almost hear him smiling over the phone line, his tone of voice was so warm. Frank's father was another matter altogether.

"What's wrong with Gianinni?" he immediately retorted. "Are you ashamed of your Italian heritage?!"

"No, Dad; it's not that." Frank explained our desire for a new family name.

"Humpf!" was the only reply we got.

Of course Frank's mother was pleased with the connection to her Irish heritage. On the spot, I thought to offer a compromise. "How about if we used Giannini as the baby's middle name?"

"Ah, now you're talking!" said Lenny.

"Lovely," Alice joined in.

Now we are fully ready to welcome the birth of Sean Giannini Kumara, I thought.

CHAPTER NINE

I was sitting quietly outside my little cottage when all of a sudden I heard what sounded like a stampede of horses. But it turned out to be a herd of escaped goats. Before I could even get up out of my porch chair I heard a sound that I imagine a swarm of locusts might make devouring a crop, only deeper. I looked up and right in front of my eyes, the herb garden of Olive Branch was reduced to rubble. Only a faint smell of crushed herbs lingered briefly in the air. Oh no!

I knew immediately there was going to be trouble in the community. I remembered the contentious discussion about if we should even have goats. It went something like this.

"No way should we have a herd of goats!" yelled Mindy at a community meeting.

"They are nasty, destructive creatures. They eat everything in sight," Tom chimed in in a milder laconic tone.

Jake countered the naysayers. "But they would keep down the brambles along the forest trail and we have extra grazing meadows. We could make goat cheese for our own use and to sell. Besides, they are so cute."

"How are you going to make sure they don't destroy the herb garden, or even the flower gardens in front of our cottages?" asked Mindy.

"I'll volunteer to build solid, secure fencing for them," Will said.

"And I promise to keep a careful eye on them," Jake confirmed.

Joy was facilitating the meeting. She was one of the founding members, now middle aged, known for being very levelheaded. After some more discussion, she brought it to a vote.

"All in favor?"

It was a close vote, but the ayes won by about five votes.

Now what will happen?

"I told you they are nasty destructive creatures!" Mindy was hollering again at the community meeting.

Jake pleaded. "I'm so, so sorry this happened!"

Furious, Mindy went off. "Well, sorry is not enough. What are you going to do about it? Is the goat dairy going to compensate us for our losses? How did it happen anyway? And most importantly, how are you going to make sure it never happens again, or are we all going to enjoy goat stew for the rest of the year."

Joy was facilitating the meeting again and slowed us all down. "Let's break down the issues. First, let's settle the issue of compensation."

"The goat dairy is offering to fully compensate the herb garden for your losses," said Will.

"And help you replant!" Jake added.

Lots of nods around the room as the knitting needles clicked. (We used to joke that members went into community meetings with a ball of yarn and came out with a sweater.)

Mindy consulted with her crew. "Okay, that's a good start, but I want to know *how* did this happen in the first place and how can we prevent it from happening again?"

Jake stepped in. "We aren't really sure. Someone didn't latch the gate properly. Maybe the children were in there? They do love the goats."

Up jumped Sarah. "Don't you go blaming the children! They know not to go into the enclosure without a grown-up."

Many head nods. Silence.

Joy spoke up. "I'm going to call for a ten-minute break. During this time I ask that anyone who knows something about this matter consult their conscience. I ask all members to calm themselves, remember that no one here would have done this maliciously, and be prepared to forgive. May I remind you all that honesty, humility, and forgiveness are core values of ours."

When we came back together, Joy asked that everyone enter into silence to allow whoever needed to be guided by their inner light to have the space to do so.

After a few minutes Josh slowly stood up. Head hanging down, shoulders stooped, he quietly said, "It was me. I love hanging out with the goats, and I had smoked a little weed. I didn't latch the gate properly when I left to go get something to eat. I'm very sorry."

Straightening up, he looked Mindy in the eyes and said, "I'd like to contribute one month's allowance to help buy new plants, and I will work with the goat crew to replant the herbs. I will also help mulch the herb garden and donate my labor after school to them for the next six months."

You could feel the sigh of relief all around. Joy said, "Is it the sense of the meeting that this issue is now resolved?" All nodded.

Some folks went over to Mindy, some to Jake and Will, and some to Josh.

As Frank and I walked home we wondered if it had not been someone born in the Olive Branch Community, would the members have been so understanding. Although we had been accepted as members, not having parents or grandparents in the community was sometimes difficult. But we were relieved that the conflict had been resolved peacefully and with apparent agreement from all.

CHAPTER TEN

"Marissa, I'd like to make sure you get good prenatal care." We were sitting in my sunny kitchen, our favorite place to hang out.

"Would it be okay if I called my OB/GYN to get you an appointment?"

"Sure, Mom. Thanks!"

I picked up the phone and called my trusty OB/GYN.

"I'd like to make an appointment for my daughter? She's pregnant."

"We don't do abortions," the woman on the other line said.

What? I thought. *You call yourselves a woman's health care practice and you don't provide abortions? And why are you presuming she wants one? Now, with our constitutional rights to control our own reproductive systems undone, this conversation bothers me even more.* But I forged ahead.

"She wants to keep the baby."

"Oh, okay. I have an appointment next Tuesday with Dr. Green. She needs to bring all her insurance information with her."

"Okay. Thank you."

How very different from my own experience!

New Zealand has free universal health care. I didn't have to worry about insurance. There was a publicly funded nurse right at Olive Branch who did much of my prenatal care. I could choose to go to a birthing center in the nearest town or to a large hospital in Nelson. I chose the birthing center as I wanted as natural a birth as possible, but with backup in case anything went wrong.

Now all the young women I know, including Marissa, have been convinced that they can't possibly stand the pain and need an epidural. In my day, we thought surely things would change with more women doctors. But sadly, they apparently become brainwashed in medical school.

But perhaps I was a bit brainwashed myself. I read lots of books on the beauty of giving birth and how it is a completely natural process. These books seemed to have the thesis that the pain just came from fear. If you knew what to expect, and could do some relaxation exercises, you wouldn't feel much pain.

Shirley, the community nurse, gave me breathing exercises to do, but unfortunately she was the kind of person that when she said "relax," I had the exact opposite reaction. One of my friends said giving birth naturally had been a "peak experience" for her, so although I was a bit nervous, I was completely unprepared for the actual pain of contractions. This had nothing to do with fear, but everything to do with a physical process that just hurts like hell.

It was around eleven o'clock at night when my water broke. I had gotten up to go to the bathroom but before I got there, a stream of fluid poured down my legs.

"Frank, *Frank*, wake up! My water just broke!"

"What? Huh? What should I do?" he mumbled, just coming into consciousness.

"Call Shirley. Tell her my water broke."

Shirley was the community nurse and the same person who had made me so nervous when attempting to teach me relaxation exercises. But now, her calm, cool presence was reassuring.

"I'll call the birthing center in Motueka and tell them to expect you in about half an hour. There's no need to rush or panic. First births usually take at least eight hours.

"Frank," she continued, "go get the community van. Brooke, do you have your bag packed?"

On the way to the birthing center, Frank looked over at me and said, "Brooke, I have something to tell you."

Puzzled, I gave him a quizzical look in between grimacing with the building contractions.

"I'm excited."

Well! This man who had never admitted to being excited before, even when we were getting married, was finally excited.

"Me too," I said.

We arrived at the birthing center and were shown into a room. I hated that they shaved my pubic hair "just in case." *Just in case, what?* I thought.

I was beginning to have strong contractions and Frank was trying to encourage me to "breathe," but mostly I was taken aback by the intense pain.

At some point a doctor came in, looked at me with pity, and said, "You read all the books, didn't you?" and then gently stroked my back. That did help a bit. He also suggested "a cocktail" that would calm me down and speed up the process. I agreed to it, so it wasn't a completely natural birth. The medications did both things.

They moved me to the labor and delivery area, which turned out not to have private rooms, just curtains separating the women giving birth.

This meant that much to my surprise, Frank couldn't stay with me. I was left alone during transition, yelling my head off. The woman next to me was doing the same.

After about forty-five minutes, a midwife came in, checked me, and said, "You are fully dilated. It's time to push."

Although dubious at first, I was able to push out what felt like a rounded flagstone. *Now I understand why they call this labor.* It was hard work, but not impossible. The pain had stopped, but I almost forgot what was happening. When the baby was born, and they briefly showed him to me, I shouted out, "It's a baby!"

When he was placed in my arms, I disassociated the entire experience of giving birth, perhaps because it was so painful. I felt that someone had just given me a baby. I looked at the baby, looked at Frank, who had been allowed back in, and said, "Sean."

Frank left to call the family, and Sean and I were moved to a room with several other mothers and babies. I was the only first-time mother and I loved listening to the more experienced moms talk. I closely watched how they held and nursed their babies. Each baby was next to their mom in a little plastic bassinet and the feeling was very friendly.

CHAPTER ELEVEN

It was assumed the babies would be nursed and no one traumatized us with "before and after weighing" like is being done today by so-called lactation consultants, Brooke grumbled as she wrote.

All the mothers ate together in a communal dining room. I was envious of their relaxed confidence in their mothering abilities. *Of course, now I have that ease and confidence around babies and children. It's something that comes with experience.*

Our unit was filled with light and had windows where we could look out on a beautiful garden. It was planted with bougainvilleas growing on trellises that shaded the stone benches and a small pond.

A few days later, I went home. Shirley came to check on me and gave me a good piece of advice. She asked, "What did they tell you about feeding the baby?"

When I mumbled something about "every four hours," which I already intuited wasn't realistic, she said, "First of all, never wake a sleeping baby. Second of all, feed him when he wants to eat." She told me how the previous generation had taken the "every four hours" advice so literally that both mothers and babies would be crying as they waited the prescribed four hours.

I still hear doctors telling this to new mothers. Then they wake their babies up, wondering why they don't eat vigorously. And they don't produce enough milk because of this. So they start supplementing with formula. This in turn means that the baby nurses less or refuses altogether because the artificial nipples are easier. And then they give up. Ugh. Brooke continued to ruminate.

I was lucky and Sean nursed well until he was three months old. Then he refused because my milk production had not quite kept up with his demand. Shirley was away and no one knew what to do. He went many hours without eating or drinking and then finally took a bottle. And my milk dried up. I now know this is called a "nursing strike" and can happen when the baby is going through a growth spurt. La Leche League suggests putting a bit of something sweet (not honey) on your nipples to encourage the baby to keep sucking, which will stimulate more milk production. It can take up to twenty-four hours, though, which seems like an eternity when you have a hungry, crying baby. So at three months, Sean began drinking from a bottle.

CHAPTER TWELVE

Frank and I were so enthralled with Sean. He was a mellow little guy who would wake up cooing to the hand-knitted toy hanging above his bed. He liked to share his food with the other children in the community daycare, enthusiastically saying, "Yum!" while trying to feed his picky friend fresh peas.

One morning when Frank was getting ready to head out for the day's work I heard him yell, "Ouch!" He was putting on his work boot. When he turned it upside down, out fell a spoon. Sean had just learned to crawl, and enjoyed depositing small objects into unexpected places.

Once he began walking, we would go on adventures in the community. First to see the baby lambs. This happened almost every day! There is nothing more delightful than baby lambs frolicking in a meadow, when your own little one is learning how to frolic. We also explored the apple and pear orchards to pick up fallen fruit that was not too badly bruised. I loved making apple and pear sauces from our own orchards.

It still amazes me how much fruit and nuts go to waste in the U.S. Some of my children have learned to glean and cook from scratch from me and some not so much. But take it from an elder—there is free food to be had if you keep your eyes open.

CHAPTER THIRTEEN

Work was another story altogether. I got six weeks of maternity leave and then went back to work half time. Remembering Mindy's remarks when I got pregnant I was determined to prove her wrong now. It was accepted practice that if someone needed to leave during work hours to nurse their baby, that was *not* minused out of their work hours. But out of sheer stubbornness, and fanaticism, I would subtract any time away from the vegetable garden. This meant that instead of working 8:30 a.m. to 12:30 p.m., I would work 8:30 a.m. to 1:30 p.m. Sometimes just to prove I could, I would work until 3:00 p.m. when the whole crew went home (they had started at 6:00 a.m.), or until I literally saw black. I was working myself to the bone. "I'm going to prove her wrong, I'm going to prove her wrong" was my internal mantra.

But I would take a long lunch break, especially when I was still on maternity leave. One day I was sitting in the dining hall long after most people had gone back to work. My friend Susan stopped by my table. "I see the chairs have gotten a lot more comfortable," she said, smirking and cracking up.

"What do you mean?" I asked.

She then proceeded to mimic me the last few weeks of my pregnancy, squirming around on a chair, groaning and sighing, rubbing my back and saying, "These chairs are just *so* uncomfortable!"

I got pretty embarrassed and laughed along with her.

"I guess it wasn't the chairs," I admitted.

Now, watching Marissa struggle to balance motherhood, work, and school, I try hard not to place such a burden on her, while at the same time encouraging her to be responsible. It's quite a balancing act. She's good at asking for help, possibly too good. I keep having to learn how to set reasonable boundaries.

The conflict between myself and Mindy did not go unnoticed in the community. One day an older member stopped me and said, "Don't let her do this to you, Brooke. We all know how hard you work. You don't have to prove anything." But I couldn't stop. The conflict between us never resolved.

* * *

Brooke was sitting in her living room, rocking Seth to sleep in her favorite rocking chair. It was a very sturdy chair that she had received as a gift when Marissa was born. The afternoon was waning and the sun bathed the room in a warm glow. It was a cozy room, painted in a Southwestern pallet, with turquoise walls and brick red trim.

I'm a grandma, she thought. *This new little being has wiggled his way into my heart. I was there when he was born, but I was more focused on his mother. And biting my tongue about the medical care she did and didn't get.*

After he fell asleep and she was able to lay him down in his crib, she returned to her memoir. *I want to capture this feeling while it's still fresh,* she thought. And she began to write.

* * *

Falling in love with my grandson didn't happen right away. But as he got a bit older and I could hold him and sing him to sleep, something almost magical happened. He just entered my heart. The sweet way he would snuggle into my shoulder. The aroma of milk breath that new infants exude. The way he seemed to understand what I was saying to him way before he could talk.

For instance, he had a hard couple of days once. He had to get some shots and he fell off the bed. I sang him a song that I had adjusted from "It takes a Worried Man" by Woody Guthrie.

It takes a worried baby

to sing a worried song.

I went to the doctor

to get me a shot

I went to the bed

I fell down on my head.

He kind of startled and looked at me intently.

I remembered very vividly when Sean fell off the bed. He had not been able to turn over even the day before. I set him on our fold-out sofa bed and turned my back to do some small task. All of a sudden I heard a thump. And then a whimper. There was Sean on the floor. Luckily the bed was low to the ground, but still, I picked him up, heart pounding, and cried along with him.

"I just feel terrible," I told Frank and then Sally, his daycare worker. Sally was sympathetic and told me not to be too upset. "This happens to every baby at some point or another. You can't protect them from having bumps and bruises."

Nonetheless, it was a traumatic experience at least for me. When I was pregnant with Lucinda I was frantic to have a crib for the baby so I would never be tempted to leave her on the bed.

But truth be told, I couldn't protect Lucinda completely either.

Perhaps we never get over that motherly panic, Brooke mused as she continued reminiscing and writing.

There was that time Lucinda had eaten some laundry detergent.

I had found her sitting in the laundry room with white powder all over her mouth. Without thinking, I put some of the mysterious powder in my own mouth only to spit it out immediately. Laundry detergent! Yuck! *Boy, that was stupid,* I thought afterward. *What if it had been something poisonous? We would have both been poisoned.*

Marissa seems more calm than I was. And also more calm than many of the young mothers I have worked with in the library over the years. It's something I admire about her. I'm so glad I didn't pass on all that panic to my children. Marissa is also so much more on top of things like doctor appointments and shots. She is a warm and loving mother to Seth, but takes the little bumps and bruises in stride.

Hmm, thought Brooke, *this narrative is awfully full of babies. What about your affair with Jake??*

CHAPTER FOURTEEN

As Sean grew out of infancy and babyhood to becoming a toddler, I returned to working full time. I came out of the intense motherhood cocoon and recovered my body. With that came renewed sexual energy and desire.

I had always been attracted to Jake. We worked together in the vegetable garden after the goat incident. He worked hard to repair the damage. His long lanky frame was so enticing. But I never let on that I liked him. I thought it would be humiliating as he had a reputation of having been with lots of women. And there were other women more attractive than me openly chasing him. However, one day when working in the garden I let slip that I had an open marriage. I noticed Jake looking at me quizzically.

A few nights later, after a class on the history of nonviolence that we were both taking, he suggested a swim in the ocean. Irresistible. A balmy moonlit night, *Jake*, and the ocean? He peeled off his clothes, the moonlight revealing his gorgeous body, and dove right into the waves. I followed more slowly, having left my shirt and underwear on.

On the walk home my heart was racing. The air was cooler than the water, my shirt was plastered to my body, and my nipples were hard. I was aware of how Jake was looking at me. When we parted, he pulled on one of my curls and watched as it bounced back up, reached out his forefinger, and gently traced it down my nose and across my lips. "Good night, my dear," he said and gently kissed me on the top of my head.

I walked the rest of the way home in a daze. Did he like me? Would there be more? I could hardly breathe. My dreams were filled with tantalizing scenes of Jake and myself. But I had no idea what to do about all of this. I did look forward to next week's class on nonviolence, though.

And sure enough, after class Jake cocked his head at me, with that same quizzical look, and said, "Wanna go for a walk in the forest?" Of course I nodded, too flustered to say anything at all. As we walked, Jake took hold of my hand. It felt nice to be walking with him like this. We got to a little hut that was on the property and he said, "Come on in."

Once in, he gently began to unbutton my blouse. Our lovemaking was awkward at first. I realized there is something to be said for knowing what a person likes. This was in the days before "enthusiastic, verbal consent" became the norm for the younger generation. Before each step was asked about and communicated. I'm not sure people really do this, but some talking about what each of us liked would have been helpful. However, I found it profoundly difficult to speak of such things. Who knows what would have happened longer term if events had not intervened.

CHAPTER FIFTEEN

Frank, Sean, and I were fast asleep when we heard pounding at the door.

"Call from the U.S. for Frank!"

Uh-oh, I thought. "Get up, Frank! Your folks never call unless it's something really important. I'll throw some clothes on and come meet you."

Frank's parents could never remember the time difference between NYC and New Zealand. It was 10:00 a.m. Wednesday their time, which meant it was 2:00 a.m. Thursday our time. It's a good thing the community took turns sleeping in the office in case of such emergencies.

Normally, the volunteer slept peacefully through the night, but occasionally one was awakened with bad news.

I hurried to the office only to overhear Frank saying, "Yes. I'll come as soon as I can."

"What's happened?"

"My dad had a heart attack. And my mom is flipping out. I need to go help her and see what the situation is. She's sending money for the plane ticket."

I sat down hard. "I'm so sorry to hear this. Did she say how serious it is?"

"Not really. But it didn't sound good. I'll know more once I'm there and can talk with a doctor."

"Okay. I'll help you pack."

A day and a half later, Melinda came to get me in the vegetable garden.

"Brooke, go to the office. Frank is on the phone for you." I ran as fast as I could to the one community phone.

"Hello?? How's your dad?"

"Not so good, Brooke. He actually had a stroke and is partially paralyzed on his right side. The doctor says it could take months for him to recover."

"Oh no. That's terrible. How's your mom holding up?" I could tell I was nervous because I couldn't stop twirling my unruly hair.

"Not well at all. Brooke, she can't really handle this on her own. I think I may have to stay here for a while."

"How long is a while?"

"I don't know yet. Give me a few weeks to see."

"Okay. I'm glad she has you. I can imagine it's too much for her. She nearly fell apart just making us that afternoon celebration with the aunts and uncles after we were married and went back to the States for a visit, remember?"

"Yeah, she's depended on my dad all these years for so much. Listen, I've got to go and this conversation is costing a lot."

"Okay. Take care. Tell Grandpa and Grandma I send my love. And I love you too."

"Yup. I'll call when I know more."

I slowly walked back to work, worried and wondering what would happen to our lives if we had to move back to the States. I had wanted to live in New Zealand for the rest of my life. But family is important and Frank was even more connected to his family than I was to mine. We were both only children, so there weren't many options if we were needed.

Two weeks passed and then another phone call came.

"Brooke, my dad is now in a rehab center. They think it will take at least three months until he can move back home. I think I have to stay at least until then. I'd really like you and Sean to come join me. I miss you, and seeing Sean will cheer up my mom and dad. Would you be willing to join me here?"

"Oh, Frank, I was afraid of this. I've been preparing myself for something like this. Yes, I'll come, but I don't think I can live in NYC for all that time. And I'm worried about messing up our path to citizenship."

"Thanks, sweetie! Can you go to a community meeting and ask for a leave of absence for both of us for three months? Then we will still have one more month before we mess up our plans to become citizens. Hopefully by then we will be able to return. And I knew you wouldn't want to stay in the city. I've been looking at options out in the country of New Jersey, but not too far from the city. It looks like there is a cooperative farm pretty close by and they have some rooms available for rent."

"Oh! That sounds wonderful. Thank you so much for knowing me so well!"

"Well, I want to make it work for everyone. And my mom can send plane fare once you know how soon you can leave."

"I'll bring it up at the community meeting tomorrow and let you know. Hugs."

"Hugs back at you and give a big hug and kiss to Sean for me."

Asking for a leave of absence was the first time I had ever spoken in the community meetings. Our leaves of absence were approved. Only Mindy had anything negative to say about how she would need more help in the vegetable garden. Jake, bless his soul, volunteered.

The childcare workers helped me look for the warmest coat and several warm sweaters that we could find for Sean in the community storeroom as it was winter in New York, but summer in New Zealand. Frank would bring a coat of his mother's to the airport for me.

I tidied up our little cottage and tried to spend some time with my best friend Susan before leaving. Jake came to see me the evening before I left. He held me gently and ran his hands through my hair.

"I'm going to miss you," he whispered. "Thanks so much for all the work you've done in the vegetable garden. So many things wouldn't have happened if you hadn't done them."

I couldn't really speak, but just nodded mutely. My heart was aching. I wondered if I would ever see him again.

The next day, Susan drove Sean and me to the airport. Looking out at my beautiful country, I fervently hoped I would be coming back soon. Only two and a half, Sean did pretty well on the long airplane flight until he started clamoring, "I want to get off! I want to get off!"

I explained to him that "there aren't any stairs" and I think that was the first time he actually realized we were in the air. He looked out the window and got very quiet and sat down in his seat. A few hours afterward we arrived in New York City.

CHAPTER SIXTEEN

What a contrast! Going from sunny summer weather surrounded by meadows, forests, and beaches to a dreary November winter day. Bare dull gray tree branches. A completely urban environment made up of brick and concrete. Ugh. It was a huge culture shock.

But once we got to Alice and Lenny's home I felt better. Alice, my mother-in-law, was so glad to see us. And Sean took to her right away in that special bond that grandchildren have with their grandparents. He settled himself in her lap and she played "This little piggy went to market" with his toes. Of course she used the traditional words of the third piggy eating "roast beef" where I had substituted "tofu," but Sean didn't mind. In fact, he was happy to eat up some roast beef she had cooked for him and Frank. She had even gone to the trouble of looking up a broccoli casserole recipe to make for me. I sensed that it was a relief for her to turn her attention toward us for a while and away from Lenny.

The next day we were able to visit Lenny in his rehab center. Somehow, Frank managed to wheedle the receptionist into letting us bring in Sean; a clear violation of the posted rules. And it was so worth it! Grandpa Lenny's eyes lit up at the sight of Sean, and his crooked smile spoke volumes.

I learned from Frank not to be bullied by bureaucrats, and that has stood me in good stead.

The next day we went to Sunnyvale Farm in Manalapan Township,

New Jersey, forty-six miles from NYC. We took the Garden State Parkway southbound to Exit 123. It seemed almost too good to be true. This was a loose cooperative located on a seventy-acre farm. The main farmhouse had a vacant large room and smaller adjacent room that would work well for a bedroom for Sean. We would share the kitchen, dining room, and living room with a collection of interesting characters. The collective was in need of a driver to take their produce into NYC to various co-ops and small organic stores.

We quickly said we would like to rent the two rooms. There was a cooperative nursery school on the farm with one paid teacher and parent aides. I could help out in the on-premise store and in producing the fall products of applesauce, apple cider, pumpkin butter, and baked goods; while Frank could fill in as the driver.

If something sounds too good to be true, it usually isn't true, thought Brooke moodily as she stared at her cup of herbal tea after writing that last sentence. Sunnyvale Farm being a prime example. She continued to write about their experiences there.

A typical night in our room at Sunnyvale could sound like this:

"Gosh darn it! Mother f—ing tool." It was our housemate Jeff. About fifty at the time, with sandy thinning hair, he had a woodworking shop adjacent to our bedroom. And he was prone to not only work at all times of the day and night, which we might have gotten used to. But he was also prone to getting frustrated, cursing loudly, and throwing tools against the wall at all hours. This was more difficult.

Then there was Joy and Chuck—a nice enough couple who were very good at asking and getting help for their projects, but suddenly "too busy" to help anyone else.

"Hi, how you'all doing? Could you help us stack our wood for the winter?" asked Joy, leaning in our doorway, a friendly smile on her face. Of course we scrambled to help. A few weeks later it was our turn to stack wood.

"Hey, Joy and Chuck, could you help us stack our firewood?"

"Oh… no, we can't help. We are very busy cleaning the house today."

Then there was Jessica and Bill, also nice enough people. But so nice that they had taken in Bill's younger teenage brother who was in a growth spurt. Dan was completely capable of coming into the communal kitchen and demolishing an entire loaf of bread and a dozen eggs for breakfast. I had once seen Jessica in the grocery store throwing boxes of cereal and pasta into her cart mumbling "that should last a day, that should last a day." No one would have minded his need for such prodigious amounts of food if they had contributed to the kitchen fund, but they didn't.

There was also their bizarre birthday ritual. The core members of the community would spend the entire day telling the person whose birthday it was what was wrong with them. No stone of a fault was left unturned. "Boy, I'm glad we aren't full members here," I said after witnessing one of these birthday "celebrations."

There were some bright spots, however. The housemates down the hall were a lovely couple. Kathleen was a classic Irish beauty; porcelain skin, sparkling green eyes, and red hair down to her waist. She had spent time in Cuba and I loved hearing how they organized basic necessities by neighborhood according to need. It seemed like a place where socialism was working for the poor and working-class people. Deb was an equally stunning African American woman, dark chocolate brown skin and sculpted muscles from her work on construction crews. She had great stories about besting the macho men on her job.

Kathleen and I worked together in the Sunnyvale Country Store and would often debrief at the end of the day.

"Did you hear that customer who wanted a discount on the already discounted produce?" I said, laughing.

"Yeah. Some people have nerve! And how about Chuck? Did you notice his 'ten-minute break' that stretched to an hour?" she said, rolling her eyes.

"Oh yeah. That seems to be his *modus operandi*. Frank says he's one of those people who thinks 'what's mine is mine and what's yours is mine.'"

We'd laugh together and shrug, feeling better for having shared our day.

But the straw that broke the camel's back happened at a house meeting. Jeff said, "I'm sick and tired of finding messes in the kitchen! I've just about had it!"

He turned to us and said, "And you, Frank, are the worst! Last night you left a blender dripping with avocado, a pile of dishes in the sink, pots on the stove, and the floor littered with lettuce and tomatoes! I move that Frank no longer be allowed to use the kitchen."

"Wait just a minute, now, before you jump to conclusions. Frank wasn't even on the farm last night. He was in the city. You can check the work schedule," I pleaded.

"Nope. I know it was Frank. He's the one always making guacamole. All in favor of barring Frank from the kitchen, raise your hands."

As nonmembers we had no recourse. Katie and Deb also did not have a vote; the other members went along with Jeff, and we knew it was time to move.

CHAPTER SEVENTEEN

In all households, kitchen cleanup can become a contentious issue. Everyone is sure they always clean up after themselves and it's always "someone else" leaving a mess. In fact, this happened just the other day when my housemate Cindy complained to me about our other housemate Zoe and then noticed the very next day she herself was too tired to clean up.

The nearby town of Manalapan was charming enough that we decided to stay in the area. A community bulletin board at the local grocery store advertised a two-bedroom apartment right in the center of the town. It was near where the stream ran under a bridge, in an older neighborhood of tree-lined streets. We went to investigate.

The house was owned by an elderly Greek widow, Mrs. Zafeiriou. The apartment was on the third floor of her house. Besides the two bedrooms, living room, and dining room it had a kitchen. Given our recent experience, this was most important. The rent was reasonable and we took to Mrs. Zafeiriou immediately. We quickly moved in as we had few belongings. Most of our stuff was still in New Zealand.

I liked hanging out with Mrs. Zafeiriou. She had all kinds of elder wisdom, like how to brew a natural tea for a cough. And she seemed very taken with Sean. She was generous with her traditional Greek cookies. They were so much like my grandmother's Italian cookies and my other grandma's Eastern European Jewish cookies. All three traditions had a luscious crescent butter cookie dipped in powdered sugar. She even showed me how to make Greek lemon-egg soup.

Enticing aromas of oregano and garlic often drifted upstairs.

Frank and I laughed when she told us, "Twenty couples rent my apartment. Eighteen make a baby. Your baby be a girl. Look like the daddy."

We didn't laugh, though, when Frank brought an African friend from work home and she said, "I see a Black man at your house. Who is this person?"

"He's a friend of Franks from work, Mrs. Zafeiriou."

"Well, I just wonder what the neighbors will think," she mumbled.

"That woman tries to blame her own prejudice on the neighbors," Frank said once we were upstairs. I just nodded, shaking my head.

But all in all things were mostly working out. Frank found a job delivering pizza in the evenings, which allowed him to be with his mother and father most days. Grandpa Len was slowly recovering and we still hoped to be able to return to New Zealand soon. Sean and I would go to visit Len and Alice when we could. Len's eyes would light up every time he saw Sean.

Alice liked to take Sean to the local playground or the zoo. With her bright white hair, blue eyes, and pale complexion, she and Sean were quite a contrast. He had Frank's and my Mediterranean complexion and was still a "little brown berry" from the New Zealand summer. People used to ask Alice if he was an adopted Puerto Rican baby. At the time it seemed funny. In retrospect it seems racist.

"Humans plan and God laughs," thought Brooke. *We were so young. We thought we could decide our fate. We had little idea what was about to transpire.*

CHAPTER EIGHTEEN

One day the phone rang. It was Grandma Alice on the phone in tears. "Lenny has had another bad stroke and the doctors don't think he'll be long for this world."

We dropped everything, bundled up Sean, and got in the car heading into New York City and the hospital.

This time, Frank was not able to work his magic on the staff and so we had to take turns waiting with Sean in the patient lounge and being with Grandpa Lenny. Although very close to death, he seemed able to hear us as we told him how much we loved him. The in-house Catholic priest came to perform the last rites and comfort Alice. While she took a turn being with Sean, Frank softly hummed "Ninna Nanna," a lullaby from his childhood, as Len gently passed to the next world.

I had the distinct impression that his spirit continued to hover around us for several days. I lit a memorial candle for him and tried to explain to Sean that his grandpa had died.

"I want to see Granpa Lenny!" Sean kept insisting.

I was cognizant of the advice not to use "going to sleep" metaphors, as that can make bedtime a nightmare for young children. So I resorted to the language of my Unitarian Sunday school and said, "Granpa Lenny went to be with God." Whatever that meant.

"But I want to say goodbye to him first," Sean insisted. So we brought him to the funeral. At the end of the service, he rose up on tiptoes and whispered "Goodbye, my grandpa" to the casket, which we had insisted be closed.

On the way home from the burial he first got very quiet and then got upset, and asked, "Who will feed Grandpa Len inside that box?"

"Granpa Lenny won't need food anymore," I replied.

"But he will starve!" he cried.

I gave up and said, "God will feed and take care of him now."

"Will God tuck him in at night?"

"Yes."

"And sing him a goodnight song?"

"Of course."

"And tell him a bedtime story?"

"Yes, indeed. God tells the best stories," I answered with a smile. At that Sean was satisfied, snuggled down next to me, and fell asleep.

Alice was beside herself with grief and completely overwhelmed with all the details that needed taking care of. She leaned heavily on Frank and me to handle logistics. Since she had not gone to church in years, she had no local priest to turn to. And she had no desire for a traditional Irish wake. The most we could muster was to invite a few of Len's friends from work, the great-aunts and uncles, and his poker buddies up to the apartment the evening before the funeral for light refreshments. I baked traditional Italian cookies. Sean kept me company as I made finger sandwiches like I remembered from my childhood. Frank brewed coffee and tea. We set out bowls of fruit and nuts and sat by Alice most of the night.

"Please don't go back to New Zealand and leave me all alone here," she beseeched us. "I have been married to Lenny for forty years. He was my best friend and took care of everything," she continued and then broke down weeping again.

"We'll see what we can do, Ma," said Frank.

CHAPTER NINETEEN

We had quite a few serious discussions about giving up our dream of living in New Zealand. We listed all the pros and cons.

"To tell the truth, I like being near New York City," said Frank.

"And I like working in the Sunnyvale Country Store," I said. "But I miss the beaches, the forest, and the meadow terribly, not to mention our friends."

"I miss those also, but I couldn't live with myself if I abandoned my mother right now," replied Frank.

"I understand that," I said, sighing. I ran my finger through my hair knowing what this meant.

"Maybe we'll be able to return eventually." Frank tried to console my worry.

"Yes, but we will have to start our citizenship process all over. Our four months will be up in a week."

"I know, sweetie. Let's sleep on it. I don't want to force you to stay here if you don't want to."

We did sleep on it and in the morning I came to my decision. I also wouldn't be able to live with myself if I forced Frank to return to New Zealand.

We informed Olive Branch and made arrangements for our cottage to be rented to somebody else. Frank went back to pack up our belongings and I took Sean for a quick visit to my parents in Southern California. I needed a break from the dreariness of

February on the East Coast.

John said to me the other day that I am better at dealing with disappointment than he is. And maybe that is why I can stay hopeful. But I don't think it's that simple. I think it's from living a life full of disappointments, but then seeing what good things come next.

A House of Cards

I built this house by hand

It is sturdy

It is messy, very messy

WATCH OUT!

There are broken shards of dreams

on the bathroom floor

But big picture windows

in the living room

look out

on blue skied new goals

* * *

In Southern California it was already spring. I could smell the fragrance of orange blossoms wafting gently through the air. Sean enjoyed the warmer weather, saying, "We don't even need our coats, Mom!"

On this visit home I again got to witness the magic that happens between grandparents and grandchildren. Sean followed my mother around like a puppy and started calling her "Mommy," since he heard me calling her that. She amended that to "Mommy Claire" and the name stuck. And Grandpa Abe was totally smitten. He wrote a letter to the rest of the family saying that Sean was the most remarkable child he'd ever met.

One night right before dinner, we saw my dad trying to sneak past the kitchen. Sean was right behind him, a bowl of something grasped in his little hands. He was walking with a bent-over back and limping on his left leg just like my father.

"Abe! Are you feeding that child right before dinner?" asked my mom in an aggrieved voice.

My dad stopped walking and said with a typical Jewish shrug, "He wanted ice cream. What could I do?" a sheepish grin spreading over his face.

He then claimed to quote Mark Twain that "a grandparent is someone who when asked by his grandchild for a cookie before dinner will invariably answer yes."

"Well, I guess you're a grandparent!" I said laughing.

When we returned to the East Coast it was still the depths of winter. Snow was forecasted for the evening. Sean and I loved the snow, but he desperately needed a nap. I promised him that if it was snowing when he woke up, we would go play in it. Well, he slept for several hours and it did begin to snow. Big, beautiful fluffy snowflakes were falling lazily down from the sky. Intent on keeping my promise, we bundled up, stood under the nearest street lamp, and danced in the snow. We stuck our tongues out to let the snowflakes melt instantly. The evening seemed magical with the glow of the lamplight, the deep blue winter sky, and the white snowflakes softly falling.

CHAPTER TWENTY

One morning in April, we all slept in. When Frank and I woke up we didn't hear a thing. We started to kiss, but then got worried we would get interrupted. We had decided to try for another baby since it seemed we were going to be in the States for a while. Sean was growing up. No longer a baby or even a toddler and my arms were feeling baby-empty. Frank tiptoed out to see if Sean was still asleep.

He came back stifling a laugh and whispering, "He's 'hiding' under the table eating sugar out of the sugar jar." I quickly wiggled out of my nightgown and reached out my arms to my husband. We had all the time in the world to make passionate love. And Sean seemed quite pleased with himself when we finally came out to make breakfast and said nothing about the empty sugar bowl or telltale sprinkles of sugar around his mouth.

All seemed well for a month or two, but then, we got an unwelcome surprise. Mrs. Zafeiriou had apparently enjoyed the peace and quiet while we were away and had been weighing her options.

"I love your 'leetle' boy. But everyday 'boom, boom, boom' down the steps. Eetz too noisy for me."

We couldn't dispute this. Sean did love to jump down the stairs. We tried for a day or two to get him to stop, but it was hopeless.

In fact, Sean did not stop jumping down stairs until he was about thirty years old, thought Brooke.

We told Mrs. Zafeiriou we would move as soon as we could find another place. A friend from the Sunnyvale Country Store urged us to look into the Halle Apartments. These had been built in the 1920s with government money and were kept at very affordable rates. We lucked out! There was an apartment immediately available. This time our friends from Sunnyvale came through and helped us move, along with friends from the pizza shop. We didn't have much stuff, as Mrs. Zafeiriou's apartment had been furnished, so we were moved in within a day. We feasted on leftover pizza and strombolis from the shop to thank our friends and celebrate our new place.

The apartments were charming. There were several units connected by sidewalks. Each unit had a small "pocket lawn" in front. There were plenty of maple and oak trees. The apartments were built at the dead end of Elm Street, which meant there was no through traffic, so it was quite safe for children. An abandoned railway line abutted the other end of the property, which proved a great place to forage for wild edibles. My friends taught me to harvest the fruit of sumac bushes, which makes a vitamin C–rich tea. There were also elderberries. I tried my hand at elderberry jelly and, like Meg in *Little Women*, found it hard to get it to jell, but its syrupy goodness still tasted great on waffles and pancakes.

There was also a small old-fashioned playground with a jungle gym and a couple of swings that Sean and the next-door neighbor boy enjoyed. They were the same age and got along very well. The family was from India and had a great attitude toward children. When they got a little rowdy, they would laugh and say, "Krishna is visiting us!" Sean loved eating their chapatis with ghee and bananas. He came home telling me, "The way we say 'car' in Kanadi is 'vehicle.'"

Inside, one walked directly into a modest living/dining area, followed by a kitchen. Everything was old, but well maintained.

Upstairs were two small bedrooms and a bathroom. There was a tiny bathroom tucked under the stairs on the ground floor. All in all, it fit our needs and our budget.

I had always assumed if I needed help my parents would come through for me, but this had not proven to be the case. During the winter when my mother had asked what she should send for Sean for Christmas, Frank had scribbled in an additional note, "Brooke could use some gloves," to which she had replied, "If Brooke needs some gloves, why doesn't she just buy herself some?"

Truth be told we were very tight on money. Delivering pizzas is a better job for a teen who wants some discretionary money than for an adult trying to support a family. And the Sunnyvale Store closed between Christmas and New Year's. That year I wore socks on my hands.

This is why I try hard not to be like that with Marissa, thought Brooke. *I don't want to be that person. But on the other hand, she has no idea how to live within her means.*

So, there was no point asking my parents for help furnishing the apartment. We scoured the local thrift store and found a serviceable dining room table and chairs. But then we realized how close Princeton is to Malanapan and how common it is for students to leave furniture on the street when they move. We found a great bed for Sean, a futon for us, and even an old sofa. Of course it was a hideous yellow and green tweed, but that meant we could easily let Sean jump on and off it. A few board and brick bookcases, a few milk crates for toys and we were set.

CHAPTER TWENTY-ONE

One afternoon in early July my friend Elsa was visiting. I noticed that my breasts were swollen and feeling very sore. I thought, *Hmm, I wonder if I'm getting my period?* I'd always been irregular and very bad at keeping track. What with moving and all, I had forgotten about trying to get pregnant.

I looked at the nature calendar hanging on the wall that marked my last period. I had to turn back two months. "Elsa, I've got to be pregnant!" I said excitedly. "How could I not have known? Why didn't bells go off in my body? Especially since I've done this before." But I had no morning sickness this time around, so I guess that could explain it.

The next day, I made an appointment with my doctor. Sure enough, I was almost three months pregnant. We were so happy! And I kept assuring myself that the work in the store was so much less strenuous than in the vegetable garden that I should be able to do it.

But it was not to be. One day at the store, the cement floor began to whirl beneath my feet and soon afterward the walls with their country decorations also began to spin. Luckily I managed to sit down right before I fainted. Kathleen came running over.

"Are you alright? You turned white."

I was shaking. "No, I almost fainted and I'm all clammy. I think I need to go home."

"That's okay. Go home and take care of yourself. I'll hold down the fort here," said Kathleen, looking very worried.

I made an appointment to see my doctor the next day. At first he didn't seem very worried, but then I told him that this was the time in my last pregnancy I started bleeding. He turned pale and leaned against the examination table.

"Oh. That's a different story. I think you need to quit your job. Be careful to drink enough water and rest immediately any time you begin to feel tired. It's probably okay for you to take walks as long as you don't overdo it. We want to keep that baby inside you."

Well, this wasn't as bad as I had feared. At least he didn't put me on bed rest. I called the store and explained my situation. Frank was generously offered the job of delivering food again, which helped our finances.

I began sewing little stuffed animals for the new baby. I also now had more time to read than I'd had in a while. I began devouring feminist books, *Of Woman Born* by Adrienne Rich and *The Mother Knot* by Jane Lazarus. These led me to Grace Paley and Tillie Olsen. During my time on bed rest in New Zealand I read a lot of nonviolence theory, earning I suppose my reputation for "an ability to read boring books," as Frank put it. But these subjects weren't boring to me.

I was thrilled when I saw in the Unitarian Universalist Congregational bulletin a group of women was starting a conscious-raising group. I missed out on this before and was very curious. I learned at the first meeting that "they had been so busy working to get the Equal Rights Amendment passed in New Jersey in 1972 and then on other campaigns that they didn't even really know each other."

This is such a common pitfall of organizing, thought Brooke. *I've encountered it again and again. We are so busy working for our causes that we neglect building the relationships that would pull us through hard times, defeats, and setbacks. Kind of like the current state of affairs when it seems as if so many of the things we fought for are being undone. But I refuse to give up! At any rate, that group was so enlightening.*

The women met weekly, usually at the pristine and very bourgeois house of Maud. The white carpets and brocade-covered furniture were a bit intimidating for me. The women were all decades older than me. So it was a rich mix of learning about and from each other. I learned how they couldn't even open up a bank account in their own name without their husband's permission. "And honey, that isn't even the half of it," said Maud. She was a woman in her early fifties, steel gray hair, impeccably coiffed, always dressed in tailored clothes that must have come from some kind of expensive store I had never been in. She continued, "You can't imagine what we went through if we wanted to start a business, get a loan, or rent an apartment!"

Reciprocally, they learned from me about not shaving my legs, the wonders of breastfeeding babies, not identifying as heterosexual, and having an open marriage. Once Lucinda was born, they loved having her attend our meetings, as she would usually sleep quietly in her little removable car seat.

One day Maud announced that she had been approached about being on the mayor's advisory board for women. "Oh, goodness," exclaimed Gretchen. "Isn't that just tokenism?"

"I may be a token, but it gets me on the bus!" laughed Maud.

That sentence has stayed with me these many years, mused Brooke. *It's a kind of pragmatism I admire.*

The women in this group did not just sit around and talk. They were also busy organizing for paid family leave, a cause close to my heart. I learned how to knock on doors and engage people with an issue. We also set up a table in the local mall with a big cake to celebrate the anniversary of New Jersey passing the Equal Rights Amendment. We used this as an excuse to gather signatures on our petitions for paid family leave. The ladies had slyly arranged for the cake to be decorated in red, white, and blue.

Maud laughed in response when I questioned this. "Equal rights for women *is* patriotic!"

"And it keeps the security guards off our backs. Especially when we give them free cake," added Gretchen.

The fact that malls are considered private property and therefore there is no guarantee of free speech in them is still a problem, thought Brooke. *They function like the commons. It makes organizing efforts difficult.*

CHAPTER TWENTY-TWO

One day when I was about four months' pregnant a letter came from Jake. *Jake!* He was exploring intentional communities around the world. Could he come and visit? And would we be interested in joining him for a trip to one of the most successful communes on the East Coast—Black Mountain Farm, near Asheville, North Carolina?

Yes. And yes. Frank's work was interested in networking with other like-minded folks and I could go along for free. There was even room for Sean up in the cab with us. My breath was shallow and faster than normal just thinking about Jake. Someplace near my solar plexus was fluttering. It would be good to see him again.

Jake arrived mid-August. We would stay up late talking and touching after Sean and then Frank went to bed. Jake had a way of giving intense attention that was very seductive. His touch was gentle and he seemed a bit in awe of my slightly rounded belly, bigger breasts, and darker nipples.

After about a week we had all the plans for our road trip. My pregnancy was more stable by now and my doctor gave me the go-ahead for the field trip. We would camp along the way, and Frank would contact food co-ops and organic markets to build his network. We were taking Sunnyvale honey, jams, and applesauce for people to sample and hopefully stock in their stores.

At my first glimpse of the Blue Ridge Mountains I suddenly understood the name for these old, weathered, worn-down mountains—so different from the Sierra Nevadas I grew up with. They actually *did* look blue! The weather was that beastly East Coast humid until we reached the Skyline Parkway. Then there were blessedly cool breezes in the evening. We were camping in a magical place aptly called Floating Heaven, outside Roanoke, Virginia.

It was very cozy with all of us in one tent. I felt surrounded by the people I loved. Jake would get up early in the morning to make coffee for everyone. Frank would cook breakfast over the Coleman stove, and I would cook supper. Sean loved being in the campgrounds. We took five days to get to Black Mountain Farm, which is about twenty-five miles from Asheville, near Black Mountain.

The road got more and more winding as we bypassed Ashville and approached the farm. The hills were a deep lush green, so different from the way the hills of California turn brown in the summer.

"Is this the community of our dreams?" I wondered as we approached. There were small outbuildings housing the various crafts they produced and residences that varied from typical ranch-style suburban brick houses to log cabins, a tepee, and a yurt. All nestled at the foot of lush green hills.

I had always thought I needed the ocean to be happy, but the mountains gave a very similar feeling of unbounded natural beauty.

During our tour several things happened. While walking from the children's building toward the dining hall, emerging from woods along a sawdust-covered trail, I caught a glimpse of a high pasture glowing green in the afternoon sun. *Oh*, I thought. *I could get attached to that view.* It was a thought I had never had anywhere in the United States since returning from New Zealand.

Listening to the many ways this community organized work and community decision-making was inspiring. They had more systems in place than Olive Branch. I wanted to learn more.

But hearing about their strict restrictions on how many children could live in the community, I regretfully decided this was not the community for us, even if we could figure out something for Grandma Alice.

I had enjoyed our stay there, as had Frank and even Sean, who made friends with Jose, a little boy just his age, immediately. They had taken one look at each other and walked off together to play in a sandbox. Wistfully, I looked back on the sheds holding the various craft shops, the herb garden, and the deep green hills as we made our way back to New Jersey. Jake stayed on at Black Mountain Farm. That seemed appropriate to me, even though I would miss him. I knew that my life was with Frank and Sean. They were my sustenance, while Jake was like a delicious decadent dessert.

CHAPTER TWENTY-THREE

Back in Manalapan I joined a "free university" class for pregnant women, called Nine Essential Exercises for the Childbearing Year. When I went into Princeton to purchase the book with the same title, I had a disturbing experience that stayed with me all these years later.

The young woman at the cash register saw my book, looked me over, and said, "Ugh. Isn't it creepy to be pregnant; like another being has taken over your body?" I was so taken aback that I don't even remember if I said anything back to her. In those days it was still difficult for me to speak up on my own behalf, especially when I was caught off guard.

I guess this is how some women feel, mused Brooke. *But it's not a great thing to say to someone who is pregnant. Maybe ask what it's like for them. I've learned over the years to ask more questions and try to approach issues with a sense of curiosity. But that's only been since my sixties. I guess I should let that young woman off the hook,* she thought, smiling ruefully.

It was good to be in a class with other pregnant women, especially after that encounter at the bookstore. I became good friends with Pat, the teacher, who was just a couple of years older than me and also pregnant. There were about ten women in the class and we all got together after our babies were born.

One surprise was that Pat and I had picked very similar names for our babies even though we had never discussed names. My new little girl was Lucinda, meaning "illumination" in Latin. Lucinda was the mythological Roman goddess of childbirth and giver of first light to newborns. Pat's new little girl was named Lena, meaning "torch," "bright," or "ray of light" from the Persian.

Hearing everyone's birth stories was quite a roller-coaster ride of empathy, disbelief, and envy. One tiny woman had twenty hours of labor and a forceps delivery as her baby, Lucille, had a huge head. But another woman meditated on an image of a waterfall while she gave birth. As someone who once again "read all the books" but hollered my way through childbirth anyway, I found this hard to believe. But perhaps the birth that left me speechless with envy was the young woman who "felt a little queasy" as she went to take her last exam, thinking, "Maybe it was that McDonald's egg and cheese biscuit she had eaten for breakfast," only to realize she was in labor. Forty-five minutes later she gave birth!

Life just isn't fair; it just isn't, Brooke thought as she recalled these stories.

CHAPTER TWENTY-FOUR

Lucinda was a completely different baby from Sean from the very start. While he had been mellow, she made her wishes known vociferously. When she was three days old, I picked her up to nurse her, but as she was completely soaked, I decided to change her diaper first. Oh my goodness, this tiny being screamed so loudly that she turned as red as a tomato down to the soles of her feet. "Well, you are sure of your own little self," I said to her, laughing. Everyone told me my next one would be a screamer and I guess they were right.

I'm glad she was my second child. I was much more relaxed with her, having had the experience of watching a baby grow into a child with resilience despite bumps and bruises.

We took her back to Mrs. Zafeiriou and said, "See, she is a girl and looks like her daddy."

We had noticed that Grandma Alice had seemingly lost her vitality after Lenny's death. We were hoping that a new baby would revive her. She did buy the basic diapers, sleepers, and receiving blankets for Lucinda. That seemed to revive her a bit.

And she was enthralled to see Lucinda nurse. "She knows just what to do!" she said delightedly when Luci nuzzled into nursing with gusto.

Alice's generosity was a contrast to my own mother. I remember how my mother huffed, "I would have done that if she hadn't," about the basic baby supplies that Alice bought. Yet she arrived empty-handed. Later, when my father came for a visit, she asked what I needed, but when I told her "Some sleepers with feet because the baby keeps pulling off her socks!" she whined, "I wouldn't know what size to get."

"I could tell you what size," I said, but no answer and no clothes.

In person she was a huge help, though! She cooked, cleaned, and played hide-and-go-seek with Sean for hours. Generous with her time if not her money.

Sighing, Brooke thought, *I aspire to be both.*

My mom even baked a special cake for Lucinda's welcoming ceremony that we held in our home. I borrowed symbols from the Jewish and Christian sides of our families and incorporated language from the Unitarians Universalists. We lit candles to wish that she would embody the illumination that is the meaning of her name. We drank wine to turn sweetness into joy. We washed her feet, as our ancestors Abraham and Jesus had washed feet, as a symbol of our love for her. We broke bread together to commit as a small community to help nurture and guide her through her life. And we anointed her forehead with scented oil to signify the holiness of each new life. Grandma Alice loved the Stephen Gaskin quote, "When a child is born, the entire universe has to shift to make room."

But then she seemed to succumb to a lack of interest in life in general. She wasn't eating much and her physical health began to deteriorate along with her mental health.

We had been debating what to do when we got a call from the police that a neighbor had called when she didn't open her door. They found she had died, apparently peacefully in her sleep. We were simultaneously heartbroken and relieved.

"Poor Alice. Her whole life was tied up with Lenny's life," I sighed as I went through her clothes, preparing what to donate.

"Well, at least she got to see her two grandchildren," Frank responded.

"And she died without pain," I added.

We buried her next to her beloved Lenny and allowed ourselves some time to grieve. But now, we had no compelling reason to stay in Manalapan. I began to dream of returning to New Zealand. Frank was not as keen to leave the United States again.

"We'll have to start our citizenship process all over," he said. "Why don't you write Susan and see what she thinks? Things may have changed since we left."

Two letters came within days of each other that changed our lives. The first was from Susan.

CHAPTER TWENTY-FIVE

Susan wrote:

I don't advise that you come back to Olive Branch. The community is in turmoil. The founding members are afraid the younger generation will not take care of them. And the younger generation don't trust the founders to continue the services like childcare now that they don't need it themselves. It looks like all that will be held in common is the land. We're closing the communal dining room. I'm not even sure if I will stay here.

My heart sank reading these words. As much as I loved the landscape of New Zealand, I loved communal living more. Was it worth going halfway around the world for beaches and forests?

While we were still pondering Susan's message, another letter arrived. It was from Laura at Black Mountain Farm.

Dear Frank and Brooke,

I am writing from the Children's Council to officially invite you to apply for membership in our community. Your children Sean and Lucinda are just the right ages for our two small children's groups. Sean would fit in with Jose and Nigel. And Lucinda is almost the same age as Topaz and Sunshine.

You would be sponsored by the Children's Council as provisional members for the first six months of living here and then the members will give input and come to a consensus on full membership.

Please let us know if you are interested at your earliest convenience as we are also reaching out to other families who have visited in the past year.

Looking forward to hearing from you.

Warmly,

Laura

for the Children's Council

"Oh my goodness, Frank. This is amazing! Even though people told us to go ahead and apply for an exception to their child rules, I didn't want to do that. They had severe limits on how many children could live in the commune. Members even had to ask permission to get pregnant. But this! This is asking us to come because of our children! I think it's fate," I said excitedly.

"It seems like a really good chance for us!" replied Frank.

I was almost in a dreamlike state thinking we could live communally in a beautiful rural setting, where our whole family was welcomed and seen as an asset.

Even though we had made friends in Malanapan, living as an isolated nuclear family had never been our dream. Frank gave notice to Sunnyvale and I began to pack.

And this closes one part of our life and another opens, thought Brooke as she wrote those words.

CHAPTER TWENTY-SIX

Brooke sat down to begin writing again.

Have I left out anything important from the time in Malanapan? Maybe I should include that poetry anthology I volunteered on when Lucinda was a baby? It did help me keep my sanity as a stay-at-home mother.

Or maybe the Three Mile Island protest? Yes, that's a bit more compelling, she thought.

When Lucinda was about three months old it was the anniversary of the Three Mile Island near nuclear disaster. I remembered listening to my dad on the phone when the news broke that there had been a partial meltdown of the nuclear reactor in Pennsylvania. My father recalled an incident in the past that he'd been intimately involved with.

"I was working on the Cobalt machine that delivered radiation to cancer patients. We were always afraid that radiation would escape from our lab, so we often had Geiger counters with us. These are handheld devices that can detect radiation. One day we were taking a break and throwing around a baseball when the Gieger counter started going crazy. We got really worried and went back to the lab to check if there were any leaks. Nothing. We went back outside and again got high readings of radioactivity."

"What was it?" I asked.

"We finally figured out that there had been above-ground

nuclear testing a few days before in New Mexico and it had rained in Chicago. The rain had left a residue of radioactive material on the surfaces outside."

"Oh my goodness, what did you do?"

"Well, we tried to alert the Nuclear Regulatory Commission, but they didn't want to 'alarm the public,' so they did nothing," he said in disgust.

"Then we tried going to the press. We had simple suggestions like that pregnant women should stay indoors for a day or two, and people who came directly in contact with outdoor surfaces, such as window washers, should be warned, but to no avail. No one would carry the story," he sighed.

"That's awful," I said.

"Yes. But it led to the founding of the Concerned Scientists organization and together with the Ban the Bomb ladies, we did get that nuclear testing stopped.

"But I hear the same lies coming out of the mouths of officials now," he continued. "No need to 'alarm the public,' therefore not even minimal precautions are being taken." Another deep sigh. "We had such hopes that a peaceful use for splitting the atom had been found. These people are sweating bullets on TV as they're lying through their teeth about what's going on at Three Mile Island."

That conversation stayed with me. So when my friend Elsa invited me to go with a bunch of antinuclear protesters to Three Mile Island, I said yes. I packed an ample diaper bag and snacks for Sean and we got on the bus from New Jersey to PA.

It was a pleasant spring day and Lucinda was very content to be held and nursed with no distracted mama trying to get laundry or other chores done. Sean liked riding buses and seeing lots of people.

We just had to make sure he didn't wander off. Elsa's little one was still in a stroller, but kept throwing down his bottle or pulling off his shoes and throwing them down while we were marching. This led to the famous chant, "No nukes, no shoes, no bottle!" which Sean enthusiastically joined at every opportunity.

It was the first time I'd been to a demonstration as a mom. I found out that kids are great to have with you. I got interviewed by a local public television station just because of my cute children. And I do think that thinking about future generations is such an important message in peace, justice, and environmental work. I didn't feel bad at all for my children being used as props. Later I had some qualms, but not that day.

Much later, thought Brooke. *I loved when Lucinda was on the front page of the* Asheville Gazette *with her golden curls and her cute red pinafore drinking a cup of "million-dollar" lemonade when we were protesting Reagan's "Star Wars" missile defense boondoggle. Our motto was "SDI- lemon in the sky." I hadn't planned on her drinking the lemonade, it was just one of our props, along with an umbrella that had 25 percent of its surface cut out in little holes to demonstrate the ridiculous system. But it was a hot day and she was thirsty. It made for good street theater. Only way later did I question this use of my children in this way. My friend Becky raised the issue.*

"I'm not sure it's fair to our children to use them for photo opportunities at demonstrations," she said. "If they didn't choose to be there with us it's a kind of exploitation."

"Well, I never thought of it that way," I replied.

"I'll have to give this some thought. On the one hand, I think involving them in political activities can be empowering. On the other, just bringing them in the hope they will boost our appeal *is* probably exploitative."

CHAPTER TWENTY-SEVEN

We rented a small trailer to haul our stuff to Black Mountain Farm. We would each have our own small room in the community. The children would sleep in the children's house most nights, depending on how they did.

I couldn't believe our good fortune! Although Frank was a good husband and did more than his share of the house cleaning and was also a good cook, I felt stifled as a stay-at-home mother. We couldn't afford daycare for both children. As it was, I had bartered my labor for Sean's nursery school.

At Black Mountain Farm I could pick multiple work areas and arrange my own preferred schedule. Frank also looked forward to being in a group of like-minded people, learning new skills such as woodworking, and having folks to play music with. And truth be told, I think we were both intrigued by the idea that at Black Mountain we could live openly as a non- monogamous couple.

With our own rooms and other people who signed up to be one-on-one adults with our children during some of the evenings, we each found some other partners. It was very liberating.

One of my relationships was with one of the very few African Americans living in the community. The first thing that attracted me to him was a very thoughtful position paper he had posted on the community bulletin board. I'm always attracted to thoughtful people. The second was he walked with a bounce in his step. I still thought this denoted optimism, which might have been true in his case, but it's no guarantee. And it turned out, he was attracted to me.

I remember asking him if it was hard living in such a "white community."

"What do you mean?" he asked sarcastically. "Like they should play more Motown music over the loudspeakers in the dining room?"

"Well, that would be a start," I answered.

Sometimes an affirmation is revealed in a denial.

We didn't talk much about race, but did share differences in our families. I learned that everyone in his family had a nickname. His was JR. No one used his given name of James. Most people didn't even know what it was.

The first time we slept together, I was shocked by the texture of his hair. It felt magical that his hair could have that same thick, soft consistency as the lambs I had loved at Olive Branch. I was way too embarrassed to say anything about that, as I knew the expression "wooly headed" was used in a derogatory manner throughout the South. But I loved the texture of his hair. I worried that this made me racist.

And maybe this will offend people, thought Brooke. *I know African Americans do not want random strangers coming up to them and touching their hair or even asking if they can touch their hair. I even read a book with the title* Don't Touch My Hair! *But for me, in an intimate relationship it was kind of like how Jake marveled over my curls. It's part of falling in love with someone, I think, to fall in love with their particular attributes.*

JR seemed to like the contrast in our skin tones. Sometimes he would hum "Ebony and Ivory" by Stevie Wonder when we lay in bed with our legs and fingers entwined.

That optimistic song seems needed now more than ever, mused Brooke, *now that we have a president who came into power by fanning the flames of racism.*

Even though there was a lot of passion in our relationship, it didn't last. I wanted more conversation and that seemed to push JR away.

I'm always wanting more conversation it seems, even with John. And we've been together now for over seven years. But at least it doesn't drive him away. He just says, "I'll have to think about that" when he isn't ready to talk. And I've gotten more accepting of differences.

Getting the children settled into this new life had its ups and downs. I had worried that even though Lucinda was on the verge of walking before we moved, the change would set her back, but it was the exact opposite. The first day we arrived, all of a sudden she lurched across the entire main room of the children's building.

Come to think of it, maybe it was because it wasn't strewn with toys the way our living room was, wondered Brooke as she reminisced.

The childcare at Black Mountain was complicated. On the one hand there were amazing folks working with the children, like Laura, a trained Montessori teacher. Laura also practiced a kind of active listening inspired by Haim Ginot and used the PET (Parent Effectiveness Training) to build a system based on respect.

But there were others on the team who leaned toward authoritarian methods of childrearing that seemed totally antithetical to the values and practices of the community. I realized that if I wanted to have both a say and some influence, I would need to work in the children's program more heavily than I had anticipated.

One of my pet peeves was the folks who insisted the children eat whatever was put in front of them and if they didn't, it got held over to the next meal.

"It's the height of hypocrisy," I argued at our weekly meeting, waving my hands in the air.

"I cook a dinner a week for the whole community and have to

leave some aside for our adult member who doesn't like onions, and make sure to remember that Sue doesn't like raisins, not to mention the no dairy, no eggs, no cinnamon folks."

In fact, one time Frank put out a pot of hot water labeled "no onions, no eggs, no dairy, no raisins, no meat, no sugar, no cinnamon" just as a joke.

"Well, we are trying to raise less picky eaters," retorted Brenda. And that was that as far as she was concerned. That ended the official conversation.

But one of the other caregivers, Starship, pulled me aside, saying, "Sign up to do afternoon shifts with me. I never let the children go hungry. Nor do I force them to eat something they don't like."

And sure enough, he would quietly put the cold congealed scrambled eggs in the compost and ask the children what they wanted for a snack. The choices were all healthy, like peanut butter and jelly on homemade wheat bread, popcorn with nutritional yeast, or homemade yogurt with homemade granola. No one starved. No one ate unhealthily and the children's wishes were respected.

I learned that sometimes it's better not to make an issue of something if it's within your power to quietly fix it.

Overall, the children seemed happy and mostly well adjusted. Except Nigel. That boy's head was in the stratosphere. One time I found him on a second-story porch that had no railing claiming, "I can jump off this point and fly!"

I tried reasoning with him, but he was stubborn. He was also too chunky for me to pick him up and carry him down a flight of rickety stairs. So, I said, "Fine. I'm leaving now. If you fall and crack your head open it will be your responsibility."

And I walked down the stairs hoping against hope that he

wouldn't jump.

Now, if this were a fictional account, it would be very dramatic to have the child jump and have to live with that guilt the rest of her life, thought Brooke. *But, I'm trying to write a truthful account. I'm filled with gratitude that he didn't jump and a bit appalled that I took that chance.*

Another time I was making the boys' lunches once they started going to the cooperative school down the road. Nigel's dad, Bill, came into the kitchen and started yelling at me.

"Nigel says his lunches are shit! He can't eat them! You never pack anything he likes and he even had Laura fill out his index card with his favorite foods."

Bill had a reputation for being difficult. I just looked at him and handed him Nigel's food preference card.

"Stones, dirt, sticks, bugs."

"He's right. I don't pack what he requested," I said dryly.

Bill quieted down.

"I try to find foods the boys like. As you know, our resources are limited. There is no separate budget for their lunches. I have to make do with what I can find. Today they are getting leftover macaroni and cheese, carrot sticks, and watermelon cubes. Macaroni and cheese is Jose's favorite. If Nigel can get me a reasonable list of foods he likes, I'll be happy to include them in the rotation."

Bill couldn't quite get himself to apologize, but shrugged and said, "Well, thanks for trying."

Whew, I was glad when he left. I found myself shaking after that encounter.

My other work was more satisfying. I loved making herb sachets that we sold in town and at craft fairs, along with our scented candles and macramé plant holders. I was hopeless at macramé, but decent with the other crafts. Once summer came along, I signed up to harvest food from the garden for the cooks. This was the best! I got to work in the garden but didn't have to get up early.

I also did one laundry shift a week, which was a pleasant, meditative job, as we hung out the laundry, weather permitting. It could be done at any time during one's twenty-four-hour assignment. I loved the flexibility of having a variety of work at hours that fit my late-night rhythm.

Cooking dinner for the entire community was challenging. Besides all the food preferences, there truly was a limited variety of raw materials, especially in the winter. Once I had come in for my shift planning to make spaghetti only to find no onions in the pantry.

"How am I supposed to make spaghetti sauce with no onions?" I yelled out loud, waving my hands in the air, not thinking anyone was around.

"I'm sorry. I really try hard to have basic foods stocked," said Frisco, the food manager, who had appeared out of nowhere.

Boy, did I feel bad. Frisco was a sweet soul.

"The veggie delivery was delayed," he continued.

"It's okay, Frisco. I found some potatoes and carrots. I can make a nice stew with these and our own tofu," I said, nervously twirling a finger through my hair. After that I was careful not to complain out loud in the kitchen.

"Oh, yeah," Frank said, laughing.

"Frisco is always hanging around eavesdropping. The same thing happened to me last Saturday when I was making breakfast for the community. There wasn't any granola to put out. But that wasn't really his fault. The team was behind on their production."

"The other thing I can't understand is why I always end up cooking with Peter," I said to Laura one day. "He's very hard to work with, so critical and impatient."

"The reason you always end up with Peter is because everyone else writes 'not with Peter' on their work assignment sheets that go to the work manager," answered Laura.

"What? That seems so un-communitarian!"

Laura just shrugged. "I guess you'll be cooking with Peter then."

There was one good thing that Peter taught me, though. "Make a meal you like, how you like it, so that way you know at least one person liked it."

Frisco, Starship, Topaz, Sunshine. This community loved odd names as much as I did. They even named their vehicles and buildings. I felt right at home, although the little ones couldn't pronounce my name and called me "Book." Then they would make jokes by holding a picture book and saying, "I'm holding you, Book," and laugh.

Frank got inspired one summer evening to change his name. "I'm going to change my name to Firefly," he said.

"I like it. It fits you. You do tend to bring light into dark situations with your sense of humor," I answered as we watched the fireflies flitting about on the summer lawn.

"I'm going to catch you in a jar," joked Sean.

"Fiware fwei?" asked Lucinda.

The name stuck for quite some time.

CHAPTER TWENTY-EIGHT

Holidays at Black Mountain Farm were always a big deal and followed my own pagan leanings. We had a huge bonfire on the fall equinox, Yule logs at Christmas, painted eggs and delicious brunch at the spring equinox, and wild parties for the summer solstice. We also had many dances to celebrate almost any occasion. I can still hear all the guys shouting out along with the Stones, "You make a grown man cry-aye! You make a grown man cry-aye!"

Oh, those were fun times! A room filled with long-haired, bearded men in skirts, women in flimsy dresses and tank tops, unshaven armpits, kids dressed however they wanted, all rocking out to great music. You just jumped right in. No waiting for a partner or to be asked to dance. Flowing in and out with anyone and everyone.

"Eh, too much 'cock rock' for my taste," said my friend Lisa.

"Oh, I guess I just don't care as long as there is a good beat," I answered.

I'm still like that. I give a lot of passes to music that can get me up and dancing, or even rocking out in my wheelchair.

So why was I so internally judgmental when Marissa wanted to go out dancing with friends? Was it because there was drinking involved? Like there wasn't drinking at Black Mountain? Because she might come home with a guy? Like I wasn't experimenting with multiple partners? We elders forget what we were like when we were young.

But as much as I liked Black Mountain Farm and as much as I

learned there, I ended up leaving. It was all because of a dog. The community had a strict limit on how many dogs could live there. But we kept making exceptions for new members that we liked who insisted they had to bring their dog. Kind of like how the community dealt with children. There were already too many dogs for my liking. They ran in a pack, disturbed the chickens, tore up the flowerbeds, and left poop on the trails.

And then prospective member Tim arrived with a dog.

"Please make an exception to your dog rule for Goldie. She's getting old and I can't find another home for her," he wrote in his application for membership.

The dog lovers rallied around him. As did the plumbing crew, because Tom was a certified plumber. And we were always short on people who could fix our antiquated systems. I was opposed. But I was in the minority.

So Tim arrived with Goldie. It turned out that Goldie was losing her sight and her hearing. This made her snappish. I was terrified she would bite one of the children. I brought up the issue with the Children's Council. We were divided.

"Let's just make sure that Goldie is nowhere near the children's building or the main dining room," suggested Starship.

"But our children go all over the community," objected Laura, who was on my side.

"But we let Tim join along with Goldie," said Brenda.

"What about if Goldie is limited to Singing House"—the adult-only residence—"and its enclosed yard?" suggested Lisa.

We agreed to that proposal and brought it to the general meeting.

"This just seems really unfair!" protested Tim. "Goldie can't help it that she's nervous."

"But the safety of our children is also important," pointed out Laura, speaking for the Children's Council.

"The landscaping crew likes this idea," said Lisa, who served on that crew.

All the other dog owners opposed the measure, but it passed. Quiet was restored for a time. But then one day, Goldie escaped. She ended up in the main courtyard and bit a visitor who did not know how to approach her.

The matter came up again at the general meeting.

"I propose that Tim find a safer place for Goldie, off the farm," said Laura.

"What if that had been one of the children? Some of them are too young to be taught how to safely approach her," she continued.

"If Goldie leaves, then I leave," threatened Tim, standing up abruptly.

"How about if we just be extra careful to keep her confined to Singing House and that yard," offered Starship.

That proposal passed with a small majority.

I just couldn't live with that decision. It had always been challenging for me to know there were people who cared more about their dogs than the children, and this just poured salt into that festering wound. I decided to leave the community.

Firefly wanted to stay. We had been growing apart. I wasn't always happy with his childrearing ways. Sometimes I thought he was not attentive enough to the children. And he would try to motivate them with promises of sweets if they would clean up their toys, a practice I considered bribery. I had also been promised sweets as a child, and that had set me up to "reward" myself with sweets in an unhealthy way.

I'm sure he wasn't happy with my nagging. I had lots of demands. "Play Uno with Sean when he wants. Tell Lucinda a bedtime story about whatever she wants, or read the same storybook over and over, even if it *is* boring."

"Are you even listening to me? Or do you just nod and say okay and then do whatever you want?" I stormed at him several times.

We decided to separate. It was a very amicable separation. We divided our meager possessions and wrangled over who would have the kids when.

We agreed it would be less disruptive for them to stay at Black Mountain Farm during the week. I would come to visit with Lucinda on Monday and with Sean on Wednesday, and I would pick them up on Friday to spend weekends with me once I got settled in Asheville.

I think we deluded ourselves that this would have minimal impact on the children, mused Brooke. The pictures of them before and after our divorce tell a different story. They looked so happy before. And then there is something like a shadow of sadness on their faces after. Sigh. Some things we can't change or take back. It is a regret of mine that pursuing my own happiness and feeling of freedom impacted them so badly. I know they were both hesitant to enter into serious relationships all through their twenties, maybe because of this.

MAY

"People speak of hope as if it is this delicate, ephemeral thing made of whispers and spider's webs. It's not. Hope has dirt on her face, blood on her knuckles, the grit of the cobblestones in her hair, and just spat out a tooth as she rises for another go."
—Matthew @CrowsFault

CHAPTER TWENTY-NINE

But, move I did. I found a cute little house in a working-class neighborhood of Asheville. The house was a sage green with the perfect front porch to sit in and watch the world go by. There were azalea bushes bordering the front lawn and a dogwood tree by the front door.

Many hippies and activists lived in the neighborhood, as evidenced by the brightly colored houses, yard signs for progressive causes, and clothes hanging on clotheslines in backyards.

It was walking distance to downtown and a five-minute drive to the Blue Ridge Mountains that surround Asheville.

The rent was reasonable and my part of our savings covered the first month. I borrowed money from my folks for the security deposit and began to job hunt.

I was very excited that the local Peace and Justice Center had an opening for a staff person. I applied but did not get the job. During the interview, one of the board members asked me if I didn't think it was a concern that I was so new in town. I allowed that this could be seen as a drawback. And because of this, they didn't hire me.

I learned a very valuable lesson: never admit anything about you or your experience is a drawback when applying for a job.

In that instance, I wished I had said something like, "Being new to town is an asset. No one has any history or preconceived notions about you. That was the advantage Martin Luther King had when he arrived in Montgomery, Alabama. And because of that, he was able to organize the whole community."

No experience? You bring a fresh perspective! Older? You bring your experience! Disabled? You are an expert on inclusion. Never admit to a drawback. Single mother with several children? You have amazing managerial skills.

I did get hired to do landscaping and I volunteered to teach Sunday school at the local Unitarian congregation. This meant I got free membership and the kids got another community. My needs were modest, so I managed to scrape by, especially after adding a housemate to help with the rent.

That first year was hard, but several opportunities arose afterward. First, I was asked to direct the Sunday school—a modestly paid position. I did not feel qualified, but everyone around me thought I'd be great. My guiding principle that first year was to think about what I wanted from an education director and do that. I ended up giving teachers materials, ideas, lesson plans, and lots of leeway to use their own creativity.

I also set up weekly meetings for teachers to each share a success. This facilitated peer learning and reduced the complaints that can overwhelm any meeting. I limited the complaints to one teacher each time who could pose a problem and we would all brainstorm solutions.

I thought I had trained them well to focus on the positive and learn from each other's successes. But the only time I couldn't be there, I asked one of the teachers to lead the meeting. When I returned I was presented with a yard-long list of complaints. Old habits die hard, thought Brooke.

As tensions between the Soviet Union and the U.S. rose and nuclear treaty talks stalled, I got frustrated.

"What the hell are they thinking, these men in power? It'd be a good idea to blow us all up?" I fumed, throwing pots and pans around the kitchen.

"There's a meeting to form a nuclear freeze group happening at the Peace and Justice Center this Thursday," remarked my housemate, Lynn, in a kind of dry nonchalant tone of voice.

I've wondered over the years how much of that suggestion was due to her shared concern about the issue and how much was motivated by a desire for quiet. It doesn't really matter; it got me to the Peace and Justice Center.

So putting aside my resentment about not being hired there as staff, I went to the meeting. I found a wonderful group of volunteers who quickly decided on actions and divided the work. No drama, no egos, just an earnest group of concerned people working together.

"Who will design the flier?"

"I will."

"Who will write the press release?"

Another hand goes up.

"We need to set up at the park."

"Happy to do that."

I volunteered to get speakers for our first action and a teach-in at a local park. I already knew my Unitarian minister would join, and she put me in touch with the local *Pax Christi* Catholics, who suggested we also invite the Baha'i community. We had a Japanese lantern–making activity for children, petitions and postcards for folks to sign, speakers, and music.

During this time, the board of the Peace and Justice Center noticed that the staff person they hired never seemed to be where they were supposed to be. And that those of us volunteering were doing all the work. They ended up quietly firing the current person and offered me the job. It was a sweet moment. As staff, I was on the lookout for more volunteers.

That is how I recruited Harold to the Peace and Justice Center. It wasn't a hard sell at all. He was looking to get involved in progressive politics. He arrived at the event and asked someone, "Who organized this?"

"They pointed out a small café au lait woman," he recalled.

"And you are like a delicious bar of milk chocolate," I answered. Tall, with close-cropped natural African American hair, fine features, and wearing wire-rim glasses, Harold was a good-looking man.

We got to talking and I found out he had canvassed for Concerned Citizens and wanted to volunteer. Excellent!

As we worked together, I noticed how competent, intelligent, and attractive he was. But he was much younger than me. Would he even be interested in me? One day, I wore a forties-style sundress to work, black with a pattern of small sunflowers and small green buttons running down the front. My neighbor had given this dress to me. It fit my curves perfectly and for once, I thought I looked good. Harold happened to come in that day.

"Wow! You look beautiful!" he said.

"Thank you," I answered, smiling to myself, thinking, *Maybe there's a chance after all.* That night at home I mulled over the exchange. *It can't hurt to ask him out. The worst thing that can happen is he'll say no.*

The next time Harold was in the office I took a deep breath and said, trying to sound casual, "Hey, would you like to go out to dinner sometime?" *Ugh, so awkward.*

But he said, "Sure. How about this Thursday?"

"Yes. That works," I said, heart pounding.

He took me out to a restaurant I had never been to. It was clear we were both nervous as could be, startling at every little sound. When the waiter handed me the wine menu and I said I didn't drink, Harold looked abashed. "My mom doesn't drink either," he said. "She thinks drink is the work of the devil."

"Well, I don't believe in the devil, so go ahead and order yourself something," I said, trying to be gracious. Even though I didn't approve of alcohol on the grounds that it impairs judgment.

Then came the dinner menu. It was all meat entrees. Perhaps reading something from my face Harold asked, "You're not vegetarian, are you?"

"Well, yes, I am, but I'm sure I can find something to eat."

Poor guy, he looked unhappy. "I should have guessed. A lot of the white women I went to college with were vegetarian. I never really understood it."

"You had no way of knowing that. I actually love macaroni and cheese."

I ordered a salad and a side of macaroni and cheese.

Once the food came, dinner went really well. I found out Harold was also interested in joining the Unitarian congregation. He'd left his mother's Baptist Church that he grew up in in Asheville.

Harold explained, "Once I went to college, I became much more of a free thinker. I still believe in some kind of Creator, but I'm not even sure I'm a Christian anymore. I don't like the way Christianity was used to keep my people docile for so long. Although I also know it helped sustain us through hard times. I'm interested in exploring other religions."

"Sounds like the Unitarian Universalist congregation might be just what you're looking for," I answered. "It's a nice, caring community also."

After dinner, he asked if I wanted to go dancing, but I had to bake cookies for a Peace and Justice Center bake sale.

"I'd love to help with that," he said smiling.

"Wow, thanks," I said, thinking what a nice guy he was.

Hmm… first and last time he ever helped me bake, thought Brooke.

After the cookies were done, I was thinking, *That went pretty well. Maybe I'll ask him out to lunch next week,* when he leaned in for a kiss. This took me totally by surprise!

"Don't you want a boyfriend?" asked Harold.

"Well, yes, but I had thought to take it slow," I answered.

He shook his head, smiling. "You are an exceptional woman. I told a friend about you. He encouraged me to ask you out. I hadn't quite gotten around to it when *you* asked *me* out. I think this is my lucky day."

"Well, this changes things," I said shakily.

I sensed this now had a potential for being serious. I wondered what it would be like to be an interracial couple in this supposedly liberal, but still Southern town.

The first time we went to bed, we spent hours telling our histories to each other. We shared a middle-class background, but Harold had three sisters, a brother, and a close extended family, most of whom lived nearby.

When we finally made love I shook from my insides out, like a leaf in the wind. The thought that this could become something serious, when I had perhaps been deluding myself that I just wanted a casual relationship, took me by surprise. My last thought before falling asleep in Harold's arms was, *I think I could love this man.*

CHAPTER THIRTY

I now had two part-time, poorly paid but enormously satisfying jobs. All I needed were a few more friends.

Enter Rachel. One day a small woman with unruly brown hair came into the Peace and Justice Center office.

"Hi. I'm Rachel. I read your last newsletter and wanted to meet you. I'd like to volunteer. I have experience doing community organizing in California."

The answer to my hope for both more help in the office and a friend! We had so much in common. Rachel's oldest child was the same age as Sean, her middle daughter close in age to Lucinda, and she had a toddler also. Rachel shared not only my political values but also my childrearing values. Maybe they go together, being based on respect for all and a healthy disregard for any kind of authoritarianism.

And now, forty years later, we're still friends. We've been through so much together. I wonder if young folks know how important it is to find good solid friends that share your values and see you through the hard times. Folks you can call up and talk to no matter what is going on. We've spent every Thanksgiving together for all these years. Up until the pandemic, that is.

Thanksgiving at Rachel's was a different experience from how I grew up. In my family my mother did all the work. Here everyone brought a dish to share. Rachel would always invite a large group of people and be especially thoughtful to invite anyone she came across who had nowhere to go.

There was the traditional turkey, dressing, and gravy, but also a huge green salad, homemade mashed potatoes, which was my specialty, along with homemade cranberry sauce and raw cranberry relish, also my specialty, Indian biryani rice, roasted root vegetables, pecan and pumpkin pies, and Rachel's poached pears.

Before we ate, Rachel would invite anyone who wanted to share a blessing from their tradition. Then we would go around the table and share something we were grateful for. And then sing several rousing choruses of a gratitude song, with harmonies, arms waving in the air "conducting," and much table pounding.

After dinner we'd sing folk songs. Some people would disappear for a while and come back a bit "pungent."

I remember one Thanksgiving in particular. There were such interesting conversations happening all around the room.

"I went to a world peace conference a few weeks ago. It was so inspiring!" said Betty, eyes shining. "There were people from around the world and the Dalai Lama sent a videotaped message!"

"Wow, that does sound amazing," replied Terry.

In another corner of the room Harold and Micah were discussing how to integrate environmental concerns into urban planning.

"It's important to make bike paths," Micah said excitedly.

"Yes. Absolutely. And I'm working with counties across the country to build low-income housing and stores close to transit and bus lines," replied Harold. "Of course, here in Asheville, there is not much public transportation to speak of," he continued, shrugging his shoulders.

I was talking with Rachel about a book I had recently read on racism, *Beyond the Whiteness of Whiteness: Memoir of a White Mother of Black Sons*, by Jane Lazarre.

"Oh yes," said Rachel, nodding her head sagely, "I read her earlier work, *The Mother Knot,* years ago. She's a good writer."

And so it went until people finally said good night and headed home.

"That was a really nice Thanksgiving, wasn't it?" I said, yawning and snuggling down with Harold late that night.

"Yes. What a nice group of people," he answered, right before he began to snore.

CHAPTER THIRTY-ONE

It was a hot August day in 1990 when I got a call from my father.

"Brooke, I've got bad news. Your mother has been diagnosed with cancer of the esophagus. It doesn't look good. There are limited options for treatment. She is going ahead with surgery, but the success rate is very low."

"Oh my goodness. That's awful. Is there anything I can do?"

"Not at the moment. Let's wait and see how the surgery goes. Would you like to say hello to her?"

"Of course. Please put her on." My eyes were filling up with tears. Even though my mother and I had our difficulties, she *was* still my mother.

"Hi, Mom. I'm so sorry to hear this."

"Yes. It's not looking good. I want you to know that I love you," she said, her voice quavering.

"I love you too. Let me know if there's anything I can do."

"Thanks, sweetie."

I hung up the phone feeling both sad and numb. My mother wasn't that old, but she had been a smoker from age sixteen until forty. When the information about the cancer-causing properties of cigarettes hit the headlines, she made a valiant effort to quit. It took her several tries, but she had done it. It really sucked that it had caught up with her all these years later.

A few weeks later, my dad called again.

"Brooke, you'd better come out. The surgery didn't help and we don't think your mom has long to live. We can reimburse you for the ticket."

"I'm so sorry to hear this, but could you send me the ticket? If you just send me the money it might mess up my food stamps."

A big sigh on the other end of the phone. I could just imagine my father's worn and worried face. This had to be hard on him.

"Just get your own ticket, Brooke. I have too many other things to deal with."

"Okay. I'll come as soon as I can make arrangements. Please tell Mommy I love her."

Sighing in turn, I ran my hands through my hair. My thoughts were racing through my mind and my heart was aching. "Oy, what am I going to do? I'll have to take off work and arrange for someone to take care of Sean and Lucinda. I'm pretty sure Harold can hold down the fort with the kids. If I go midweek, I could be back for Sunday school. And tickets should be cheaper."

Within a few days I was on a plane to California. I dreaded seeing my mom in such bad shape but was determined to give her as good of attention as I could. She'd always been quite anxious.

But when I got there, I was in for a surprise. My mother was calm. She'd had a vision of gentle voices beckoning her and the aroma of roses wafting through the air. My mother loved her rose bushes, which she tended carefully. There couldn't have been a better predeath experience. She taught me how to face death with grace and dignity.

"Brooke, it's so good to see you! Is it okay if I don't get up? Is it okay that I'm still in my nightgown?"

"Of course, Mom. Of course!" I said, trying not to cry. "You stay right there. I'll come sit next to you," walking over and holding her hand. We sat that way for a while in silence. Then she needed to go back to bed.

The next day she told me about her vision. "I'm really not afraid to die. I'm just sorry that I had that surgery. It added nothing to my quality of life."

I rushed in to reassure her. "But at least you know you did everything possible to stay alive!"

Now I have a different perspective. I'm aware of the medical profession's abhorrence of death and the general population's abhorrence of death. The idea of "doing everything you can" has taken hold and often functions to put more money in the hands of the hospital than actually cure the patient. And I guess it assuages the doctor's conscience and the family's conscience if the patient dies. But many times it seems like it merely prolongs suffering.

The next day my mother was feeling worse and starting to fade. My father arranged in-home hospice care. We took turns sitting next to her, holding her hand and letting her know that we loved her. My father took care to let her know he would be okay and she could leave this plane of existence with no worries about him.

In one moment of lucidity, she looked right at me and said, "I know I wasn't always the best mother. I want you to know I'm sorry about that. I have always loved you." Then she slept for a few more hours.

This apology of hers meant a lot to me. I held it to me like a comforting blanket, close to my heart.

Around midnight two days later, her breaths came more and more slowly. I smoothed her brow and began to hum "Swing Low, Sweet Chariot." At 12:05 she took her last breath. The room had an oddly calm, heavy feeling to it. I could sense her spirit hovering above me. I went quietly to get my dad.

He asked to be alone with her for a while, which of course I obliged. I could hear him sobbing softly. She had been the love of his life. Eventually he came out of the bedroom and called the hospice nurse. She arrived and confirmed the time of death.

The next day, my aunts swooped in and took over everything. I couldn't even get the use of a car. I felt like a character in a Chekhov play—the one who can never get a horse and carriage. But I know they were just trying to help.

We had a memorial service in the Unitarian Universalist congregation that my parents had belonged to all these years. My father, the atheist, shared a Jewish legend about the "lamed vavnikim," thirty-six hidden individuals whose loving kindness redeems the world. He felt my mother was one of these righteous people.

I spoke about how hard my mother had worked, trying to have a career outside the home and also living up to the ideal of a fifties housewife, cooking every meal, including homemade desserts.

We sang an original song written by a friend of mine. It was written for her own mother, but was true of my mother also: "Do you know / how many songs you sang to me / even though you always said you couldn't sing."

But what struck me most was how many people came. People we did not necessarily know. Her hairdresser. Folks she had befriended on her daily walks around the neighborhood. I realized my mother had a whole life that did not involve me and that she was exceptionally good at making friends. It was eye-opening and humbling. I got a totally different picture of my mother.

When I returned home I began journaling all my good memories of my mother and telling Sean and Lucinda stories of her good qualities. It's not that she all of a sudden turned into a saint. More like I wanted to have a more balanced view of her.

It took me many more years to truly forgive her for the daily criticism and ridicule I grew up with, and her unwarranted stinginess toward me. But now I have been able to understand the vast pressures she was under, especially sexism. Here was a woman who had wanted to be a doctor. She gave up that dream when reminded of the prejudice she would face. Here is a woman who told me once she didn't pursue a Ph.D. because she thought it would be too hard for my father's "weak ego." Here was a woman who did all the cooking and cleaning in the house and made my father's lunch every day he went to work. No wonder she lashed out.

And sure enough, I lost my food stamps. I got called into the Social Service office and they said, "We see here you received a large check."

Sigh. "Yes. My mother got very sick and then died. My father sent me money for a plane ticket home. I can show you that receipt," I said, knowing in my heart it was probably hopeless.

"Well, if your father can send you money for a plane ticket, he can surely send you money for food for your family," the social worker said snootily.

I just looked at her and thought, *That's not how it works in my family. They think that since they have paid taxes all these years, the least the government can do is help out poor people, including me.*

"Yeah, well; he is not going to do that," I said dejectedly.

"Well, there is nothing I can do to help you. We are not giving food stamps to people who have money in the bank," she said as she opened the door so others waiting could hear.

When I was younger this would have been humiliating to me, as I'm sure she intended it. But now I just rolled my eyes and said under my breath but loud enough for those in the waiting room to hear, "Yeah, money to go to my mother's funeral."

Folks shook their heads in sympathy. If you have ever dealt with the so-called welfare system, you know what it's like.

And if you've ever tried to assist someone to get the help they are entitled to, you also know how hard that can be. Our "helping our neighbors" committee at the Unitarian Universalist congregation tried to assist a homeless family and almost went crazy. The family were homeless, but they had to provide every document imaginable. It took weeks to get a replacement Social Security card. Then the office was closed exactly at lunch time when folks like me could drive them there. Then after submitting all the paperwork, the social workers "lost it," and they had to start all over again. Folks learned to get and keep receipts for every document.

Harold was a very active member of this committee. He turned out to be the best at prying benefits out of the system. He would put on a suit and tie and say he was there to "represent" the family. He had learned over the years how to function in white society out of necessity. We figured out later, the social workers probably thought he was a lawyer! Maybe someone has managed to "cheat the system," but more times than not, "the system" cheats the people.

CHAPTER THIRTY-TWO

Not long after my mother died, the Peace and Justice Center hosted a talk by two women from the Women's Peace Movement of Northern Ireland.

I sat riveted to my chair hearing about the cross-community work they were doing with women. They did this work despite endless "stop and searches," by both the British army and the Royal Ulster Constabulary (RUC)—the overwhelmingly Protestant police force. And they persisted despite threats to their lives from both sides.

"Fear is the main problem we have to cope with in our community, but all it takes is just one person to say, 'I won't stand for this,'" declared Eileen Semple, eyes blazing, fist coming down on the table.

May Blood agreed. "When you get a group of very strong women together who have a real aim in life, there's very little that stops them, even a threat." She laughed defiantly.

"How can we help?" I asked, burning with a desire to join this nonviolent women's movement.

"Well, we are putting together a delegation of women to come to Ireland to witness our work and then come back to the U.S. and share what we are doing," Mary answered with a twinkle in her eye. I don't think she thought I was up to the challenge. But I took her information down and went to work to see if I could answer the call.

"Frank, would you be able to hold down the fort with the children for a week if I get accepted to join this peace delegation?" I asked, holding my breath. "It's during spring break so you wouldn't have to worry about getting them to school."

"Sure. I'm happy to support you in this way. I'll round up some extra help and they can stay at Black Mountain the whole time."

"Thank you!" I gave him a huge hug. I wouldn't have been able to do this without his support.

At home, I began to worry. "I always thought I'd have to wait until the children were grown to do something like this," I confessed to Harold. "What if I get killed in a random bomb explosion or crossfire? Is it irresponsible of me to take this risk as a mother of young children? Lucinda is only five."

"There is much less violence there now, in 1985, than in the '70s, although a bomb did go off at the airport a few months ago. They've tightened up security considerably since then," Harold replied. "People are bad at risk assessment. You are probably in more danger driving our mountain roads at night than going to Northern Ireland."

These words turned out to be more true than either of us could guess at the time.

After things were in order, I sent in my application and was accepted to join the women's peace delegation.

Now my next task was to figure out how to raise the money for the plane ticket. We would be hosted in homes, so the flight was the only major expense. Of course, on the pittance I was paid by both the Unitarian church and the Peace and Justice Center, I had no savings at all. I barely made it month to month.

"I'd love to do a fundraiser for you at the Peace and Justice Center," said Rachel the next day in the office, pacing the floor, with her usual abundance of energy. "How about an Irish-themed dinner and raffle? I can donate my labor and potatoes and cabbages from my garden. I have more vegetables than I know what to do with. And I can get some corned beef wholesale. I'll just have to research a vegetarian option," and she was off and running before I could even say thank you.

My friends at the Unitarian congregation organized an "Irish Tea" in my honor, serving authentic Irish breakfast tea, scones, homemade shortbread, and Irish soda bread. There was a basket set out for donations in typical polite Unitarian style.

Between the two events we made enough money to buy my plane ticket and some children's books for one of the women's center's libraries. I had a good time picking out books about Gandhi, Martin Luther King, and Mother Teresa. But to sort of camouflage these, I also bought some children's illustrated Bibles and some classic stories, such as *Corduroy* and *Crow Boy*, that emphasized kindness and understanding.

The preschool at the church donated some supplies, as did the children's program at Black Mountain Farm. After researching the weather, I was ready to pack. It turned out that Northern Ireland in March was just slightly colder and wetter than Asheville in the spring. My winter jacket and a few thermal undershirts would suffice. But that is when a major panic attack hit.

"Arghhh! Help! I don't know what or how to pack all this stuff! I need to be able to manage on my own. What if I forget something?" I was hyperventilating and almost in tears.

"What's going on, Brooke? You've traveled before, even to New Zealand," said Harold, looking concerned with furrowed brows and speaking gently.

"I don't know," I wailed. "Why would I ever leave my home? Why? Only if the Cossacks were coming," I blurted out.

"Oh! Hmmm. Seems to be a message from my ancestors," I said, somewhat surprised and abashed. I took a few deep breaths. "I guess I can get this all to fit in my suitcase and book bag."

The next day, Harold drove me to the airport. He kissed me at the airport and said, "You'll be fine, Brooke. Just remember to treat everyone with respect."

I nodded, hugging him back. "Thanks for everything. See you in a week."

Then I slung my book bag over my back, grabbed my suitcase, straightened my back, pulled my shoulders up, lifted my chin, and took two deep breaths as I walked resolutely toward the ticket counter. I would be meeting the rest of the delegation in NYC for orientation and training. Then we would travel together to Northern Ireland.

We met at a beautiful retreat center, located in an old stone mansion surrounded by huge mature oak trees and a sloping lawn. We got to know each other. We practiced suffering a pat down and answering questions that might be posed to us at a checkpoint. We worked on getting our stories straight about our "cultural arts tour" of Ireland.

We had been encouraged ahead of time to think about any of our ties to Ireland. I would be invoking my mother-in-law, Alice. The various authorities had no need to know that I was now divorced from her son, nor that she had passed away. My story of why I was coming to Ireland was that I was inspired by her and was planning to bring back real Irish linen and lace to brighten up her old age.

Our guide explained to us that we would follow the advice of our hosts, especially if a situation turned dangerous.

"In case they say we need to leave right away, we will leave right away. No discussion. No voting. No consensus building," she stressed.

"Everyone needs to agree to this now, or leave the delegation."

Whew! I was so relieved to have this spelled out explicitly and unequivocally.

I had seen enough stupid, mostly young men, or maybe agent provocateurs, escalate situations. And there was no guarantee a woman couldn't do the same.

There were a few raised eyebrows and a bit of grumbling, but in the end everyone agreed to this stipulation after being asked rhetorically,

"Do you want to be responsible for someone's death?"

"Well, neither do we," said our guide, Sarah.

"There have been way too many deaths already. Our mission is to demonstrate another way. The way of peace. And if you think martyrdom will move things forward, think again. Even the deaths of ten brave souls who went on a hunger strike in jail did not change the situation."

A quiet fell on us; some shed tears. We were getting the orientation we needed. Tomorrow we would fly to Northern Ireland and if all went well, we would be allowed into the country.

CHAPTER THIRTY-THREE

We arrived at JFK International Airport three hours early for our 10:45 p.m. flight. The lines were long going through both check-in and security, but we faced no difficulties. I was actually glad they made sure that each bag that was checked in at the counter had a corresponding passenger boarding the airplane. This was after a plane had blown up taking off from Northern Ireland not too long ago.

We got pushcarts for our luggage and made our way to the gate. Luckily, we had made sandwiches and packed fruit for the flight. The airport food was outrageously expensive, and by this time most places were shut. And since this was an overnight flight, there would be no meal provided by the airline.

Things would be tighter at Heathrow where we had a stopover. In Heathrow passengers were allowed only one piece of hand luggage, including a book or umbrella. I was grateful for the L.L. Bean book bag Harold had lent me that had room for my book, umbrella, scarf, sweater, and lunch along with my passport and wallet.

Once at Heathrow our luggage was searched and we were all patted down. I was glad I had put the illustrated children's Bibles on top of and interspersed with the other books I was bringing in. We were questioned closely about our purpose in visiting Northern Ireland. Thankfully, we had practiced our answers to these questions during our orientation and were believed. Even though we were going to support the women's peace movement, we knew the British did not look kindly on any movement that supported Northern Ireland independence and better conditions for the Catholic population.

We did it! We made it into Belfast, where we would remain for our stay. I was so proud of us. We had been strategic. We had dressed modestly, and kept our stories straight. Now we were exhausted. Some of us had been able to sleep on the overnight flight, but many of us only dozed a little bit. We were too excited and nervous to sleep much.

We were met at the airport by Grace, Sadie, and Maggie from the Women's Coalition. "Howya," Maggie asked as they shook our hands and grabbed our luggage to load onto a cart.

"I bet you're knackered from your long flight," said Maggie, patting me on the back.

I wasn't sure what that meant, but I was sure I looked like "death warmed over," to borrow an expression from my mother.

"We've got some taxis waiting to take you first for some breakfast and then to your homes," said Grace.

"Don't get all rattled if we get stopped by a peeler or two on the way. They've got 'security gates' up all over town."

And indeed we did get stopped twice, but our hosts got us through easily. Thank goodness because I don't think any of us could have dealt with the police at that moment.

We stopped in a little café where we ordered scones, Irish soda bread, porridge, and eggs for breakfast. I guess some of us had bacon or sausage but no one was up to a full traditional Irish breakfast that first morning. Then we drove to the various homes that would be putting us up so we could sleep for a while, and freshen up. We needed to be ready for our first adventure later in the afternoon. Surprisingly, most of our hosts were Protestant. But later we figured out that the Catholics lived in such run-down and cramped quarters that it would have been far more difficult for them to put us up.

Around two o'clock we began walking toward the Women's Center of Shank Hill. We had distributed the books and nursery school supplies among us. I wondered why other people hadn't thought to bring some donations, but didn't say anything. By distributing them, no one had too heavy a load to carry, so it turned out for the best.

As we walked, I found myself shivering. It wasn't because of the overcast sky and damp cold, though. It had suddenly occurred to me that I was entering a war zone. There were stones scattered on the sidewalk from street fights, and burn-smudged buildings among the two-storied brick apartment buildings. Armored trucks were cruising the streets, and we could hear the rattling, clanking sounds of a tank or two. There was graffiti on the walls of buildings with conflicting messages.

"Remember the murdered," listing loyalist names. Then in contrast, a memorial mural for Bobby Sands, the IRA political prisoner. He was an elected MP who had organized a hunger strike in prison, from which he died. Some were hard for me to decipher. "The murderers have a choice: their victims have none." Which murderer was this referring to: Protestant? Catholic? All?

Our hosts were chatting, but also looking around frequently, checking for anything that might seem out of place.

"There's a checkpoint up ahead," said Grace, pointing her chin in the direction of two soldiers holding guns and wearing the green and tan camouflage and black berets of the British army.

"Okay, ladies, keep calm, breathe," said Sadie.

I grabbed Maggie's hand. "It's okay," she said softly, "we go through this all the time."

"Hello, boys," said Grace, smiling and nodding at the men.

"Keeping us all safe, are ye?" with a teasing tone in her voice.

The two men stared at us. I felt a chill roll up and down my spine.

"Well, well, well, what do we have here? Gaggle of nannies out for a stroll?" said one of the soldiers sarcastically.

"These are a group of ladies come here to learn about Irish culture. We're taking them to the Irish Arts Center," said Grace.

"We have to pat you all down, you know," said the second one grimly. "Never know who might be smuggling a bomb in."

"Yeah, yeah, yeah, we know. You're just doing your job," said Grace.

We let them pat us down slowly, one by one. First, Grace, Sadie, and Maggie. Then each of us in turn. They examined our passports and the contents of our purses. I held my breath the whole time I was being patted down. No amount of practice could have prepared me for the feeling of being a small animal caught in a trap, dependent on the mercy of my captor. Those moments seemed endless. I couldn't tell if I was slowing down the time out of fright or it actually was taking forever.

The only time I had faced anything remotely like this was being stopped by police in L.A. outside my own house. They obviously didn't think I belonged in my lily white neighborhood, thought Brooke as she relived these experiences.

"They took their bloody time, now didn't they," said Grace when we were finally through.

"Yes," replied Sadie. "They have to show how in charge they are, the manky melters."

So it wasn't just me, I thought, relieved that I hadn't just disassociated.

Finally, we were at the Shank Hill Irish Cultural Center. Housed in an unassuming beige brick building at the end of a street of row houses, the cultural center offered many opportunities for what our hosts called "cross-community work." Our guide that day was named Rose and she greeted us warmly. We gave her the books and supplies we had brought.

"Why, isn't that grand," she said. "Thanks so much."

We toured the center and nursery school.

"We provide classes and preschool to all the women and children who want to participate," explained Rose. "Both Protestant and Catholic. As the women learn together, they also realize they have much more in common than they thought."

"Yeah—like lousy housing, lousy health care, and lousy husbands," quipped Grace.

"Well, yes. Especially the first two. But we do also offer discreet domestic abuse services," replied Rose. "And as you can see for yourselves, the children get along fine with each other. By building friendships and trust across communities at this early age, we hope to be building a more peaceful future."

We bought some lovely lace hankies and a few pieces of Irish linen from their gift shop. The income was divided between the women who crafted the items and the center for its ongoing work. The additional income was a welcome bonus for these poor and working-class moms.

Then we headed "home." I was very relieved we didn't have to go through any more checkpoints that day.

"Well, you must all be craving your beds by now," said Grace. "See you in the morning."

The next day our first stop was an apartment in a Catholic neighborhood that had recently been "investigated" by the army. In actuality, it had been almost demolished.

The furniture had been dumped in the bleak dirt yard, their kitchen dismantled, and floorboards ripped up. Nonetheless, our hosts insisted on serving us tea from the small camp stove they had set up. We knew that to be polite, we had to accept.

"The fecking soldiers use any excuse to destroy our property," said Sam, the husband of the household.

"They think they can break our spirits that way. But we will not back down in our demands," he continued.

"They use the excuse that our son is suspected of cooperating with the IRA," added his wife. "But we are all SDLP—Socialist Democratic Labor Party—in this family. But even if he had gotten mixed up in that mess, why not just arrest him? Why destroy our home?"

We shook our heads and had nothing much to say to comfort them. I felt a sense of despair looking at the destruction. But perhaps having witnesses to the injustice helped.

The contrast between this neighborhood and the one where we were staying was great. It didn't take knowing all the statistics to see this area was vastly poorer. And the graffiti had changed also. Now we saw much more radical messages such as "Revolution," "Break Thatcher's back," "PLO and IRA: same struggle," "End British Rule," and "Belfast says No." There were no trees or shrubs to be seen, and the apartments were tiny and cramped, although all of them seemed to have attempts at beauty—wallpaper, a picture on the wall, lace doilies covering the arms and back of worn furniture.

After listening to several families, we made our way toward another women's center. This time we were stopped by the RUC, the overwhelmingly Protestant police force. Once again our bags were searched and we were patted down.

"Huh, more like felt up," said Grace after that encounter.

"Yeah, that hallion squeezed my bum," complained Sadie.

"Mine too," said Maggie ruefully.

"Apologies for our countrymen. Let's go ahead and continue our dander. It's almost lunchtime and we can eat with the pensioners," continued Maggie, turning to a more cheerful topic.

The delicious aroma of potato soup greeted us, and the brown bread slathered with rich Irish butter did cheer us up. We also enjoyed the good-hearted banter of the older woman who had come for a hot meal.

Then we were treated to a cooking class where we learned to make barmbrack and each got to take a loaf home. As we baked, we spoke with the other women there, hearing their stories of the Troubles. Many had experienced demolished homes and the daily indignities of being a minority. Some had lost husbands, brothers, or sons to the conflict. All had decided there must be a better way, a peaceful way, out of the conflict.

The next day was Sunday, a day to rest, or go to church with our host families if we chose. I decided to journal about my experiences so far. The weather had turned nice and some of us went for a walk in a nearby park. After the intensity of the past few days, it was a relief to have a day off.

* * *

Thinking about taking advantage of the nice weather took Brooke traveling through her memories back to the present for a moment.

"Marissa! It's a beautiful day! Take that baby out for a walk. Babies need fresh air, and the exercise will be good for you too," she hollered.

"Oh, I'm too tired, Ma. Besides, I'm busy," answered Marissa, rolling her eyes.

"Too busy doing what? Texting some new boy? Posting selfies on your phone?" Brooke retorted, grimacing and running her hands through her hair in annoyance.

Laughter. "Yeah, something like that."

How on earth did I raise a child that doesn't like to be outside? Why, I even remember once when the Sunday school was running a day camp at an organic farm, she didn't want to go, saying, "I don't like to get my hands dirty!"

Shaking her head, Brooke thought, *Well, at least I didn't force her to go to that camp. Unlike my mother, who sent me to several sleep-away camps when I didn't want to go.*

She turned her attention back to her writing about Ireland.

* * *

The next few days were spent meeting with local elected officials and representatives of the Women's Coalition.

One woman said, "We have opened doors in the walls dividing the communities through which the women can walk, but which the men don't see."

Another said, "We can see that if we don't work together and speak up, there are going to be very few female voices around the table negotiating the future for Northern Ireland."

"More female voices can bring new perspectives and a positive dynamic," said a third.

And that turned out to be true, thought Brooke. *Although it took another thirteen years to get to the Good Friday Agreement. Most people don't realize how long struggles for peace and justice actually take. And the Women's Coalition was at the negotiating table, contributing to a vastly better settlement.*

On our next-to-last day, we were treated to an "Irish Culture" day, starting with a full Irish breakfast, including beans, grilled tomatoes, and mushrooms, along with eggs, bread, butter, and a bottomless "pot o' tea." Some people were brave enough to try the blood pudding, but not I. It culminated in a cultural performance at Falls Women's Center featuring traditional music, dance, and poetry. Of course I loved the children's performances the best, but the room was filled with talented adults as well. I also liked the peace dove painted on an outside wall with a rainbow-colored background.

Our last day in Ireland, we mailed our notebooks plus all the pamphlets, bumper stickers, and buttons with revolutionary messages back home from the postal office. We had no desire to deal with British customs officers over anything that might arouse suspicion. We packed our clothes and bade farewell to our host families. We would leave early the next morning for the U.S.

When I got back to the United States I missed Ireland immediately. All I wanted to eat for breakfast was baked beans on toast with grilled tomatoes and mushrooms. And it seemed that Lucinda had overheard talk about "checkpoints" because she set up a cardboard box barrier in the kitchen door and wouldn't let me pass unless I "paid" her. Luckily for me, she would accept paper clips, buttons, or small candies. Although her "checkpoint" was more like a toll booth, and was kind of funny, it did remind me of the thing that was most difficult for me.

I never got used to the "stop and search" checkpoints on foot or in a vehicle. Each time, my heart would beat faster and I would often hold my breath until we were through. People thought I was brave, but what I realized is that "bravery" in the moment can be accompanied by feelings of fear. And yet a determination to do what one had set out to do can overcome that. No one in our group wavered. We were well aware that the people we were meeting had to deal with this daily. They would not be returning to the United States.

* * *

Brooke hummed and sang an anthem written by Naomi Littlebear Morenas as she wrote this last bit. It was a song they had sung during the nuclear freeze movement, and it was known in the Irish Women's Peace Movement also.

We need more songs now, she thought. *Singing brings people together, uplifts spirits, and gives one courage.*

CHAPTER THIRTY-FOUR

One day in February when Lucinda had just turned five and Sean was nine, I woke up to the sounds of happy children playing right outside my window. I got up and looked outside. It had snowed overnight. It looked like about four inches, a good amount for Asheville. And there were my children sliding around in it and attempting to make a small snowman.

Wow. When they were toddlers I never imagined a scene like this. Or even now to be honest. It looks like Sean helped Lucinda get all bundled up and out they went without even waking me up! Glory be. Wonders never cease. And oh, it was sooo nice to sleep in on a snowy day. The snow muffles all the usual noises and covers the sky with clouds, so it is beyond lovely to snuggle down under the covers and go back to sleep. I never thought a day like this would come.

In some ways, I marked that day as the turning point of my life when it got easier as a single mom. Of course there were still interventions that needed to be made on behalf of each child at school, but the children themselves were so much more capable of doing their daily life tasks without me. They also helped cook and do various chores.

However, it was hard to see Lucinda struggle with all the arbitrary rules her first year in kindergarten. It seemed like every day she came home with a new one: "We can't run our hands along the walls of the hallway. We can't sit with our legs tucked up under us in the cafeteria."

Well, these seemed ridiculous to me and I told her that, but I also told her that her life would be easier at school if she went along with the rules. *Sigh.* I'm not sure that was the right advice.

By first grade she was so quiet the teacher didn't even seem to know she was there. I tried talking with the teacher, who had no complaints about Lucinda, but said the class in general was "wiggly as worms in hot ashes." So I could just imagine her saying things like, "Class, settle down," and my poor kid wondering how she possibly could be any more quiet. Stop breathing, perhaps?

At the end of the year, I took her to the parent-teacher conference, as she thought she was doing badly in her studies. When I directly questioned the teacher, she said, "Lucinda is doing fine." Lucinda skipped all the way home saying, "She said I'm doing fine! She said I'm doing fine!" That was helpful to her, but it didn't satisfy me.

On Lucinda's report card, everything was marked "satisfactory"— the equivalent of a C—and I knew she was doing better than that. The school had administered standardized tests to all the students in her grade. Her scores came back in the high 90s percentiles. Armed with this and her report card, I made an appointment to speak with the principal. He was a courtly old Southern gentleman who truly cared about each child. I remembered when Sean was given the honor of getting to "eat lunch with the principal"; he came back from that experience glowing.

I showed Mr. Beaufort Lucinda's report card and her test scores. He looked them over and then said, "Why, this is neeeglect! Every student deserves to be appreciated. I promise you she will not have another year like this."

Wow. I could not have asked for more. I left very much relieved.

And sure enough, from the very first day of the new school year,

Lucinda's teacher saw her clearly and encouraged her creativity. Lucinda blossomed that year. I have no idea what the principal said to the teacher, but it worked. At the end of that year, the teacher wrote how pleased she was to have Lucinda in her class and that she "had never had such a unique child as Lucinda in all her years of teaching."

This actually broke my heart and I wanted to write back and say, "Every child in your class is unique. You have never had anyone like them in your class either," but of course I didn't. It reminded me of research I had read that when teachers were told this year's class had "exceptional" students, all the students thrived, even though in actuality, they had previously tested as "average."

Things went better for a year or two, and then Lucinda got another teacher who was not encouraging. And also gave her grief if she tried to read a book of her own choosing after completing her other work. But once again, a simple conversation, this time with the teacher, made a difference. The teacher agreed that Lucinda could read any book from the class library after she finished her work.

And now, she's so grown up! We finally have an adult-to-adult relationship. I think the first sign of that was when she called to ask about a recipe.

"Hi, Mom, can you tell me how you make your stuffed mushrooms? I'm having some friends over for dinner."

"Sure," I said, smiling and thinking, *It's a huge deal when your young adult children think you have something to offer them.*

Now, she calls weekly and we have a nice chat. But her teen years were rough.

Meanwhile, Sean had his own struggles in school. Although his fifth-grade teacher was wonderful and saw all his strengths, including his kind and caring nature, sixth grade was another story. One day I got a call from his teacher.

"Hello? Mrs. Kumara? I'm calling because I'm having difficulties with Sean in my classroom. He's the rudest student I've ever had."

"Sean? Rude?" I asked, running my hands through my hair. "Are you sure you have the right student?"

"Yes, of course I have the right student. On our first day of class, when I wrote the classroom rules on the board, he raised his hand and asked if we could vote on them!" she said in an exasperated tone. "And he is always asking why he has to do a particular task."

Breathe, Brooke, breathe, I told myself.

"Well," I said. "Sean has been raised in communal settings most of his life where people do vote on everything, so that just seems normal to him. I'm sure he didn't mean to be rude. And I also have raised him to think that there are good reasons why I want him to do something. He's a very rational person and I think you will find that if you tell him why you want him to do something, he will be very cooperative." *Breathe, breathe, breathe.*

"Well, Mrs. Kumara, this is quite unusual but also interesting. It's my first year of teaching and I was not prepared for this in my teacher training program. I'll try it out and get back to you."

Whew. "Well, thanks for calling," I said gently, hanging up the phone. Of course, she's a first-year teacher, and of course she didn't learn how to have a democratic classroom in her teacher training program. I wish I could afford a good alternative school. But then I remembered how a friend's child was made to write a hundred times "I will do what the teacher says no matter what I think or feel" at a pricey, supposedly progressive private school. *There's just no guarantees of a good, respectful education.*

As it turned out, Sean's teacher became a great advocate for him and even went out of her way to write to the next year's teacher that

"Sean needs to be told the reason for assignments."

I wish I could write that it always turns out well to advocate for our children, but it never went as well when I tried to do so for Marissa, the child I eventually had with Harold. Her school counselors seemed to routinely dismiss her, sometimes even making things worse, and definitely did not seem to have her best interests in mind. I couldn't help wondering if it was because she is biracial. Confronting racism is an ongoing struggle.

During those earlier years, I continued to date Harold, but it was hard to envision a future for us given our age difference of ten years. I wasn't worried about the interracial aspect of our relationship. But perhaps I was in a bit of denial about how it might impact us.

I decided to "live in the moment" and not worry about the future. We enjoyed hiking together in the mountains surrounding Asheville and doing political work together. Harold had good technical skills and brought those to the Peace and Justice Center. He was also much calmer under stress than I was when there were deadlines for getting out the newsletter.

The children were now spending weekends with Frank, so Friday night we almost always went out to dinner, Harold paying. He had a good-paying techie job and was happy to foot the bill. He thought this helped balance out our age difference.

"It's so nice to get to eat my own cucumbers out of my salad. When I take the kids out for a rare occasion to get pizza, I always first give them my croutons, which I don't mind, but if the meal has still not arrived, I hold them off by giving away my cukes," I said, smiling up at Harold.

I like to appreciate the little things in life. "And this eggplant parmigiana is the best! I love it like this, very thinly sliced, and layered with ricotta cheese along with the sauce and mozzarella. It's almost as good as my mother's, and it's so much work to make it myself."

Now I guess this appreciation of small things would be called "a gratitude practice," but then it was just my way of staying happy.

Harold would stay over and it was nice to have that private time together. But in those days, we were often woken up at 8:00 a.m. by his mother.

"Would you *please* tell your mother not to call so early? It's the only morning I have to sleep in," I grumbled or possibly even snarled at him. But he never would.

Maybe that should have already been a warning sign, that Harold would never speak up for me. Or maybe I should have learned way earlier to speak up for myself. And, perhaps it was his greater respect for his mother and for his elders in general.

On Saturdays we often indulged in brunch. The Blue Lagoon was our favorite place. Harold would read the paper and I would read the comics.

"I worry enough about the world during the rest of the week," I would always say.

"Yes, but listen to this, Brooke. Reagan has decided to reduce our nuclear weapons stockpile!"

"Wow! That's amazing. Let me see." This put me in a good mood, so I decided to share a speculative question that tickled me.

"Harold, you know when I see the leaves turning colors in the fall, they look so beautiful but they are actually dying. It makes me wonder if we look beautiful to the worms as we are decomposing. Do they sit around saying 'now that is a beautiful show'?" I said, laughing.

Sometimes I crack myself up.

"That's not funny," said Harold, which is what he often said to me when I would make jokes involving death.

"Oh, Harold, I'm going to be on my deathbed and I'll crack a joke and you'll say, 'That's not funny,'" I continued, heaping coals on the fire, shaking my head and giggling.

"That's really not funny," he said, causing me to laugh so uproariously, the people at the next table looked over at us.

In those days I had a macabre sense of humor. Maybe it was my way of dealing with the prospect of a nuclear war. I loved the bumper sticker I had put on my car, "One nuclear bomb can ruin your whole day." It still makes me laugh. I routinely put cartoons in the Peace and Justice newsletter like the one that pictured earth enveloped in a mushroom cloud with two cockroaches sitting on top. The caption was, "I thought they'd never leave."

"Do you really think that's funny, Brooke?" asked Mary, one of the board members.

"Well, maybe the thought of cockroaches taking over the world will motivate people to get more involved," I answered a bit defensively.

Or the time I put in a cartoon of a middle-aged man and boy standing together. The man asks, "What do you want to be when you grow up?"

The boy answers, "Alive; if it's not too much to ask."

Tyler, usually an ally on the board, thought that one was "rather grim."

But I notice I'm not laughing at all about the climate crisis. I would like to think perhaps I've matured. But I'm afraid I'm just more numb. Which isn't all that helpful. However, I did just hear a climate joke that made me laugh.

"Help! I need someone who can read astrology to tell me which planet is making me sad."

"Well, I'm not an astrologer, but I think it's earth."

In the afternoon we would often hike in the Blue Ridge Mountains. One of our favorite hikes was to Crabtree Falls.

It was beautiful every season of the year. Fall brought bright yellow from the tulip poplar trees, orange from the oaks, and flaming red from the maples. In winter, the views were spectacular through the bare branches. Spring brought the pale pinks of the lovely mountain laurels and dogwoods. And summer, ever-deepening greens. From spring through fall there was an ever-changing array of wildflowers. Queen Anne's Lace, with its feathery white blooms, is a favorite of mine.

And sometimes we would stop and visit at Black Mountain Farm on the way home. It was good to see old friends and enjoy a fresh tomato from the garden, sliced on a piece of homemade bread with a bit of mayo. I've never been willing to put in the time to make my own bread. And I gave up trying to grow tomatoes in my tiny garden when the deer come along and chomp them down every darn time I try. So that was always a treat.

Another favorite hike was to the Rainbow Falls in the Pisgah National Forest. This waterfall was even more beautiful and there were other falls along the way. When it was sunny, you could indeed see little rainbows shimmering off of the water.

In those days, I could still hike. I miss that, but I can still get to beautiful lookouts along the Blue Ridge, so that is some consolation.

If the day was rainy, we might go see a movie, play Scrabble, or go back to bed. But always by early evening I had to turn my attention to Sunday school the next day.

"You work entirely too hard for what they pay you, Brooke. How many hours have you put in this week?" Harold would demand.

"Yeah. I know. Way too many. But I had this great idea to do an intergenerational program with various stations on understanding disability. I still have to make signs for each station." Or I'd say, "I know, I know, but Shelley is sick and I need to find a substitute." It was always something.

I had no boundaries. I was always having a "great idea" that demanded hours of work. I was terrible at delegating, so I was perpetually overworked. Luckily, I have finally learned how to set reasonable expectations for myself and to ask for help. But that only happened after I turned fifty.

Often I would have nightmares on Saturday.

"Oh, Harold, I just dreamt a Boy Scout troop was running wild through the building," I said as I pulled myself out of a dream.

Or, "This time it was a whole circus that took over the Sunday school."

"Well, running a Sunday school is sometimes like a circus," Harold would laugh and go back to sleep.

In my waking hours I loved my education director's job. We had a great curriculum that was inclusive of many of the world's religions. So our students got to study and participate in "Holidays Around the World," learn "Wisdom Stories from the World," and of course learn "Bible Stories of Our Ancestors." The education was very hands-on, participatory, and grounded in respect for each student.

And I loved joining the larger community for our worship services. The sanctuary had wonderful acoustics and beautiful stained-glass windows.

"What was that song you sang in choir today? *'We will rise like the ocean / we will rise like the sun'*? It made me cry and feel happy and defiant all at the same time."

"It's called *Common Threads*, by Pat Humphries. I like it too," said Harold. "She's part of a duo called Emma's Revolution. They come to Asheville sometimes. Would you like to go see them?"

"Oh, yes! That would be great."

The Unitarian Universalist Sunday school and congregation was such a contrast to the public schools. No wonder my kids never minded going there. It was a welcome respite from all-too-common authoritarianism.

And the only conflict was what calendar to follow—the University of North Carolina's or that of the local public schools.

We were sitting in a classroom. The bulletin boards were decorated with children's drawings of Thanksgiving and pumpkins. It was a school committee meeting. There were about six folks in attendance.

"I'd like to suggest that we follow the university calendar," said Matthew. "So many of our members work there that it just makes sense."

"But not all of us work there," said Doug, who taught at the local community college.

"And the other colleges in the area all have different calendars," added Trina.

"Not to mention the private schools," said Jane.

"If we continue to follow the local public schools, I think that is the least elitist," chimed in George.

I could see that Matthew was outnumbered and tried to keep my face and voice neutral. "All in favor of continuing to follow the public school calendar? The ayes have it.

"Now let's discuss plans for our winter celebrations. Do we want a candlelight Christmas Eve program again? And light Chanukah candles at the same time, since they coincide this year? What about solstice?" I asked.

"Don't forget Chinese New Year, please," piped up Jane. "It's my favorite!"

Matthew was perhaps smarting from being outvoted on the calendar issue.

"I don't like the idea of combining Christmas and Chanukah. They are two completely different holidays."

"Except for the fact that they both are winter solstice replacements," said Jane, smirking.

"Well, yes," agreed George. "But I also prefer to keep them separate."

"But three school holiday celebrations in one week is a bit much, especially for our overworked ed. director," added Trina to my grateful smile.

"Let's alternate which winter holidays the school will celebrate and which we will do as a whole community. That way, the program and ritual committees can take some of the burden off of the school," suggested George. "Which holiday do you want to focus on this year, Brooke?"

"Me? I'd like to organize the Christmas Eve celebration. I have a lovely story I've been wanting to tell and the children are already so excited for their nativity play."

I was smiling and so relieved. Maybe for once I wouldn't have to do it all.

"Okay. I'll speak with the program and ritual committees to see which they each can plan. Thanks, all," said George.

As I left that meeting, I thought, *I wish meetings with the Peace and Justice Center were so easy. They've always been a bit fraught for me. There's just not much trust between me and the board.*

CHAPTER THIRTY-FIVE

When I got home, I broached the subject with Harold.

"I've never really trusted the board at the P and J Center. They seem too fucking polite. I never know what they're really thinking. They seem satisfied to just do very symbolic actions to make themselves feel better, without looking at how to be effective. And now that Hugh has joined, I'm sure he has a hidden agenda to fire me and hire his wife."

"Whoa, Brooke, don't jump to conclusions. Why do you say this?" Harold looked at me over the edge of his glasses.

"Because, when I first proposed joining the Jobs with Justice campaign to build more connections with the African American community, he was completely opposed."

"'What does this have to do with peace?" he asked.

"And half the board was in agreement. Until Tyler spoke up and said, 'Well, we are the Peace *and* Justice Center.'

"So they agreed and then when it was a great success, Hugh says in his sly and slimy way, 'Why aren't we doing more of this?'

"And not giving me any credit, and not admitting he was wrong. I'm telling you, he's up to no good," I said, slamming my hand down on the table. "Mark my words, before the year is over, he will get me fired and his crazy wife installed as staff."

"Well, why don't you try talking to some of the board members that you like or have built a relationship with? Find out what's going on?" said Harold, still not convinced.

I decided to call Tyler.

"Hi, Tyler. Thanks for standing up for our participation in the Jobs with Justice campaign. Did you happen to notice how Hugh backtracked on that? Do you know what's going on with him?"

"Well, yeah. It happens, Brooke. When I worked at the War Resisters League I got laid off when a new person came on board. Hugh doesn't think you're qualified. He's going to suggest you just do clerical tasks."

"Tyler, you know that's absurd! I hate the clerical stuff and love the organizing," I said, running my hands through my hair until it was standing straight up. "Can't you do anything?"

"Well, Brooke. Maybe it won't be so bad. You will still be contributing."

Sigh. "I see. Okay. Thanks for letting me know what's happening," I said, sighing some more as I put down the phone.

Next I called Mary. I got a similar response: "We still want you, Brooke, just in a different capacity." *Yeah, sure,* I thought.

"There doesn't seem to be anything I can do," I confided to Rachel. "And you know Nancy, Hugh's wife, is completely disorganized. She runs everything at the last minute out of fear and panic. She thinks if you don't do the same, you are not 'committed' enough," I said.

Rachel also didn't know what to do. "It's just a shame, Brooke, after all you've done."

Within a few weeks, the board had met without me and voted to offer me a much-diminished job, filing papers and such. So I resigned.

"Now what am I going to do?" I wondered out loud. I decided to confide in the minister of my congregation.

"I really don't know what to do. My part-time education director job here is just not enough to sustain me."

"Would your parents help?" Melissa asked.

"Yeah. Maybe. If I could think of something that had potential to earn a living."

"Think of what you love to do and what you are good at," she wisely suggested, smiling kindly.

"You know I love educating and I'm good at it, but I just can't imagine working in an oppressive institution like a public school."

"How about becoming a librarian? You love to read, and librarians often do educational programs also. Your parents would surely support that," suggested Melissa.

"Hmm... that's intriguing. I think I'll investigate that option after the holidays. Thanks."

I was determined not to let losing my job at the Peace and Justice Center ruin our holidays. I had joined a peer counseling group a few years back and did my crying and raging with my peer counselors. That left me free to celebrate with a lighter heart. My friends also rose to the occasion. Both Laura and Lisa had left Black Mountain Farm and moved to Asheville. Laura came by one afternoon to bake Italian Christmas cookies with us, bringing along Topaz, so she and Lucinda could help. Lisa, her children, and I had often celebrated a night of Chanukah together and we did so again this year.

I still regret that year when her young son cried when I wouldn't let him blow out the candles. Now I let Seth blow out the shamash and relight it as many times as he wants.

I had Sean and Lucinda gather pine cones and hickory tree pods for Christmas decorations. With some cotton balls, glue, and glitter, we created a winter wonderland with the pine cones for our mantlepiece in the living room. Lucinda particularly loved sprinkling glitter all over the cotton dotting the "branches" of the pine cone "trees."

And I had learned from my friend Becky the local custom of creating ornaments by gluing toothpicks onto the hickory pods to look like stars and then spray-painting them silver and gold—a job Sean enjoyed. Then, some of those also got sprinkled with glitter by an exuberant Lucinda.

So what if my sidewalk and living room floor sparkles, I thought, *it just adds to the festive feeling.*

Rachel also came with her kids for a night of Chanukah, and Harold made delicious latkes, crunchy on the outside, soft on the inside, just like the ones from my childhood. Luckily I had my paternal grandmother's recipe.

"They're really just glorified hash browns," Harold said as he dipped his in ketchup.

One thing I did not do was succumb to overcompensating by buying a lot of expensive gifts I most certainly couldn't afford. The children still got one useful gift a night for Chanukah, including the traditional socks and then a hat, a pair of mittens, a scarf, a book, some of the See's Butterscotch Lollipops my mom had always sent, and that my dad continued to send, one toy or electronic device from the grandparents, and one gift to share, like a board game. This year it was Parcheesi and they played that for years.

Although Lucinda always complained that Sean cheated in Parcheesi. I defended him at the time, saying, "No, he just sets up these annoying roadblocks." But later, I found out he actually did cheat!

Christmas Eve, Harold stayed up late wrapping gifts for the kids and me. He learned from his mother how to wrap things beautifully, whereas I was somewhat famous for recycling wrinkled wrapping paper and bunching it all together with lots of tape. I had asked him also not to go overboard but to think of things that would be treats for us, like a coupon for pizza. So under our Christmas tree, there were a variety of presents.

Early Christmas morning, Harold kissed me on the forehead and left to go to his mother's. Sean, Lucinda, and I slept in, like we prefer, and had a very leisurely Christmas morning, sipping hot chocolate, nibbling on cinnamon rolls, and taking turns unwrapping our presents.

Harold had done a great job thinking about each of us. There were coupons for pizza and also for the movies, a book for each of us, and best of all, a promise of a "supermarket sweep" for me. He knew I always dreamed of winning one of those chances to rush through the aisles of my favorite grocery store, throwing item after item into my cart of all the things I normally couldn't afford.

Around 1:00 p.m., Frank showed up with a homemade lasagna and goodies from Black Mountain. Herbal sachets, goat milk soap, and a macramé plant holder for me. Wooden bookends for Sean and a darling wooden seal for Lucinda. We had a nice meal, went for a walk, and then he left. As the children played with their gifts, I took a well-deserved nap, drifting off to sleep, thinking the holidays had been very successful.

On the day of New Year's Eve, I got to do my supermarket sweep. But Harold told me to take my time and get anything I wanted. Wow! I chose all kinds of imported cheeses, some sparkling apple juice, crackers, grapes, and of course, chocolate. We went back and spread these delicacies over my bed for an indoor picnic, followed by lovemaking. *I could die content right now,* I thought as I drifted off to sleep.

This is one of the advantages of having a younger lover. I'm sure I read somewhere that males reach their peak sexuality in their late teens, while women come into their own in their midthirties. We were both just a little past that. So completely attuned and compatible.

SUMMER: GROWING, RIPENING

If you are on your way to the goal and stop to throw stones at any dog that barks at you, you will never reach that goal.
—25 Basic Rules of Life, Fyodor Dostoevsky

JUNE

The very existence of libraries affords the best evidence that we may yet have hope for the future of man.
—T.S. Eliot

CHAPTER THIRTY-SIX

After the holidays, I began to explore my options for a new job. I found out that our local public library had part-time positions that did not require a degree. It was mostly shelving books and helping with checkouts, but it was a foot in the door and paid a bit above minimum wage. The hours were reasonable also, and the head librarian was okay with having Lucinda hang out in the library after school while I worked. Sean preferred the after-school program at his school.

I realized I would need a B.A. before being able to get an M.A. in library science. Community college seemed like a good place to start. However, my first visit to the local community college was a disaster.

"I'd like to take this women's literature class," I said to the clerk.

"Oh no, you can't take that without first taking English 101," she replied haughtily.

This can't be right, I thought, and decided to approach the head of the department.

"I wrote an essay a week for English and an essay a week for history all through high school, have helped edit a poetry anthology, have been producing the Peace and Justice Center newsletter for several years, and write a monthly column for the church bulletin. I know how to write," I protested.

"That may be true, but we have changed how we do footnotes," he replied. I left disgusted and demoralized. *Surely I can look up how they do footnotes*, I thought. That can't take an entire semester.

I was complaining loudly about this to Becky, who told me to check out the adult study program at Hoover College, a small private liberal arts college in the area. Asheville is blessed with a total of seven colleges, both public and private institutions. I was trying to find the most economical way I could accomplish my goal of becoming a librarian and a program flexible enough for my schedule. A program designed for adults sounded promising.

I learned that the adult degree program of Hoover College was designed for folks just like me. They understood that adults have lives. You could go as fast or as slow as necessary (which in my case turned out to be extremely slow), and get credit for "prior knowledge and life experience." And, they had a cooperative degree program with my local community college.

So I trudged back to the community college, this time bypassing the general office and finding the Hoover College office. As I walked in I noticed a page from the Asheville Peace and Justice Center tacked up on a bulletin board. *Wow*, I thought, *that seems like a good sign.*

"Hello, may I help you?" asked a middle-aged woman sitting behind a desk.

"Yes, I hope so," I said nervously, taking a deep breath. "I'm interested in the adult degree program. My name is Brooke Kumara," smiling, heart pounding.

"I'm Jean Richardson and I direct the cooperative program here at Asheville Community College. I recognize your name from the Peace and Justice Center. We would be happy to have you in the program. You're a shoo-in."

"What do I have to do to be accepted into the program?" I asked.

"Fill out these forms, and write an entrance essay. That's it. I'm here to guide you in your course selection so that everything you take here will transfer to Hoover."

"Wow, that sounds great. Will I have to take English 101?" I related my previous experience.

"Oh, no," Jean said laughing. "You can CLEP out of that and History, Art, and Humanities 101 courses easily!"

"What's CLEP?"

"It's the College Level Examination Program run by the same folks who design the SATs. They are multiple-choice questions and you only have to pass them. Really anyone with basic knowledge should be able to pass them. I'm sure you will have no trouble."

Well, I went home pretty excited that day. I talked it all over with Harold.

"Go for it, Brooke. I'll help in any way I can."

And the next day he came home with a little Mac computer for me.

"Oh my God, this is amazing! I can move around paragraphs and it has a spell checker! Boy am I glad I waited until computers were invented to go to school. Otherwise I would have had to hire someone to type my work for me! Thank you so much!" I was feeling hopeful.

But there was still the issue of paying even for the modest community college tuition. Sigh. I would have to ask my father.

I steeled myself for a difficult conversation.

"Hello, Dad? I've got great news. You know how you've always said, 'If you want to go to college, the money is there'? Well, I've decided to become a librarian and I found a great adult degree program that I can do to begin the process at my local community college," holding my breath, literally.

"Ah, Brooke. I don't have the money. There's not really any money put aside."

What?, I thought, not entirely surprised. "I don't think that is fair. You've always said you would pay for my college and this is so inexpensive. I want to hold you to your word," I said, shaking.

"You have a point," he said, sighing. "Get me the information, I'll think it over and see what I can do."

"Thanks," I said as I set down the phone. I was still shaking and so angry. I was also crying.

I really don't know why both my mother, when she was alive, and now my father, won't help me. I've tried to be so good all my life and I live by their values and they are never as poor as they make themselves out to be.

I remember a conversation with my mother where she was moaning about having to replace an Oriental rug in her living room that their dogs had ruined. God damn it, if they could afford an Oriental rug he can for sure afford community college tuition and books at the very least. What if I had wanted to go to a state university??? And live in a dorm? How many times have I heard them say, "You know, if you want to go to college, the money is here," while never helping me with anything else. He had better come through.

With a mixture of grim determination, nervousness, and beating heart, I went ahead and filled out the paperwork to apply to the adult degree program. Harold bought me a practice book for the English CLEP exam. It all seemed doable, except that they had invented some kind of weird analogy questions that I had to learn how to answer. I studied for a weekend and then took the exam. I kept telling myself, "You only have to pass; you only have to pass."

I notice that I have a habit of giving myself little positive mantras to get through life. It's weird that I never realized I did this. But I actually think it's helpful.

Well, I scored in the 96th percentile, so that helped boost my confidence. When I looked at the sample questions for the art exam, I laughed out loud. Really?

Q. Who is a famous architect?

A. Vincent Van Gogh

B. Beethoven

C. Frank Lloyd Wright

I think I can take this test right now. The general Humanities exam was equally simple. Yay! I didn't have to take English 101! I signed up to take Women in Literature and an ethics class.

And, my father begrudgingly agreed to pay for my tuition and books. I had a bunch of peer counseling sessions on that and on any lingering fears about starting school in my midthirties. I bought my books, some notebooks, pens, and a backpack. I was ready to start this new adventure!

Since Lucinda was now eight years old, I figured she could stay at home alone for a few hours if she happened to get sick and I could still go to my classes.

I loved my literature and philosophy classes. Thanks to the adult degree program, I wasn't the only older student. We adults tended to sit close to the front of the classroom and participate fully. I admit to being annoyed by some of the younger students who didn't seem to take their studies seriously. They'd sit in the back of the class, brushing their hair and snapping their chewing gum, and brag about how they didn't do the readings, just read the Cliffs Notes for English or looked up the philosopher in the encyclopedia.

Maybe education really is "wasted on the young," I thought. But then I had some of my biases challenged. There was a fairly young woman who sat in front of me in my Women's Literature class. She had blond "from the bottle" hair, curled into long Farrah Fawcett curls, and lots of mascara. She didn't speak much and when she did it was with a heavy Southern accent. I couldn't quite figure out what she was doing in this class.

One day our professor said, "Please divide yourselves into some small discussion groups." Wendy turned around and drawled, "Brooke, you'll join us, won't you?" Surprised, I agreed. Heidi turned out to be a serious student who was studying to be an English teacher. We became good friends. We did eventually talk about our different upbringings.

One day I asked her, "Were you raised to think you had to be pretty?"

"Oh, yes! My mother would not leave the house without putting on her face," she answered.

"Well, I think if you want to be taken seriously as a high school English teacher, you might want to rethink that," I said.

"Yes. This class has really opened my eyes."

So that is how she had been raised to look like a Barbie doll, I thought. *I'm glad I said something.*

There were other interesting differences between us. One time I confessed, "My children have unfortunately learned to curse from driving around with me."

"Ah know what you mean. My children probably think the other drivers on the road are called 'idiots,'" said Heidi .

I didn't have the heart to tell her what I called the other drivers. But I sure laughed about it at home with Harold, who was not nearly as amused as I was. He actually disapproved of my swearing and had warned me that I couldn't speak like that in public in the South.

* * *

Brooke was interrupted in her writing when Marissa stopped by her door.

"Mom, I think I'm ready to go back to work. Seth is eating solids now and drinking from a bottle, so he doesn't need me here all the time. I would like to start earning some money."

"That sounds good, Marissa. What kind of work are you going to look for?"

"I already applied at the Starbucks near here. I have an interview tomorrow. Will you help me pick out something to wear?"

"Sure. Let's see what you have that might be suitable." *Nothing with holes, hopefully. Nothing too tight. Nothing too revealing. Does she even own anything suitable?*

"How's this?"

A button-down shirt, a pair of intact jeans, and a pair of ankle boots with spiked heels.

"The shirt and jeans are fine. I don't know about those boots. They're not very practical."

"Well, I wouldn't wear them to work, but they make me feel good about myself for the interview," Marissa said, preening in front of the mirror and smiling.

"Fair enough," I said, thinking, *I never liked heels, but I did buy a pair of platform shoes once.*

* * *

Unfortunately, my scientific knowledge was not enough to CLEP out of a 101 astronomy class to fulfill my science requirement. The class was right after lunch in the summer. Taught by a teacher I dubbed "the Southern Mr. Rogers." I had a huge struggle staying awake in that class! The worst was when the teacher would show films of the solar system. Backed by calming music and a sonorous voiceover narrator, the films inevitably lulled me to sleep. It didn't help that my father had told me astronomy facts as bedtime stories, so I associated astronomy with sleep.

And even when the teacher lectured, I had to resort to biting the inside of my lip, pinching myself, or asking questions to stay awake. It's a wonder I passed that class.

The other class that was a struggle was algebra. I wanted so much to actually understand it, but that was not to be. Harold offered to help me and he gave it a valiant try. But I just couldn't grasp the underlying concepts. After a few frustrating sessions he said, "You do know how to follow a recipe. How about if I write down all the steps to use for each kind of equation and you just follow them? You will probably make a few computational errors, but most professors will just take off a couple of points for stuff like that. The exams are open notes, so you should be fine."

So this became our process. Harold would read the chapter in the book out loud to me, making empowering comments as he went along. "Oh, 'it is clear that…?' Sure it is. That's why it took mathematicians centuries to solve it." Or "Hmm, so-and-so's theorem? I guess he got a Nobel Prize for this; so I don't know why you can't understand it!" I would laugh, feeling much relieved.

Then he would write the steps to the equation down. Then I would follow them to do my homework. Then he would look it over and say, "Oops. I left out a step. Here you go." And I would do them again. In this painstaking way I managed to get a B in algebra even though to this day I could not tell you what a "function" is.

The other thing I noticed was that I avoided doing the algebra work like the plague—or like Covid-19. I would spend hours and hours looking up every reference to a character in a book I was reading, but do the absolute bare minimum for algebra. In fact, Harold would have to bribe me to do the work. "Come on, I'll take you out to lunch and we can do some math," he'd say. I would groan and reluctantly agree. My notebook was littered with images of dogs jumping through hoops as a metaphor of how I felt about the math requirement.

I recently saw a meme titled "How to do math"

1. Write down the problem.

2. Cry.

This is perhaps more accurate of my true feelings and experience.

During this time, I took a history class from one of the church members who also served on my Education Committee, Doug Green. He invited me to a party at his house. Most of the other guests were history professors. It turned out to be kind of a bust. First of all, there was little to nothing I could eat except potato chips. The ham biscuits, shrimp cocktail, and crab cakes were obviously not vegetarian. The liquor was flowing freely, but since I also don't drink, that was useless. *(Too bad there wasn't any grass, that could have helped.)* But worst of all, one man approached me and asked what I taught. When I told him I was a student of Joe's and did not yet even have a degree, his eyes widened, his mouth dropped open, and, speechless, he turned and walked away.

When I recounted this to Harold he said, "Next time say your first degree was in communal living."

I laughed and that is indeed what I have done in similar situations ever since.

I hate that kind of elitist snobbery, especially from folks who are supposed to be progressive. I'm convinced that this disrespect is what got us our worst president. Of course the lousy policies of so-called neo-liberals like Clinton, that shipped good-paying union jobs across the border and overseas, didn't help. Even though Trump's policies were even worse and his interests totally aligned with his wealthy friends and donors, he spoke like a friend and ally of working-class people. I watched him once on T.V. speaking at a rally. He leaned close to the people and said, "I see you. I hear you. You are not forgotten." We're sunk, I thought at the time.

CHAPTER THIRTY-SEVEN

Harold got inspired by my studies and decided to go back to school himself. Even though he was making a great living as a computer engineer with just a B.A., he wasn't sure that was what he wanted to do for the rest of his life.

He applied to a master's program in mathematics in the Midwest.

"What shall we do about our relationship?" I asked. "Since you don't think you want children until you are much older and by then I will be too old, I don't think it makes sense to make any commitments now."

My heart was breaking, but there was no way I wanted Harold to feel tied down. Once when eating breakfast he had said to me, "You see this egg? The chicken 'was involved' with our breakfast. You see this piece of bacon. The pig was 'committed.'"

"Let's see how it goes," said Harold. And so come that fall, he went off to the Midwest.

I had attended a woman's retreat with the church that summer. At the evening culture share, someone had sung "Give Yourself to Love" by Kate Wolf. Tears rolled down my cheeks as I began to weep. At that moment I decided to keep my heart open to Harold. I can still love him even if we are not together, I told myself.

Well, only a few weeks passed and then Harold called.

"Would you be willing to consider having a baby with me?"

Though surprised, my heart skipped a beat. "Yes," I said, excitedly running my hands through my curls.

"Good to know. I'm trying to figure things out. There are several very nice and very smart women here who seem interested in me, but they are so immature compared to you. They went directly from undergraduate to graduate school. And you are the first person I've ever met who doesn't treat your children like pets or pests," he said.

"Well, keep me posted," I said, wondering where this was going.

I reminded myself that I had decided to keep my heart open. *It's not easy, but I think it's the right thing for me. He's young. I have to give him time to figure out what he wants. Hmm. Another baby. I would love that.* I had given up hope, but that had not stopped the longings.

A few weeks later Harold broached the subject of marriage.

"Would you consider marrying me?"

"Well, that's a much harder question. I really don't want to fall into the 'wifey role,'" I said pensively.

I was twirling a curl around my pointer finger. "I don't really like the idea of marriage. How would that even work with us? We're both terrible housekeepers. The house would be a disaster. How about if we just lived next door to each other? We could buy two small townhouses and even cut a door through one of the walls so our kid could go back and forth."

I was getting caught up in this idea.

Harold paused for a moment and then said, "No, I don't think that would work for me. Think about it, Brooke. There's no rush and I'm not going to pressure you."

Well, I did think about it. I played out scenarios in my mind. I thought about if it was possible to have an egalitarian marriage. After about six months of deliberating, I said to my friend Becky, "I haven't even lived with him. How can I decide if I can marry him?"

"Living together and being married are two different things," she replied.

That statement shocked me, but also had a ring of truth to it. *A marriage has a completely different level of commitment,* I thought as I went to sleep that night. I woke up about 2:00 in the morning, thinking, *I could marry Harold.* The next morning I sat with the idea, sitting in my homey kitchen. The decision seemed solid. I picked up the phone and called Harold. Taking a deep breath, I said,

"Hi. I've decided I can marry you."

Silence on the other end of the line. *Hmm… I thought he'd be overjoyed,* running my hands through my hair. I waited.

"Well, now I have to think about it," he answered.

Taking another deep breath I said, "Okay. That seems fair," thinking, *Well, he did just ask me if I would consider it.*

This is so different from all the romantic fairytale garbage most people write about. I wish young people knew it's possible to be honest and take their time in making such decisions. Of course, I was now almost forty. It's not like I knew this the first time around.

It didn't take Harold long to decide to go ahead and get married. We told his parents and my dad. I was worried about his mother. She obviously didn't think a divorced woman with two kids was the best possible match for her eldest son. At least I knew it wasn't because I was white. Their family had every human shade from practically albino to midnight. But, they put up a good front and had us over for a little celebration.

My father laughed and said, "I'm not surprised! You kept saying it wasn't serious, but you would be on the phone with him for hours every night you were here."

This is what comes of having a psychologist for a father, I thought. *Sometimes they know more about you than you know about yourself.*

Our friends were all overjoyed. They also weren't very surprised. We started referring to ourselves as "clueless in Asheville," after the movie *Sleepless in Seattle*. We set the date for the end of August when we would both be done with our school work for the year.

"Should I get you an engagement ring?" Harold asked one day.

"No, no, no, no!" I shouted. "We don't believe in that kind of thing in my family. Especially not diamonds. They are all mined by essentially slave labor. In fact, my father didn't even want to get my mother a wedding ring because they symbolize the husband owning the wife," I continued. "He only did it to appease her family."

"Well, I have a different understanding about a wedding ring," he said. "To me it means you will never be alone."

This still makes me cry. If only it were true. Writing about this is kind of painful.

My father offered to pay for the wedding, giving us a very modest budget. But that was okay with me, because although I wanted to invite a lot of people, especially from the congregation, I didn't want a fancy wedding; just a joyous one.

Luckily, my best friend Rachel had a catering business at that time and could get me all the linens, cutlery, and plates, wholesale. And for our wedding present, she donated a huge roasted turkey.

"It's a good thing I'm not such a strict vegetarian anymore," I remarked to Harold. "I think your family would hate it if we didn't have anything they could eat at our wedding."

We paid Rachel to make deviled eggs, ham biscuits, and a huge chocolate cake.

"I'm sorry if it's more traditional to have a white cake for a wedding," I said. "But also, why reinforce the notion that white is better or symbolizes purity? Seems like internalized racism to me."

"It's okay. My mother will live with it," Harold said. "She's not as rigid as you think. And she really appreciates it that you agreed to no alcohol."

The rest of the meal was potluck style, provided by the women's auxiliary of the Unitarian Universalist congregation, with Trina and Jane from the Education Committee taking charge.

Rachel wisely advised us to keep the menu limited, because otherwise everyone wants to taste everything. So we had lasagna (to honor my Italian heritage), noodle kugel (to honor my Eastern European Jewish heritage), green salad, and potato salad. I made a huge bowl of my mother's potato salad to feel her presence at our wedding.

I thought we did a good job of including both of our families' traditions. It was quite a feast and I'm sure no one went hungry. This was before the days of veganism.

Although I don't advise doing your own cooking the morning of your wedding, the way I did! The phone kept ringing, I hadn't ironed my dress yet, and there I was dicing potatoes, celery, and olives, up to my wrists in mayonnaise.

I found a book about "creating a big wedding on a small budget." It had great ideas, many of which we followed, such as borrowing friends' house plants to spruce up the church social hall and placing a disposable camera on each table and having guests take their own pictures.

Of course nowadays people can take pictures on their phone. But it would be good to delegate one person per table to do that.

I asked one friend to videotape the ceremony and another to take photos. We spent a portion of the money to hire a live "old-timey" band composed of local friends. Harold made a dance tape of Motown and rhythm and blues to get everyone up and dancing.

I really hate how weddings have become such a business and so expensive! I loved our DIY festivities. But, now I'm about to attend Sean and Amara's massively elaborate Unitarian/Hindu wedding this spring. His fiancée's family are pillars of their community. At first Amara and Sean thought they could do it themselves, but it became apparent that they had too many guests and too many expectations from the community for that. Luckily, they found a beautiful all-inclusive venue with a view of the Blue Ridge Mountains, an arbor that can serve as the Hindu wedding canopy, and a large tented pavilion that can accommodate their 250 guests. Her parents are paying for most of it, but I'm also contributing. I'm trying very hard not to be a critical mother-in-law, making things difficult for everybody.

CHAPTER THIRTY-EIGHT

After the wedding we drove into the Blue Ridge Mountains for a short three-day honeymoon. Chimney Rock was at that time a tiny town near Chimney Rock State Park. It's one of the most beautiful parts of the Blue Ridge, with spectacular views and lots of hiking trails. We stayed at a quaint Victorian-style bed-and-breakfast. Our room had a rickety queen-size bed, an antique nightstand, and an easy chair covered in flowered material.

The first night we brought all the presents and cards up to the room and had a great time seeing what we got. But truly the best present was that my father and Harold's parents had helped us buy the house I had been renting all these years.

And, since we now owned the house, I could put up the metal sun, moon, and stars sculptures we had received as a wedding gift right on the house itself. It would make it easy for folks to find us, and it cheered me up every time I came home.

With the house located right off of Montford Avenue, we were so lucky to buy it back then. Today, the price would be out of reach. Even then, there were mature trees on the property. I had always loved sitting on the front porch. With its overhanging roof, it was usually shaded. I had a couple of wicker chairs and a small table there. It was a nice place to read and watch the world go by.

Plus, I was so relieved not to have to move. Harold had transferred to the University of North Carolina, Asheville when we decided to get married. He was a bit worried that he was moving into what had essentially been my space for years, but I was sure I could adjust and it would work out.

We fell asleep completely cuddled up to each other, with a soft breeze wafting through the gauzy curtains. The sounds of a hoot owl and the high-pitched buzzing hum of late-summer cicadas was so familiar and soothing. And the aroma of summer roses lulled us to sleep.

The next morning, Harold tried to get me to get up for breakfast, which was being served far too early for me, so he went downstairs and brought up breakfast in bed for me. Our host was none too pleased about this, but I truly didn't care.

Then, he climbed back into bed, took off his glasses, and said, "You know, we're married now. We don't have to be careful anymore."

"Mmm…shouldn't we wait a little while?"

"Why? And anyway…" caressing me and kissing me, "…it's a safe time."

I was too far gone to think at this point how he would even know this as my periods were not regular, or to remember that with my body, there was no "safe" time of the month. And that's how Marissa was conceived on our honeymoon, on the first day of our married life. There's a picture of me hidden somewhere in this house that Harold snapped right afterward, my bare shoulders showing under the patchwork quilt, a beatific, satiated smile on my face.

Later in the day we went hiking in the state park. There was no one else on the trail. Most hikers prefer to hike earlier in the day during the summer. And it was a weekday. At some point I stopped by a huge oak tree and sat down to catch my breath. Harold was looking at me with glittering eyes. He reached under my flimsy summer blouse and, cupping my breasts in his hands, began to roll my nipples between his fingers.

"Harold! What if someone sees us?"

"There's no one here," he said grinning wickedly and proceeded to unbutton my khaki shorts. By this time my breath was catching in my throat and I was pulsing with desire. As he entered me, I had to put my own hand over my mouth to stifle my moans of pleasure.

Whew, thought Brooke. *I'm sure glad I'll probably be dead by the time my grandson can read this book! It's embarrassing, but I'm trying to paint a true portrayal of my life. Besides,* she grinned to herself, *it's good for young people to know their elders had some fun in their day.*

We returned to our bed-and-breakfast for showers and a nap and then ventured out for dinner. Way back then, there really was nothing for vegetarians on the menu. So, I threw caution to the wind and ordered pork chops and mashed potatoes smothered in gravy. And peach pie for dessert.

Harold was looking at me strangely.

"When in Rome…," I said laughing. "Besides, it's my honeymoon. Why not live it up," I said, smiling and winking.

The next morning I managed to get up in time to have breakfast across the street from our bed-and-breakfast at a small diner and again shocked Harold by ordering bacon with my eggs and biscuits.

"I like bending my own rules occasionally," I said. "It keeps me from getting all self-righteous about what I eat. And even at home I'm not a complete vegetarian anymore."

We spent that day at Lake Lure and had a late picnic of leftovers from our wedding. The next morning we headed home.

When we got home, we began making the house more accommodating to Harold. We added bookcases everywhere, even in the bathroom, and another desk in my spacious upstairs bedroom.

The one thing I wasn't willing to compromise on, though, was a television. I had never had one in the house and wasn't about to start now.

"I hate the noise. I hate the commercials. I hate the arguments about programming and how much or how little the children can watch."

Harold did remember the time I had thrown away his remote control after his T.V. had been temporarily at my house to watch the presidential debates.

"You're lucky I didn't smash the whole damn thing! That lying, fake-smiling ex-actor drives me crazy," I had said at the time.

"Hmmm… you're the one who's acting crazy," said Harold, but he let it go for the time being.

Sometimes we would take a walk in the botanical gardens of UNC or the arboretum. It is a beautiful bit of nature right here in Asheville. I had not ventured onto the UNC campus before this, even though those spots are open to the public. Somehow having Harold be a student there made it seem more accessible.

I was hoping to finish my time at the community college that year. Classes had already started and I had left messages all over the English Department for my World Literature teacher that I would miss the first two days due to my honeymoon.

However, when I arrived on Friday for my first class, one of the first things she said after going over the syllabus was, "I want to remind you that two or more absences will lower your grade to the next grade down. This class is based heavily upon class participation."

I panicked. I stayed after class to talk with her.

"Did you get my messages?" I asked shakily, thinking, *There goes my grade-point average.*

"No," she said. "I didn't get anything. Where have you been? You've already missed the first two days."

"Oh! I left a message on the department voicemail and spoke to the secretary and asked her to leave you a note in your box," I said desperately. "I just got married and we went on a short three-day honeymoon. I had no idea of your policy or I wouldn't have done even that."

She looked at me and smiled kindly.

"Congratulations. Don't worry about your grade. I just start off the year sounding tough because otherwise the younger students don't take me seriously. They think I'm their age and that they can walk all over me. I've never had that attitude from the adult degree students. Just don't share this information," she said, nodding at me.

"Oh, thank you so much!" I said, greatly relieved.

About six weeks later, I realized I had missed my period.

"Harold, I think I might be pregnant," I said with both trepidation and anticipation.

"I'll run out right now and get a pregnancy test," he answered excitedly.

Oh, boy, I thought. *I had wanted to wait a few years. At least get my B.A. before we got pregnant.* But then, smiling to myself, I thought, *Babies come in their own time. Wow, it would be wonderful if we didn't have any trouble getting pregnant. A baby!!!*

CHAPTER THIRTY-NINE

When I was about three months' pregnant, I was in the social hall after services one Sunday chatting with my friend Trina from the Education Committee. Trina was also pregnant, a bit further along than me.

"You know," she said, "the doctors want me to do an amniocentesis test, but I'm not going to do it. If I had a child and it was injured in a car accident and became disabled, would I somehow not want it?"

"I agree with you," I said.

"But I'll tell you what," she continued. "I'm not sure having a thirteen-year-old and a baby at the same time is such a great idea."

She had a daughter who was in Lucinda's class at Sunday school.

"Well, I wasn't gonna tell anyone quite this soon, but I'm also pregnant," I said, laughing.

"Oh, you're going to love it!" she said, in the quickest about-face in history.

But a few weeks later, I started spotting and was put to bed. I realized I needed to take a leave of absence from my education director job and from the library. Everyone was very understanding, and Jane agreed to step in to run the school for the rest of the year. I hoped to be able to finish the semester. I dictated one paper to Harold from bed.

But then, after the bleeding subsided, one night I woke up with contractions in my fourth month. We rushed to the hospital, where they, of course, put in an IV to give me extra fluids, as they so love to do in hospitals. They took my medical history, and despite the fact that I had told them I had childhood asthma and chronic bronchitis, they prescribed a magnesium steroid to stop the contractions. This medication can interfere with breathing.

The contractions did stop, but my breathing became very, very labored. I needed extra oxygen. Harold went to the doctor and demanded that he take me off this medication that was doing me in. They hooked me up to an EKG machine without explaining the procedure at all. In my weakened state, I had the bizarre idea that they were going to give me small electric shocks to see how well my heart would handle it. But when I mentioned this to the nurse, he laughed and reassured me that I would not feel anything.

My EKG was normal. They took me off the medication but wanted me to stay in the hospital for several more days. And the annoying IV was still in my arm. Within another day, I had an infection going up my arm from it.

"Why do I need this IV?" I asked one of the nurses. "I can make sure to drink plenty of water."

"You are also getting some antibiotics through the IV in case the contractions were caused by an infection," she answered.

"Can I take the antibiotics by mouth?"

"Yes. I don't see why not."

"Good, then please take this IV out of my arm right now."

When Harold came that day to visit me, he looked at my chart.

"Hmm… this is interesting," he said, looking over the top of his glasses at me. "They have you down as a drug abuser."

"What? Just because I said I experimented in my youth with marijuana?" I exclaimed indignantly. "I don't smoke, I don't drink, I don't even use caffeine. That's ridiculous!"

"Not only that, they said you are a noncompliant patient because you 'refused the IV,'" he continued.

"I'm really done with this hospital. If the doctor doesn't discharge me today, you're just gonna push me out of here. They can't keep me against my will," I told the long-suffering Harold.

I learned something from this. Never admit to any past recreational drug use to medical professionals. And, no matter how logical or calm you are in asserting your rights about your own body, if you don't do what they want they will label you "noncompliant." Nonetheless, you do have rights and should not be afraid to ask questions and make decisions based on what makes sense to you.

This episode brings back memories of some bad experiences with medical professionals from earlier in my life and probably explains why some people are so hesitant to take the Covid-19 vaccines. In that case, the evidence is clear that it protects against hospitalization and death, but I can understand the skepticism.

Luckily, the doctor did discharge me that day, and we went home with strict orders for more bedrest and to stay hydrated. Harold, being the scientist that he is, went and found a high-risk pregnancy nursing manual. From that he learned that it would also be helpful if I laid on my left side. I had been prescribed an off-label medication that calms the uterus, but it raised my heart rate to such a point that my hands shook, and my voice was higher than normal. I found I couldn't do my schoolwork. I had to take incompletes for two of my courses.

Sean, now in high school, made up a work schedule for himself, Harold, and Lucinda to take care of the house, but Harold was none too happy about that. Instead, he hired someone to come clean once a week and bought a lot of takeout food. Lucinda was kind of freaking out from the whole scene. She had been the baby of the family for quite a while. She asked to go live with her father, and after putting up an initial fight, I acquiesced. I think in the long run it turned out for the best.

The Unitarian congregation arranged meals to be brought once a week to me. My friend Becky baked delicious cakes and chocolate chip cookies over several months. We had once had a discussion about my heightened sense of smell during pregnancy. I had said there were many worse smells in the world than good ones, but she had answered,

"Think about honeysuckle. Think about cinnamon. Think about the smell of chocolate chip cookies, fresh out of the oven!"

Well, she was right about all those delicious smells. And those cookies were very appreciated.

Harold was very good about reading to me out loud in the evenings during this difficult time. He selected *The Fire Next Time* by James Baldwin, and I selected *Their Eyes Were Watching God* by Zora Neal Hurston.

I found a midwife group, so I didn't have to go back to that first hospital. My father offered to pay for a doula once the baby was born, since my mother was no longer alive to come and help out like she had in my other two pregnancies.

It was a hard time, but I had been through similar hard times and knew that a baby would be worth it. Finally, I was far enough along to go off the medication. Within three days I went into labor. I had a whole support team, and Sean and Lucinda were there too. At some point, I kicked everyone out of the room except Harold.

When I went into transition, I grabbed his upper arm so hard he had dark red bruises the shape of my fingers afterward. And as before, I yelled my way through labor. This baby came so quickly, I didn't actually have to push. It was more like an earthquake had taken over my body and expelled her. I had meant to recite a prayer when she was born, but I totally forgot. But I believe prayers of the heart are also heard. The look on Harold's face when holding her for the first time was the embodiment of awe and gratitude.

And so baby Marissa was born to our great, great joy and wonderment. The Hebrew meaning of this name is "wished for child," which summed up our feelings perfectly.

The baby was healthy except for an elevated bilirubin, and for the first week she had to be under ultraviolet lights. They wouldn't even let me pick her up, so I had to try to express my breastmilk. At first I tried with a hand pump, which was really hard. I could only do it by looking at pictures of cute babies from the spiritual midwifery book. I finally understood pornography. But then I realized I could go to the hospital and use their pump while sitting next to Marissa. And so we got through that week and were finally able to bring her home.

We set up a bassinet in our bedroom, but I always had her sleep next to me for the first three months or so. It was so much easier. Nowadays, this is not encouraged, but I remain skeptical of Western discomfort with co-sleeping. I'm a very light sleeper and she was in no danger of me rolling over her. Harold would have been another story entirely.

Eventually we were able to buy a crib thanks to my dad. My friends at the Unitarian congregation had a beautiful welcoming ceremony for her. My dad and Harold's parents and siblings plus their spouses and extended family all came. Everyone wished Marissa many blessings, and we had some nice homemade refreshments afterward. My father had remarried, and he and his wife bought us the rocking chair I still have to this day.

That's a great gift to give to anyone who has a baby. I have also given swinging baby beds to new mothers.

Harold's mom, Edith, bought us lots of great baby clothes,

blankets, diapers, and a changing table. My friend Rachel brought by a huge box of infant clothes from a yard sale. They were all pink, but I figured it couldn't hurt an infant. But as soon as Marissa could express herself, she always refused to wear pink. Her grandmother had to go in the boys' aisle to find clothes in nice bright primary colors for her. The extreme gendering of children in the '90s took me by surprise.

I think this might be one of the reasons the younger generation has raised the issue of nonbinary and nongendered folks. We had hoped to create a world where they could just be themselves and be accepted as themselves and not put in such tight, horrible conforming boxes, but we failed.

CHAPTER FORTY

I think the first year of a baby's life is probably one of the most stressful that a couple goes through. The lack of sleep, the changing dynamics, the different approaches to each decision that seem so momentous at the time. And in our case, both of us trying to finish our degrees added an extra layer of stress. Harold admitted later that he had been a bit "crazy" to finish so he could support his new family. And that left me with the vast majority of childcare and a huge load of resentment.

One morning in that first year I woke up about 4:00 a.m. to nurse Marissa and realized we had forgotten to take out the trash. She was still awake after nursing, so I carried her downstairs with me. But looking at how much trash needed to be put out, I realized I couldn't do that and hold her at the same time. So I put her in the playpen and dragged the two heavy trash bags outside.

When I came back in, Marissa was screaming bloody murder and Harold was at the top of the stairs hollering.

"What are you doing to my baby?"

"Oh, now she's your baby? But not when she needs feeding?" I answered grumpily, picking up Marissa, who immediately settled down. "I put her in the playpen so I could take out the trash."

"Oh. Sorry. I woke up and heard her screaming," Harold said sheepishly.

"It's okay. It did sound like she was being tortured," I said, laughing and nuzzling that little one.

Since Harold was both working and going to school, while I was taking care of Marissa and also trying to finish school, I was with her the vast majority of the time. But on a lovely spring Saturday, Harold offered to take her outside for a bit. Much to my everlasting jealousy, that was the moment she took her first step. Harold came running in to tell me.

"Oh, that's not fair!" I exclaimed, although I was of course thrilled at the same time.

Sometime in that first year I realized I really couldn't get any of my incompletes done without at least a couple of uninterrupted hours of work during the week. I posted fliers at the local grocery store and library for a babysitter, "teenager okay."

I got a phone call. "Would a grandmother be okay?"

"Oh, yes! Even better!"

And so we met "Mamaw," a downhome Southern grandmother who took care of Marissa for me until she started walking. At that point, it was too hard for Mamaw to babyproof her whole house.

The next person I found was Jade, the partner of Ruth, an ex-Black Mountain member who had also moved to town. Jade was lovely and took great care of Marissa, allowing me time to finish one of my research papers. But then, they decided to move and I was stuck again.

Back to the fliers at the grocery store.

This time I found Wendy, and what a find! Wendy was the mother of five children; a white woman married to an African American man. So, we already had that in common.

When I had called one of Wendy's references, the woman had said, "I've never heard Wendy raise her voice to a child."

And that turned out to be true. I was there at odd hours and often hung out, just to soak up some goodness. I also never heard Wendy raise her voice to a child.

One day, I brought Marissa by and said, "I'm going to teach you some Yiddish: 'Hock me a *chienik*.' It means 'You're banging on my china teakettle.'"

"I'm going to teach you how to say that in Southern. 'You're pluckin on my last nerve,'" she said, laughing and taking Marissa from me.

When I came back to pick Marissa up, she said, "Yup, we were joined at the hip today."

Isn't that exactly what every mom wants from a babysitter? To take care of your kid with love? Wendy's children were like that too, treating Marissa like one of the family, where the older children all helped with the younger ones. They even potty-trained her.

It turned out that she was cutting yet another tooth that day she was so clingy. How the heck many teeth does one baby need anyway?

Here's a hint for parents of teething babies. Ice can help soothe the pain, and distracting them with something funny can help also. In Marissa's case, this turned out to be tearing up pieces of magazines and throwing them on the floor. She would chortle each time. One night we filled the whole kitchen with bits of paper before she and I could go back to sleep.

On another of the rare occasions when Harold gave me a break from childcare duty, I went to a lecture at the library. It was so nice to be with other adults without having to keep an eye and ear out for a young one. I cranked up the radio to the country station on the way home, feeling very refreshed.

Until I walked into the house and heard these ominous words.

"Oh, Brooke. I'm so sorry. She was so quiet."

"Uh-oh," I said, flashing back to Lucinda and the laundry detergent and a time when Sean and his little friends had painted the bathroom sink bright red while "being so quiet."

"What did she do?"

Harold mutely showed me my brand-new walking shoes, once white; now covered with pink lipstick.

"Oh dear. You had no way of knowing that when children are quiet they're usually doing something they shouldn't. I think I can get most of this off."

I noticed that I took this mishap with greater equanimity than I would have at a younger age.

CHAPTER FORTY-ONE

Each child is so different and Marissa was no exception. When she learned to jump over the thresholds between rooms, she would give off the most wondrous "Ah Ha Ha!" A sound of joy and power I envied. I even practiced making similar sounds in my peer counseling sessions hoping to gain self-confidence. Then I would laugh and laugh. It was very cathartic.

While I was having tea with my old friends Lisa and Laura from Black Mountain one day, Lisa said, "Oh, Marissa is eighteen months old now. I remember that time as being really difficult."

"That's funny. I can't remember it at all," I said, getting worried. "Maybe I've blocked it all out."

"Well, they are mobile, but don't have much judgment yet," said Laura. "Much like our teenagers."

So I went home and began to notice Marissa at eighteen months. It was true that she was very mobile and hated being in her stroller. I had to watch her like a hawk on walks around the neighborhood. Shopping trips usually ended with the packages in the stroller, me pushing with one hand and holding her by the collar with the other hand.

And impulse control was a work in progress. "No, no," scribble, scribble, marker in one hand, standing by the back screen door. "No, no," scribble, scribble. *It's a good thing we own this house now. These marker stains won't come off easily.*

But then one day, conscience won out. We had forgotten to close the baby gate to the upstairs where she knew she shouldn't go. She stood by the gate and screamed. I came running, picked her up in my arms, giving her a big hug.

"Good girl, Marissa! You didn't go up the stairs! I'm so proud of you!"

I quickly closed the gate and offered for her to come help me cook dinner in the kitchen.

By the time Marissa was almost two, I was very tired of breastfeeding. We were down to just one feeding at bedtime. I tried to convince her, "It is all gone," but she would say, "Let's try," lifting up my shirt.

"By the time your child can speak in full sentences, she should be weaned," I grumbled to Harold.

He just shrugged.

But my milk supply was diminishing and one night I told Marissa, "You drank the laaast drop."

And that was that. She never asked again and it was true. I had no more milk left.

Around this time, when she was two and a half, I had finished my last incompletes from the pregnancy and was ready to go back to work and school. The Unitarians ran a preschool she could attend for free as I resumed being the Sunday school director. We said goodbye to Wendy and her family as babysitters, but stayed friends and would often stop by for a visit.

Marissa adjusted well to preschool, and I was able to add afternoon hours at the library. And here is where my studies really paid off. They put me in charge of the display cases for Black History Month and Women's History Month. It was really fun to feature the books and authors I had come to love: Zora Neal Hurston, Alice Walker, Virginia Woolf, Langston Hughes.

It's a good thing I retired right before librarians began getting targeted by right-wing fanatics. I would have been a perfect scapegoat. I was always showcasing marginalized people in any way I could: story hour, book clubs, displays. I loved Nikki Giovanni's children's book about Rosa Parks. It has beautiful illustrations and lilting prose. It even included the little-known story of JoAnn Robinson and the other women who were the first ones to call for a bus boycott. And it told how the children had passed the fliers all around the Black neighborhoods in Montgomery. It's probably being banned right now in Florida, Texas, and Louisiana.

CHAPTER FORTY-TWO

As I returned to work and school I began to feel like I could breathe again. Like I was coming up out of a deep pool of water where I had been close to drowning. I was very happy. Marissa and I had a good time in the afternoons hanging out together, going to the park and playground. She would ask me, "What do *you* want to do?"

I'd jokingly say, "I want to take a nap."

"No, you don't," she would answer.

"Hmm…I want to read my book."

"No, you don't."

"I want to go to the park or go see what costumes the statues of geese in our neighbor's yard were wearing."

"Yes!" and off we would go.

Later we would cook dinner together. I'm glad all my children learned to cook by helping out in the kitchen from an early age. I even began to teach her some chants she could adjust when she was older, like:

"What do we want?"

"Juice!"

"When do we want it?"

"Now!"

But Harold had taken a job administering the University of North Carolina's computer systems and it was one headache after another. And he had a terrible boss. So terrible that Marissa would pretend to be Harold.

"Goodbye, I'm going to work!" she would declare and march out the front door.

The next minute she would come back in saying,

"The boss, rrrrrrr….."

Now I understand that he was resentful of my newfound happiness but could not figure out how to tell me, or how to negotiate the issues between us. Like many couples, we also had vastly different ideas around money. I tend to be frugal and he tends to spend more than he can afford. And the ongoing domestic chores issues ate away at us. But much else remained good.

I tried to encourage Harold to look for other work. He was very discouraged about finding something better.

"Brooke, I don't think you understand what I'm up against even in this supposedly liberal town. Most people don't see me as a viable candidate in a highly technical computing job. At least at the university I'm accepted and have good benefits."

And the ongoing racism he and his family had to deal with was challenging.

One day he walked in the door looking both dejected and barely containing his rage.

"What's wrong? What happened?" I asked immediately.

"I got pulled over by the cops yet again," he said grimly. "You know how careful I am to stay within the speed limit and obey every rule. I hate dealing with them. This time they claimed I hadn't come to a complete stop right up the street."

"Oh, Harold! I'm so sorry. Is there anything we can do? File a complaint or something?"

"No. I'm pretty sure that would just make matters worse. Then they'd have me in their mental radar and would begin to deliberately dog me. This was just a random 'driving while Black' thing."

Another time, I happened to look out the window at about the time Harold was due home. What I saw shocked and terrified me. Harold was outside our house, hands on the top of our car, with two cops frisking him.

Breathe, Brooke, breathe. You don't want to make things worse. I took a few deep breaths and then walked out the door.

"What's going on, officers?" I asked.

"This man fits the description of someone who just held up a liquor store downtown," one of them answered.

"This man is my husband and is employed by the university as their computer systems administrator," I answered as calmly as I could.

"Well, we are just trying to protect you, ma'am," said the other officer.

I had to bite my lip to not say, *Looks like I and my family need protection* from *you rather than the other way around.*

Luckily, at that moment, they got a call on their walkie-talkies that the real thief had been apprehended.

They abruptly let Harold go. But no apology. No acknowledgment that they had made a mistake.

At this point, I felt compelled to ask, "I'm wondering what the description of the thief was."

"Well, an African American male, five-foot-six, wearing jeans and a green windbreaker," one of the officers said.

I just looked at him. Harold is six-foot-one and was wearing khakis and a white sweater.

"Well, good day, ma'am," they said and got into their police cars and drove away.

"Brooke, you could have gotten me killed!" Harold exclaimed once we were inside.

"I kept very calm, I thought. I'm not just going to stand around and watch them harass you!" I answered heatedly.

At that Harold laughed. "Here, let me draw you a little graph." He took a piece of paper and drew a line across the bottom. On the far left he wrote a C and labeled it "Asheville calm." Midway he drew an X and labeled it "Asheville agitated." Way past that, at almost the far right end of the paper, he drew a B and labeled it "Brooke, calm."

"Oh," I said dejectedly, feeling rather abashed. "Yeah, my Jewish and Italian families were off the charts too. And now I understand where that phrase comes from."

Harold hugged me and said, "I know you were just trying to stick up for me."

A few days later he said, "Brooke, if you are going to do another display for Black History Month, it might be nice to feature the fact that during the Civil War, Asheville contributed a number of companies to both the Confederate army and the Union army. One would expect the Confederate army, since the wealthy professional classes owned slaves, but it's pretty cool that some folks sided with the Union.

"In fact, after first being defended by Confederate troops, North Carolina Union troops from the Third North Carolina Mounted Infantry captured Asheville. They negotiated a departure, and the twenty-seven hundred troops left town, accompanied by hundreds of freed slaves. Most people don't know there were Union troops from North Carolina."

"Wow, Harold. That is really interesting. I'll do some research and create a display. Maybe someone local has written a book about this."

I began some research.

"Harold, thank you so much for getting me started learning about the history of Asheville! There are quite a few books and some of them look very good. I'm going to make a display of those next month. And I'm going to read this one that includes tall tales. Maybe I can tell some of them during my next story hour."

Unfortunately, just as I was starting to feel better again about Asheville and its surrounding areas, I got a call one day from Edith, Harold's mother. Usually a calm person, she sounded quite upset. I asked what was wrong.

Edith said, "I just got a call from my mother's cousin, my Aunt Pearl. She's being fined seventy-five dollars for not mowing her lawn out in Candler."

"What, that's ridiculous! How can we help?"

"Well, we've already taken up a collection to help pay the fine, but do you think Harold could get out there this Saturday and mow her lawn? They're threatening her with jail if it isn't mowed within the week."

"Jail?! For not mowing her lawn? That's outrageous! Of course Harold will help, I'll tell him as soon as he gets home. Let me write down Aunt Pearl's address and phone number."

"Thank you, honey."

This incident reminded me that everywhere I had lived had both a history of racism and current-day manifestations of the ongoing struggles of people of color.

One of my friends in high school who had a Jewish father and an African American mother had a cross burned on their lawn in Southern California.

And recently my own little beach town made the national news. Bruce's Beach, a Black-owned beach resort that was seized by the city in the 1920s, was finally returned to the heirs after one hundred years.

Sigh, we have so much work to do to repair the damage from racism.

JULY

Blues on a rainy day
I cry as I drive away
The blues cry in the world just like an ocean
—Tom Davey, "Like an Ocean"

CHAPTER FORTY-THREE

"Mama, can I have my thirteenth birthday party out at Black Mountain this year? My dad said it's okay with him," Lucinda asked. "Since I moved back in with you," she added.

Sigh. *I don't like this idea very much. With all the drugs and alcohol floating around that place, it sure doesn't seem like a great place for a teenager to have a party.*

"Let me talk to him. I need to make sure there will be some adult presence there."

"Hello, Frank? Are you sure you want to do this?"

"Sure! No problem. What are you so worried about? Don't you trust Lucinda?"

Oh, for goodness' sake; he sounds like a teenager himself.

"It's not that I don't trust Lucinda. It's just that teenagers in general are apt to do stupid things when there are no adults around, especially if they have easy access to drugs and alcohol. I know Lisa won't allow Hannah to come unless there is adult supervision. And I agree with that. Can you promise me that you will be there?"

"Okay. No problem. I'll stick around."

"Thanks."

* * *

About two minutes after the party was over, my phone started ringing.

"Did you know Lucinda had a bottle of wine at her birthday party?" Lisa asked me.

"What? No! Where was Frank? I was very clear with him that he had to be there."

"Well, apparently he wasn't. Willow brought it and was also smoking cigarettes out on the back deck. It made Hannah very uncomfortable."

"I'm so sorry, Lisa. I will speak with both Frank and Lucinda about this."

The phone rang again. "Hi, this is Laura. I just thought you should know that there was wine at Lucinda's birthday party."

"I just heard the same from Lisa. Frank promised me he would be there," I said distraughtly, running my fingers through my hair. "Laura, what should I do? Now I feel like I can't trust Frank."

"Well, maybe you can't. There should be some consequences for this."

"Yes. I agree. But I don't want them to all fall on Lucinda. We have enough of a strained relationship right now. And it's more Frank that I'm upset with. He's supposed to be the adult."

"Well, some people don't grow up. Black Mountain is filled with grown-ups still acting like teenagers. That's one of the reasons I left," said Laura. "I advise you to have an open conversation with Lucinda and tell her how you feel. Try to negotiate something workable with her.”

“Thanks, Laura. I’ll do that.”

Laura was so good about parenting issues. I’m glad I had her as a friend during all those years.

Lucinda came in the next morning from her dad’s.

“Hi, Lucinda. How was your birthday?” I asked, trying to sound neutral. I was interested to see if she would mention Willow, the bottle of wine, and the cigarettes.

“Oh, fine,” she answered, trying to look innocent, but not quite succeeding.

“Well, we need to talk. I heard there was wine at your party,” I said firmly, trying not to yell.

“That was Willow! I didn’t know she was going to bring it. I didn’t even drink any,” Lucinda wailed. “How do you know about it?” she then asked.

Sigh. The odd things that people forget.

“Lisa and Laura called me.”

“Oh,” she said in a deflated manner. I could tell she was now remembering that my best friends were the mothers of her friends.

“Look, I know it wasn’t your fault, but your father had promised he would be there. And now I can’t trust him. I would like to be able to trust you. How can we move forward here?”

“I don’t know. Maybe I can promise to agree to your requirements?” Lucinda suggested.

“Well, that’s a start. It might take awhile for me to completely trust you again. I guess that’s the consequence of this. I also heard Willow was smoking cigarettes,” I said, determined to clear the air completely.

“Well, she did. But only on the back porch. You don’t have to worry about me smoking. I told her I have ‘personal’ reasons for not smoking. Because of Grandma Claire."

"Well that's real smart, Lucinda. I know that teens respect personal reasons. And if you ever need another reason to refuse things, you can use me as your excuse. Just tell them your mother is crazy and would kill you if she found out."

"Oh, I don't need that excuse! Willow wanted me to go quarry jumping a few weeks ago, but I just told her, 'No, thanks, I prefer to live,'" she said rather triumphantly.

I breathed a big sigh of relief. *Thank God she knows she's mortal. So many teens do not. And she wants to live. Thank God for that also.* I smiled at her, gave her a hug, and said, "I think you have better judgment than either Willow or your dad. Thanks for sharing that. Just please check in with me if you're going to parties or such."

"Okay, Mama." And she skipped out the door. *Whew, I'm glad that's over. And I think I handled it well. I'm comfortable being the adult in the room.*

A few weeks later, I was having lunch with Lisa and Laura in downtown Asheville. "It's so scary having our girls enter their teen years," said Lisa.

"Yes. When I think of all the risky things I did as a teen, I get chills going up and down my spine," added Laura.

"Hitchhiking was the riskiest thing I did at that age," I said. "I had to get out of a moving car once, when the driver was turning off the main highway in New Zealand. And a friend of mine got raped at knifepoint while hitching."

We had a slogan back then, "Live the revolution now!" We thought we could change the world just through the force of our alternative actions. So, if we behaved as if it was safe to hitchhike, it would be safe. And it actually kind of worked there in California for a while. So many young people were hitchhiking that even my mom started picking them up. But then, too many bad experiences happened and, on that front at least, we gave up.

"Is there any way we can keep our girls safe?" asked Lisa.

"Probably not," answered Laura. "But keeping the lines of communication open is the most important thing we can do. Hopefully they will come to us if something bad does happen."

And some bad things did happen. It's impossible to protect our children completely. Sigh. *They do need to learn from experience. And besides keeping the lines of communication open, the only other thing to do is let them know we love them no matter what,* thought Brooke in a pensive mood.

"Would you all like to go with me to the Shakespeare festival next week? It's right in your neighborhood, Brooke," asked Lisa, changing the topic to something more cheerful.

"I can't," said Laura. "I already have plans with Topaz to go kayaking on the French Broad River."

"That sounds like fun, Laura. Someday I'd like to try that. I'm free next Saturday, Lisa. And this is one of my favorite times of year. The dogwoods should be blooming in the park. I think Lucinda would like to meet up with Hannah at the Shakespeare festival also. As long as they don't have to sit with us," I said laughing.

CHAPTER FORTY-FOUR

It may sound from the last few chapters like I completely gave up any kind of activism once Marissa was born. But that isn't true. During the first Clinton administration, when he was proposing his famous "welfare reform," I was appalled. He played on every intersection of sexism, racism, and classism, and right into the hands of people who loved to talk about "welfare queens." I went to a town hall meeting at the high school with our local representative.

Sitting on those uncomfortable folding metal chairs, under glaring fluorescent lights, staring at the worn linoleum all institutions seem to use, I saw a fairly packed room. I hoped I wouldn't be the only one protesting these changes.

When my turn came to speak, I said, "As the mother of a young child, I have some questions. Do you expect mothers of newborns to return to work immediately? How much maternity leave, if any, is in this new proposed legislation? What if the mother is breastfeeding? How can women afford childcare while working a minimum wage job?"

"I really can't answer that. But I can tell you that I support the idea that anyone receiving government assistance should be working."

There were several other women there, bringing up points I hadn't even thought of.

"Hello, I'm the director of the battered women's shelter. Many women needing aid are escaping from abusive husbands. If women have to divulge the names of the fathers of their children in order to get any aid, they are endangering their life and the lives of their children."

Our representative merely scratched his head at that. "Hmm… thank you for sharing." *One of the most useless comments ever.*

At the end of that meeting, before people dispersed, I got the names and phone numbers of every person who had spoken against this so-called welfare reform. Harold helped me organize a meeting to discuss our options. The Peace and Justice Center let us use their space.

"This legislation is really horrible!" said Jessica, the director of the battered women's shelter.

"And these so-called employment training centers that pay half of minimum wage—just to be able to get a little financial help? Who the heck thought that up?" asked Lily, head of the tenants association, sounding extremely exasperated.

"Obviously, not someone who has been a poor single mother," said Joyce, a member of the local NAACP.

"So what should we do?" I asked. "Representative Howell seemed unsympathetic."

"Senator Blake owes his last win to the Black community and he knows it," said Joyce thoughtfully. "Even if he did meet secretly with our officers."

"And Senator Smiley has been a lot more moderate on many issues than the other Republicans. He supported the Americans with Disabilities Act, for instance," I added.

We decided to organize a citizen lobby to meet with our senators when they were back in North Carolina during their break. They heard our concerns and understood that there could be unintended consequences for this horrible policy change. We were able to get a better law in North Carolina than existed on the federal level. One of the key provisions was a "just cause" exemption to divulging the name of the father if it would endanger the lives of the mother or her children.

One such case happened that made the papers about a year later. This woman had raised her son who was the result of a gang rape until he was twelve. But then she got laid off from her job. She applied for cash assistance. When asked to divulge the name of the father, she refused. She still lived in the same housing project as the young men who had raped her. The agency tried to deny her any help, but she won on appeal, thanks to our work. *And all of that done from my battered kitchen table.*

CHAPTER FORTY-FIVE

But when Marissa was two, three, and four years old, Harold really took the lead of being the activist in our family. I supported him by doing childcare on the weekends. We had gone to the famous Mountain Dance and Folk Festival in Asheville to both listen to music and see what local activists were up to.

Marissa and I enjoyed Laura Boosinger and her band, with their upbeat tempo that appealed to Marissa, even if the words often contained heartbreak. I appreciated the range of traditional and more contemporary lyrics. It was also very nice that Timmy Abell played a children's set. Then we went back outside to get some snacks. This was a day I didn't worry about health. We ate peach ice cream and donuts for our lunch.

While we were enjoying ourselves at the festival, Harold connected with a group of environmental activists. They were working on shutting down the C and T paper and pulp processing mill at the entrance to the national forest. It was horribly polluting and a dangerous place for the workers also.

"Do you know how when you come around the bend on Route 197, the signs say, 'Watch out for fog'?" Harold asked.

"Yes. I've always wondered about that. It seems more like smog sometimes to me, although it can also get foggy up there," I said. "It reminds me of going into L.A. when I was young. It looks kind of yellow and my eyes sting when I pass through there. And it smells horrible."

"Well, that is indeed air pollution from the paper-processing plant. I just learned today that pulp and paper generates the sixth largest amount of industrial air, water, and land pollution in the United States. This seems like a good project to work on. I'm trying to 'think globally, and work locally.' And I really like the group of people I met today from the Save Our Forest/Save Our Workers Alliance. They're hoping to build an alliance between the workers and the environmentalists instead of pitting one group against the other. I know there are some African Americans working in that plant. Perhaps I can be a good example that this is an issue that affects everyone. Even if most of the other folks are white."

The factory ran day and night and on weekends. The Save Our Forest/Save Our Workers Alliance picketed every weekend. Harold was heavily involved. They tried to be there when the shifts changed and to engage in dialogue with the workers. Sometimes they would even bring cookies for the workers. And they were working with the Forest Service to explore expanding the job opportunities in conservation.

Since the site was so polluting, it wasn't a good place to bring a child. So I held down the fort at home, contributing childcare to the cause. I also sent homemade cookies on occasion. I'm not sure most of the activists understood my role. When they occasionally had potlucks, they mostly wouldn't talk to me or notice Marissa.

But in retrospect, they may have just been shy. Because many years later, several of them seemed really glad to see me when I spoke at a vigil for George Floyd.

The one exception to all this was Sammy. He always had a kind word to say to me and would play peek-a-boo with Marissa. He was also one of the only folks, besides me, who would actually cook something for those potlucks. Everyone else would just bring tortilla chips and salsa, or veggie sticks.

Sometimes he came to events at the Unitarian church. He was kind of shy, but also up for challenging himself with some of the sacred pagan dances we did, or other rituals. I liked him so much and invited him home for dinner on occasion. He would always insist on bringing something to share or doing the dishes. Everyone loved Sammy.

The protests went on year after year, while nothing seemed to change. Then one day, disaster struck. There was a fire at the plant caused by a freak accident. Due to the corrosive nature of the bleach used in the pulp-processing procedures, the workers had to periodically recoat the vessel walls with fiberglass and flammable resins. On this particular evening, the overnight temperatures prevented the hardening of the resin. So they had to use a curing gun to complete the application.

This is a routine procedure. But this time, one of the workers accidentally dropped the heat gun into a five-gallon bucket of resin. The fire that followed moved too quickly for the workers to extinguish. Two workers perished in the blaze, along with Sammy.

Sammy was inside the building, using the restroom, when the fire engulfed the plant. Over the years, he had built some real friendships there and someone had let him in against company regulations.

"It's just not fair! It's just not fair" I sobbed to Harold, who was also crying.

"With all the evil people in the world, why Sammy? Why Sammy? Why couldn't one of the factory owners have died? That would have been poetic justice."

Of course, even then I knew that isn't how the world works. Nor is that the kind of sentiment I wish to have. But in the moment, it was how I felt.

And now, I really understand why there just can't be that kind of "justice." If there is such a God who would mete out punishment like that, especially if this imagined God listened to people's prayers, in a short time there would be no humans left alive. Because we think the factory owners should die and they think we should die. In the end, random chance turns out to be a comfort.

When the names of the dead were printed in the local newspaper, I realized that Mamaw's son was also killed. I threw together a macaroni-and-cheese casserole and went over to pay a condolence call.

"I'm so, so sorry for your loss," I said as I sat beside her, holding her hand on the worn green-and-yellow sofa, trying to ignore the cigar smoke from her husband.

"Well, you know, when those protesters started picketing, I thought they were way outta line. But now, I think they were right," she said sniffing.

I sighed and ran my hands through my hair.

"Well, we all would rather have everyone alive. No one is getting any satisfaction from this. But perhaps the factory will shut down and the remaining workers will be able to get jobs with the Forest Service."

After a long pause, "Do you have enough money for the funeral and burial?"

"Yes. The company is paying for it all, and there is a small pension for his family. He has—I mean *had*—a wife and a little baby," she said, crying again.

I teared up too and could only sit with her, shaking my head at this tragedy.

It's weird the way a community can be brought together by death. Suddenly, there were not "tree-hugging hippies" and "ignorant rednecks," just grieving folk. Although there were individual funerals in various churches around town, including one for Sammy at the

Unitarian Universalist Church, we also held a joint memorial. All the choirs got together and sang "I'll Fly Away." Many ministers spoke, and we laid wreaths and flowers by city hall in downtown Asheville.

The plant shut down. Our air quality was clear again. Our streams less polluted. But at what human cost?

Both Harold and I pulled back from activism for a while after that.

* * *

When Seth was about two years old, Marissa came into my bedroom one evening. "Hi, Mom. I have something to tell you."

"Yes?" I said, looking up from the book I was reading.

"I've decided to move into an apartment with Belinda. We figured out that between the two of us, we can manage the rent and utilities on this townhouse that we looked at. It's just a few miles away. And there's a woman across the hall who can look after Seth when I'm at work."

"Well, Marissa, I'll miss you and Seth, but I understand that you probably want your own space. I *am* pretty set in my ways," I said, thinking, *How's she really going to manage?*

"Yeah. You are," she said, laughing. "And Belinda and I have been best friends since high school. My father said he'd pay for the security deposit."

"Okay. Thanks for letting me know. And be sure to bring that baby by for a visit."

* * *

The second Iraq War pulled us back into activism and the streets again. We stood in pouring rain with my laminated "No Blood for Oil" sign.

I think I still have that sign. You never know when it might be needed again given our government's proclivity for starting wars and our population's reluctance to give up gas-guzzling cars.

We even traveled to Washington, DC, to join protests there. Marissa was old enough to say she wanted to come with us. Harold got arrested lying down in the street. He was thrilled that Daniel Ellsberg was in the same paddy wagon as him. They apparently had a good chat.

Because we were with him, he posted bail and was let out in time to join us in a raucous demonstration from the Washington Monument to the White House. Marissa enjoyed shouting with the crowd "George Bush is 'wack'! U.S. out of Iraq!"

When we returned home, I was discussing these kinds of slogans with my friend Becky. "It doesn't seem in the spirit of nonviolence," I said.

"No, it doesn't," she agreed. "And not a great way to reach a broader section of the population. Especially the funniest ones like 'George Bush, read my labia / U.S. out of Saudi Arabia!'"

We both collapsed laughing. "Maybe the main point is to energize ourselves," I said. But I still have my doubts.

CHAPTER FORTY-SIX

I buckled down and finally finished my B.A. when Marissa was seven. Sean and Lucinda had moved all the way across the country to attend Piney Woods College in Oregon. It was both progressive and affordable. An excellent choice.

They did come home for occasional visits. One time Lucinda phoned ahead.

"I've met this really nice human. They are going to come home with me to meet you."

Hmmm…someone unusual. The nongender noun and pronoun. Should be interesting. Of course, all I want for any of my children is for them to be happy and have people in their lives who love and care about them.

Well, we met Jim and liked them a lot. On a car ride back from dinner one night, they began to explain why they were not comfortable with their assigned gender.

"A man is supposed to be tough. Never show any emotion. Competitive. Empathy is seen as a weakness. None of this is how I am or want to be."

"Well, I'm sorry that is how you were raised," I said, hoping to offer a better alternative, but the best I could come up with was, "We think all humans can embody any human characteristic."

What I didn't feel comfortable saying was that their definition of being a "man" was my definition of "toxic masculinity."

The next time they visited, their name and pronouns had changed.

Jim was now Jinny; pronouns she and her. She was experimenting with feminine dress.

"I always wanted to be on an equal footing with women, rather than deferred to, but found it almost impossible when I walked through this world as a man," she reported.

I found that very interesting.

We had taken a drive along the Blue Ridge Parkway and needed to stop at a rural gas station before heading home. I could see Jinny trembling as she got out of the car to use the bathroom in her new female attire.

"Do you want me to come with you?" asked Lucinda.

"No; it's okay," Jinny answered.

I could well understand their trepidation. So I went in also, just in case. Thankfully nothing happened and we returned peacefully to the progressive oasis that is Asheville.

Lucinda and Jinny have had various relationships over the years, some closer than others, but always remaining friends. I'm also Facebook friends with Jinny. I've watched from that vantage point her transition to be more and more female.

It has seemed torturous at times to me and like a huge failure of those of us who wanted so badly to create a society where gender roles would be open rather than tiny, constricting boxes. The backlash began with Reagan and has taken on an even more dangerous, life-threatening aspect in these years since Trump. Sigh. I truly wish people did not feel they needed surgery or hormones to be their true selves.

Jinny is not our only friend who has transitioned. Some of them are so much happier now, feeling that they can be their true selves. And I often forget their new names or pronouns. That's how I learned that using a person's old name is called using their "deadname." Ouch!

We have so much to learn about how to be human with each other.

CHAPTER FORTY-SEVEN

Thanks to my having a B.A., both the church and the library gave me raises. I was so tired of being in school that I took a break. Harold also finished his M.A. I was hoping that with both of us more free on weekends for the first time in years, we would do more fun things with each other like in the early days of our relationship.

But Harold got interested in chess tournaments that took him out of the house most weekends. I felt abandoned and like domesticity just didn't interest him. I was doing 98 percent of the dishes and laundry. My resentment grew and grew. One day when no one was home I threw a pot against the kitchen sink window, cracking it slightly.

I'd miss him all day, waiting until he came home in the evening, and then the minute he stepped in the door, I'd yell at him about something. The more I yelled, the more he withdrew. I couldn't seem to stop this cycle and neither could he.

It got even worse when I decided to go to graduate school and finally get my librarian's license. Even though I begged him not to, Harold decided to get a Ph.D. at the same time.

"You know school stresses us out!" I implored. "We are already having trouble getting along. This will make things ten times worse. Let me go first and when I'm done, I promise you I'll support you to get your Ph.D."

"No. I've put it off too long already. You've inspired me to go back to school too."

I had to go through a lengthy application process and a grueling interview to be accepted into my master's program at Hoover College, even though I had excelled in the B.A. program there. On the other hand, Harold just called up the head of the computer department, went in to talk the same day, and got offered to go immediately into the University of North Carolina Ph.D. program.

It all seemed so unfair.

And I was correct that both of us being in graduate school did put a huge strain on our relationship, including some ways I had not anticipated.

CHAPTER FORTY-EIGHT

"Brooke, I've been invited to go out drinking with some new friends from school. I know you're not into that. I'll probably be out pretty late, so don't wait up for me," Harold said one day over the phone.

Sigh. *What the heck is he thinking? That he's twenty-seven again?*

"Okay. I have a big day at Sunday school tomorrow, so I won't wait up for you."

A few days later…

"Brooke, some of these grad students are really amazing. This one young woman has designed a completely new way of doing electronic graphics!"

"Hmm. That does sound interesting."

"And she's very pretty too."

What is he trying to tell me? Should I be worried?

"Well, that's an added benefit, I guess. Should I be worried?" I asked, wrinkling my brow.

"Well, I wanted to bring this up, but I didn't know how. I'd like to renegotiate our monogamy agreement," he said, looking hopeful and grinning in a way that stabbed at my heart.

"You want to renegotiate our monogamy agreement," I repeated dully, in a kind of shock.

This man who insisted on monogamy when we began seriously dating. This man for whom I had closed my heart, and even my eyes. For years I had no eyes for anyone but him. And now that I'm "old," he's enamored of a younger woman.

"I have to think about it," I said, pulling on a curl.

Well, I thought about it.

I don't even believe in monogamy. It would be hypocritical of me to demand it now. Surely Harold loves me and this is a passing infatuation.

So I said yes, dreading this decision. How could I compete with a slim, beautiful, African American woman who was smart, in her twenties, and engaged in computer work? But I saw no honorable alternative.

During this time I went to a national conference of Unitarian educators. I had a good time and stayed up late one night singing folksongs and cracking jokes with a small group of folks mostly my age. When we said good night, one of the guys pulled on my toe and grinned at me. *Hmmm,* I thought, *maybe there are nonmonogamous possibilities for me too. Maybe I don't have to be fixated on Harold.*

A few weeks later I found Harold crying in the living room.

"What's wrong?" I asked, feeling pretty worried and wrinkling up my brow again.

"I think I have to leave the marriage," he replied.

"What? For a twenty-something grad student?" I yelled.

"No," he sighed. "It's not her. She has a boyfriend. It's that I've realized I'm not happy. I can't stand all your yelling. And, with Marissa growing up, I really want another child."

"Whoa, Harold. Let's take things a bit slower," I said with the proverbial sinking feeling in my stomach.

"I can certainly make a much bigger effort not to yell. But there's nothing I can do about this wish for another child. Are you sure you are willing to tell Marissa and me we are not enough?"

"I don't know, Brooke. I wish I could figure it out. I'm willing to give you a chance to stop yelling and see how I feel then," he answered.

I couldn't read the expression on his face. Was it defeated?

Resigned? Ashamed? Vaguely hopeful?

"Okay, I'll try really hard to stop yelling. Do you think you can do more of the dishes and laundry?"

"I'll try too. I do love you, Brooke. I don't want to hurt you. But I think I deserve to be happy."

Hadn't we been happy in the twenty years we had been married? Even with the struggles? Weren't there good times too? All the social justice work we had done together. All the parenting. The laughter, the shared enjoyment of literature, music, holidays? I felt shattered.

Well, we gave it some time. My first attempts at not yelling were just gritting my teeth and sounding irritated, which landed about the same as yelling. Then I tried walking away until I had calmed down, but that also upset Harold

Finally, I remembered friends of mine who seemed to have a good marriage. They used a lot of humor to get their points across. Even though I tend toward the serious and earnest to the self-righteous side of things, I attempted some humor.

God dammit, the end table in the living room is filled with his coke cans and coffee mugs again! Hmm… maybe this is a time to use humor.

I went to my computer and found a lovely image of some brown Hindu goddess. I put a caption under it: "The Goddess of caffeine is grateful for your offerings; however, she requires fresh gifts daily." And I waited to see what would happen.

Harold came home and after dinner he went into the living room while I put the food away. I heard him laugh and then he came into the kitchen carrying a load of his coke cans and coffee mugs.

"That was funny, Brooke," he said smiling.

I smiled back. *Hey, maybe there's hope for us after all.*

Another time I drew a picture of a fat happy mouse and taped it onto the stove with the caption, "I sure do love these yummy crumbs and grease!" That yielded another laugh and a clean stove.

But Harold kept crying. Although over the years I had tried to listen and support him in his goals, this was too much for me.

"I can't help you figure out if you need to leave me in order to have another child," I exclaimed one day, close to tears myself and feeling exasperated.

A few days later, we got into one of those stupid arguments married couples often fall into. I stomped off to work.

That evening Harold came home and announced, "Brooke, I can't do this anymore. I'm leaving the marriage."

"You're leaving me over a stupid argument?" I asked dully, feeling numb, defeated, and hopeless.

"No. I'm leaving because I can't shake the desire to have another child and the possibility that I could be happier with someone else. I appreciate the effort you have made to stop yelling, but it is too little, too late. All this became clear to me after that argument this morning."

A deep wailing, keening sound was coming out of my mouth that I had never heard before; not when my mother died, not when my father died; not even when my best friend in high school killed herself and I found her cold lifeless body.

And I was rocking back and forth, tears pouring down my cheeks, running like rivulets into my neck. I clutched a pillow to my chest and stared at our ketuba: our wedding document, which hung over our bed.

I had the distinct impression that Harold was thinking something like, "Good. Now she knows how I have felt all these years."

Well, he did leave. And I learned there can not only be life after heartbreak but love also. It didn't happen all at once. I had to grieve. I had to take some responsibility for my part. I had to learn to do things differently.

AUGUST

Some
Hold their dreams
Like blown glass bubbles
Watching the colors change
From gold to rose

Others
Might come along
And smash those dreams
Leaving shards of broken glass
To wound the unaware

But my dreams
Are liquid
Deep as the grey green river
Sometime frozen
And ever growing wider
—Rain Zohav

CHAPTER FORTY-NINE

"There's a librarian's conference on the topic of 'Libraries' role in changing social norms.' It's in Paris, Brooke. Would you like to go?" asked my supervisor at the library. "The topic is right up your alley. It might cheer you up. Take your mind off that lousy husband of yours."

My friends and coworkers were often more judgmental of Harold than I was. They didn't really know how hard the marriage had been on him and had a difficult time imagining me yelling at him the way I had. I didn't treat other people like that. Just those closest to me.

"Wow. Paris! I'd love to go. What is the cost?"

"It's not too bad. Our professional development budget can cover the conference fees. And the conference has a list of folks offering home hospitality. So you would just have to pay for your plane ticket."

"That sounds wonderful! Yes, I'd very much like to go. Thank you so much!"

I eagerly got ready to go. I filled out the form for home hospitality, and a librarian answered that he had space in his apartment for me. I recognized his name, Jacques Moreau, from articles he had published in professional journals. He had a radical background similar to my own and had been involved in the student uprisings of 1968 in Paris. And he looked kind of cute in his biopic. I allowed myself to fantasize about him.

It's not easy to get from Asheville to Paris. Every airline had two stops. I decided to go with Delta, which took me first to Atlanta and then to Boston, before arriving at Charles De Gaulle International Airport. I packed a book about the history of Asheville, figuring that would be a fitting gift for my host.

It would be colder in Paris in early October, with rain always possible, so I made sure to pack some sweaters, a light jacket, and a raincoat. *I hope I get to see the peak of fall color in Paris and then come home to the peak here too,* I thought.

Hmm. Should I throw in a pair of earrings and one nice dress? There is a welcoming dinner scheduled the evening before the conference officially begins. Yes. Can't hurt.

The conference was taking place right at the French National Library, the Bibliothèque Nationale de France. There are two locations for this library, which house every French publication. I was glad that our conference was taking place at the historic Richelieu site, rather than the modern site. The Richelieu site takes up a full city block in Paris. It includes a museum of not only books and manuscripts, but also art objects and other interesting historical artifacts. I loved seeing the Charlemagne chessmen, a group of eleventh-century chess pieces made from ivory.

I arranged to arrive early on the morning of the dinner, so I could nap, shower, and change beforehand. Jacques would be at work but had made arrangements with a neighbor to give me a key to the apartment. I tried practicing my limited French to explain who I was.

All I really know is *merci, pardon, Bon jour, bonne nuit, s'il vous plaît,* and *fromage.* So I looked up on Google Translate how to say, "Hello. I'm Brooke Kumara. I'm staying at Jacques Moreau's apartment. He said you have a key for me?" I even listened to the audio recording several times. I also practiced saying "where is?" and "How do I get to?"

Though I've always thought that as long as you know how to say "please," "thank you," and "excuse me," you can travel anywhere.

CHAPTER FIFTY

I found the apartment, a three-story stone building with overgrown rose bushes and a few chrysanthemums growing in front. The neighbor was expecting me and turned over the key. I let myself in and looked around. It was a modest space, once again reminding me how everything in the United States always seems bigger than in other parts of the world. There were two bedrooms. A note said mine was on the right of the living room.

The kitchen was a narrow galley type. It didn't seem like he cooked much. The cupboards contained a salt and pepper shaker, a half-full jar of olive oil, a few plates, cups, and dishes, but little else. The fridge held a piece of dried-up cheese, a couple of yogurt cups, and an old onion. *Looks like a typical bachelor pad,* I thought.

The bathroom had a shower, tiny sink, toilet, and bidet. *At least I know what that is and how to use it this time around. I was so embarrassed when I had to be shown the last time I was in Paris, so many years ago.*

My room contained a single bed, neatly made up, a small dresser, night table, and lamp. Very simple but very clean. I admit I peeked into the other bedroom. It was slightly larger and filled with bookcases along one wall, an overflowing desk piled high with papers, and a double bed.

On the wall were only two pictures. One was cut out from an old newspaper, showing two curly-headed youths, arms raised, surrounded by a huge crowd of protesters. *That must be Jacques and*

Cohn-Bendit, I thought.

The other showed the same two men, arms around each other under a banner for the French Green Party. I smiled. *I love it when we older people stick to our values.*

CHAPTER FIFTY-ONE

I took a cab to the dinner because it was raining and I was jet-lagged, even though the apartment was not too far to walk under different circumstances.

The dinner took place in the oval reading room of the library. What a beautiful space! The rain had stopped and the many arched windows let in the last of the sunset. The round skylights also let in this last light of the day, lending a magical air to the book-lined walls. It was a librarian's dream.

Jacques spotted me right away. He sat down next to me, asking if everything had gone well with the apartment. I assured him it had—all the time thinking, *He's much cuter than his picture, and he seems so nice.* On the other side of me sat a young-looking French woman named Vivien. We hit it off right away also.

And, oh my goodness! The dinner. It featured sole meuniere, the white fish cooked in butter and lemon that excited Julia Child so much about French cooking. Accompanied by haricots verts, a side salad, and little roasted potatoes, it was delicious.

Of course, excellent French wine was served and, even though I don't usually drink, I did this time.

After welcome speeches and dinner, dessert was served and a chamber music ensemble played softly in the background. Jacques must have noticed me nodding off.

"It looks like you are pretty tired from your long flight. Let's go home so you can be fresh for tomorrow."

I gratefully accepted.

CHAPTER FIFTY-TWO

The next day the conference started with a panel discussion on the main topic of libraries as places of social change. Jacques Moreau was one of the panelists. Each panelist spoke first in French and then either in English or Spanish. There were interpreters on hand for those who needed, but Jacques did his own translating. He did have a charming French accent and would make a few grammatical errors, but in general his English was excellent.

Lunch was then served. Another delicious meal, including fresh figs, crème fraiche, and smoked salmon.

The afternoon sessions were more participatory workshops. I attended one on the use of folktales to empower children. This was something I had noticed myself, so I had stories I could share. Vivien also attended that workshop. It was nice to sit by someone I knew.

We were on our own for dinner, and Jacques found me. "Can I take you out to a nice little North African restaurant nearby?" he asked, looking at me quizzically, head tilted to the side.

"Oh, yes. That would be lovely," I said, smiling and wondering if he was possibly attracted to me. Or was he just a charming host? Either way, I felt very lucky.

The restaurant was very unassuming from the outside, but inside the luscious aromas enveloped us, as what I would call Middle Eastern music played in the backyard.

"We have a lot of Algerians, Moroccans, and Tunisians living in Paris now."

"Yes. That makes sense. From your former colonies. I read Albert Memi's book, *The Colonizer and the Colonized*, a long time ago. It stuck with me. I thought his description of colonization was very accurate. But I still question whether he was correct that there is no place for allies in liberation struggles. What do you think?"

Jacques paused with a thoughtful look that I would get to know well.

"It's an interesting question. On the one hand, often the people leading liberation struggles come from some kind of privileged past. They have more education and access than the people who most need liberating. The most oppressed are often too beaten down to even resist."

"Yes, this is certainly true of the early civil rights movement," I answered. "Martin Luther King Jr. came from the middle class. But the movement gained strength and authenticity when folks like Fannie Lou Hamer joined."

"It's a bit of a conundrum. Should we not speak out if we see injustice? Should we not use our power and resources to aid liberation struggles?" Jaques continued, perhaps a bit defensively.

"Well, no. Obviously, I think everyone should do everything in their power to improve the world. But I do think that we who come from privileged backgrounds could do better at listening to and taking direction from those directly affected in the worst ways," I answered.

It's so nice to have these kinds of conversations, I thought. *Back home there is only a small group that has even read Albert Memi.*

"Speaking of changing the world, would you like to come with me tomorrow evening to a gala honoring Daniel Cohn-Bendit, our new European Green Alliance Party member? He's receiving the European Parliament's European Initiative Prize." Again the quizzical look, but this time with a bit more twinkle in his eyes.

"Oh my goodness, yes! I'd be thrilled. I read his book about the student uprising in 1968. Thank you. And by the way, this is the most delicious eggplant I've ever eaten," I said, sopping up the last of the juices with a piece of baguette.

"Ah, good. Would you like to take a stroll along the river and then get some coffee?"

Boy, this man seems indefatigable. And coffee, at this late hour?

"That would be lovely. But I'll have to get decaf if such a thing exists in Paris," I said, laughing and a bit embarrassed.

"Decaf? I don't know what is that?" he asked, raising his eyebrows.

I could see he wasn't just kidding me, so I explained: "Coffee that has had the caffeine taken out of it? Otherwise I won't sleep all night."

"Ah, yes. We call that 'un deca,'" he said, smiling.

CHAPTER FIFTY-THREE

The next day at the conference, I attended a workshop on creating safe space for gay and lesbian people. I felt sad that I appeared to be the only ally in attendance.

But maybe that is how it should be. I've recently heard the slogan, "Nothing about us without us." So, if LGBT people want to take the lead on this, that could make a lot of sense.

One suggestion that I found helpful was to avoid terms like "mother and father" on sign-up sheets, permission slips, and other forms. It's better to use more general terms such as "guardian." Or even "parent one," "parent two."

And then I realized that this would also benefit other parts of the population raising children, such as grandparents or foster parents. It is often the case that changes that seem at first narrowly helpful, like curb cuts for wheelchair users, end up benefiting much larger swaths of the population; like people pushing strollers or moving large items on dollies.

CHAPTER FIFTY-FOUR

After that workshop I rushed back to the apartment to change into my one nice dress for the gala. Luckily, for once I hadn't spilled any food or drink on myself. Jacques came home in a very good mood, rang the doorbell, and grinned at me. "Are you ready to go?" he asked.

When we got to the eighteenth-century hotel, Jacques seemed to know lots of people and kept introducing me to folks as "a colleague and comrade from America."

No one where I live would ever use the word "comrade." They'd be run out of town on a rail. Europe is so much more progressive than America. People were friendly and somewhat curious, but also busy getting settled for the program.

I couldn't understand much of the speeches except "*environnementale responsabilité, liberté, la diversité,* and *la nonviolence,*" which seemed to be their slogan, as it was repeated by many speakers to great applause.

Despite not being able to understand much, I loved the energy and enthusiasm in the room. And anyone could tell that Daniel Cohn-Bendit was a warm, passionate, and charismatic leader. He received a standing ovation at the end of his speech. After he was presented with his award, people started leaving and we made our way home.

When we got back to the apartment, we took turns using the bathroom and were both in our night clothes.

"Good night, *bonne nuit,*" I said, looking at this man; wondering if he was involved with anyone. I wanted to say something. I wanted to spend the night with him, but I found myself tongue- tied.

Oh, for goodness' sake, Brooke. Are you still sixteen years old? Unable to speak your mind?

He looked back at me with a similar look, as if he wanted to speak but couldn't. "*Bonne nuit,*" he answered and shut his bedroom door.

CHAPTER FIFTY-FIVE

That night I dreamt of the ocean. In my dream, the waves washed over me gently and rocked me in their swells. I woke up with the familiar thought that water was my truest lover. *I wonder what that dream was trying to tell me?*

The next day I was sitting in the courtyard of the library catching up on email. *Uh-oh. There's a message from Harold.*

He wrote, "Let me know what you think would be fair in terms of alimony."

Shocked, I began to cry silently. The fronds of the palm trees began to first blur and then become more vivid. I was acutely aware of the stone bench I was sitting on. The sounds of the birds became magnified and then dimmed.

I wrote a quick reply. At that moment, I looked up to find Jacques peering at me.

"Are you alright?" he inquired gently, looking concerned.

"No. Not really." As I explained the email, I saw his liquid brown eyes fill with sympathy.

"I'm so sorry, Brooke. Did you answer him?"

Sighing, and running my fingers through my hair I said, "Yes. I probably shouldn't have, because at this point it's not even true, but I just sent a link to Joan Baez singing 'Boots of Spanish Leather.'"

Jacques's eyes deepened with even more understanding. "Ah, I know that song: 'just carry yourself back to me unspoiled / that's all

I'm wishing for or wanting.'"

"How do you know that song?" I asked, both touched and impressed. *Another thing we have in common.*

"I'm a big aficionado of American music. Especially Bob Dylan and Joan Baez. But also Nina Simone, and lots of jazz."

"We forget we export our music and that lots of Americans come to Paris to perform. I'm embarrassed to say, I don't know many French singers, unless Jacques Brel counts. But I think he's Canadian."

"Actually, he's from Belgium, and well known here," he answered.

"Well, anyway, I already regret sending that email." I looked up at him sheepishly. "It's not even true anymore. I know the marriage is over."

"Would you like to go get some coffee?" he asked kindly, putting his hand gently over mine.

"Sure." *Coffee is the panacea for everything in this country, it seems. Waking up in the morning, afternoon doldrums, after dinner with dessert, heartbreak.*

We walked to a nearby café, passing quaint shops with brightly colored awnings, people walking their dogs, children playing. After a generous cup of café au lait and a croissant, I did actually feel better.

"What about you?" I asked. "Have you ever been married?"

"Ah, yes," he said, sighing a bit and looking serious. "Twice. The first time we were very young. I have a son from that marriage. He's a lecturer on French literature at the University of Bordeaux. My second marriage also didn't last. We tried, but we just couldn't, how do you say? Reconcile our differences. My daughter from that marriage is wanting to be an artist."

And then I got up my courage to ask if he was currently involved with anyone.

"No. There isn't anyone."

Hmmm…

After a pause, he said, "I have to go back to work for a few hours. Shall we have dinner together?" with that characteristic quizzical look.

"Yes, I'd like that," I said, feeling flustered but trying to look "calm, cool and collected," which is a phrase that I never feel describes me, although others might think so.

CHAPTER FIFTY-SIX

Around 7:00 p.m. the doorbell rang. I went to open it and there was Jacques grinning at me, holding a grocery bag and looking very pleased with himself.

"Hello, honey, I'm home," he said mischievously, giving me a big hug. "I brought us sushi for dinner. I hope you like it."

"I love sushi. Thank you. Shall I get some dishes out?"

"Oui. Merci."

As we ate, we talked about the conference and what I would do when I got home. This was my last night in Paris. I wondered if we would take the next step, which we both seemed to want.

Finally, I stood up and said, "I think it's bedtime."

Jacques stood up also and came to give me a hug. My heart was thumping as I held him close.

"I think we should spend the night together," he whispered in my ear, cupping the back of my head with his hand. Immediately, my body melted into his, before I could say anything, before my brain had consciously computed this.

"Yes. Let me go get ready. Then I'll join you," I said, barely able to breathe. I rushed into the bathroom and furiously brushed my teeth. The last thing I wanted was to have bad breath.

It's been years since I've been with anyone except Harold. I feel like an incompetent teenager again.

When I came into Jacques's room, he was already beginning to undress. *Okay. We're both adults. We know how to do this. We don't have to pretend.* I began to feel more confident. I removed my clothes also, folding them carefully and placing them on a chair. We got into his bed. As we began to kiss, I thought, *Oh, this is so sweet…*

CHAPTER FIFTY-SEVEN

Early the next morning Jacques said he had to go to work but would call me at lunch. I slept in, used the bidet, showered, and packed. I had bought good chocolate, cheese, and scented soaps to bring home as gifts for friends, family, and coworkers. Just as I was about done, he called. It was exactly noon.

"How are you?" he asked with real concern in his voice. *I guess he knows that the day after a first night together can be rocky. But I was feeling fine.*

"I'm good, Jacques. Last night was so sweet. Thank you."

"Ah, good. When is your flight out this evening? There is something I would like to show you. I think I can leave work a little early today."

"I don't have to be at the airport until ten o'clock tonight. My flight leaves around 2:00 a.m., but I have to go through customs." *I wonder what he wants to show me… Such a sweet man. I think I'm smitten.*

"Good. I'll be home around six o'clock this evening. *Au revoir.*"

We walked from his apartment to the upper side of Place de Abbesses. It's a small park with a wall engraved with the phrase "I love you" written in over 250 languages. A semi-secret gem of Paris.

"I want this to be one of your last memories of Paris," Jacques said, enfolding me in his arms and kissing me for a long time on the mouth. I'm a bit embarrassed by such a public display of passion, but when we came up for air, I saw that there were other couples similarly engaged. *This would never be acceptable in North Carolina,* I thought, nonetheless smiling to myself and then looking into Jacque's eyes.

"Thank you. You have given me back a part of myself I wasn't quite aware that I had lost."

Jacques looked at me with that thoughtful look I had grown to appreciate. But he didn't say anything.

"The wall was created by the artists Frédéric Baron and Claire Kito." It's a special place. Shall we go have dinner and watch the sun set over the Seine?"

"Yes. That would be lovely," I said for maybe the fortieth time since I met him.

You would think I'd be a bit more articulate, but I'm still shy around him.

We ate dinner at a French bistro overlooking the Seine River. I ordered a cup of French onion soup, but then had trouble deciding between grilled salmon with Hollandaise sauce and roast chicken.

"Would you be willing to share dinners so that we each have half of the salmon and half of the roasted chicken? My daughter calls that 'a bite for a bite.' It's nice when you can't make up your mind. Which I'm having trouble doing right now," I asked Jacques, smiling, pretty sure he would say yes.

"Of course, this is your last night in Paris. You should have whatever you want," he answered graciously, smiling into my eyes.

"Okay then. Let's do that and share a salad also." Over dinner I kept gazing at this sweet man, sorry I was leaving so soon.

We made our way back to the apartment for me to pick up my suitcase and backpack.

"Oh, I almost forgot! I have a small gift for you," he said, pulling out a package wrapped in tissue paper. It was a replica of the Eiffel Tower. "I thought you should have something to remind you of your time here."

"Oh, thank you. That's very cute. I know just where it will go on my desk at home," I said, putting it safely away in my suitcase.

And then it was time to leave. A good long hug and kiss, promises to be in touch, wishes for safe travels, and I was in a taxi to the airport.

CHAPTER FIFTY-EIGHT

Nine and a half hours of flight later and we landed in Charlotte. The trees had turned into a glory of fall colors, just as I had hoped. The mountains were ablaze with yellow, gold, orange, and crimson.

My friend Trina picked me up at the airport. I wanted nothing more than to shower and go to sleep, holding onto the memories of my time in Paris before I had to reenter my North Carolina life.

But that was not to be. *Have you ever noticed that the good times in life and the hard times in life can pile on top of one another in reckless disregard for our own wishes?*

On the way home, Trina broached a very difficult subject.

"Brooke, I need your advice," she said seriously. I couldn't ignore the worry in her voice.

"Sure. What's up?"

"My older daughter, Hope, has gotten involved with an abusive man. It got so bad, we had to call the police. He's in jail now for thirty days until the trial, but I'm scared to death he'll come after her and possibly me when he gets out. She has a restraining order, but I'm not sure he will abide by it. I don't know what to do. I lie in bed shaking at night feeling so helpless."

I couldn't ignore my friend's pain. "Have you changed the locks?" I asked.

"Yes. And we added deadbolts."

"Good. That's a good start. Let me take a nap and I'll come over later this afternoon to help you think things through. I'm so sorry you and Hope are going through this."

Oy, what a mess. She sounds so distraught.

So after a shower and a nap, I drove over to Trina's.

"So, Trina, you know that after that shooting at the Unitarian church in Tennessee in 2008, I've done a lot of security training. Let's make a list of things you and Hope can do to decrease your risks," I said, sighing to myself.

It's pitiful that we live in a country where gun violence is such a grave possibility that Sunday school directors become experts in security.

"Thanks so much, Brooke. That's why I asked you. I always meant to do some training but never got around to it. I never thought the issue would hit this close to home," confessed Trina.

She'd been on the Education Committee for years. I had advocated for such training but didn't make it a requirement for the committee members, just the teachers.

"The first thing you all need to do is get Hope out of this house and to an 'unknown location' before her boyfriend gets out of jail."

"Ex-boyfriend," interjected Trina.

"Yes. Ex-boyfriend," I nodded. "Make sure she gets that changed on the restraining order and that the court, or his lawyer or if he ends up with a probation officer, let him know she no longer lives here. And that this address and any contact with either of you is forbidden."

"Hope's not going to like that. She moved back in because she was having trouble paying her bills," moaned Trina, shaking her head.

"Well, I understand that. Maybe you can help her with rent. But for her safety and yours, she needs to move as soon as possible. I'm not joking, Trina. This could be a life-or-death situation," I said firmly, maybe even sounding irritated.

I was both sleep deprived and genuinely worried.

"Now let's go through every room in your house and see if you can escape from there. That's called 'run' in the security business. Your other options are 'hide' or 'fight.'

"Barricades are very useful to think about. I want you to have a plan for each room, so you are not frozen with fear if you hear something suspicious or think he has managed to break in." I looked over at Trina. She was kind of pale. "Green around the gills," my mom would have said.

"It's okay. It's very unlikely he will show up. You just have to be prepared for the worst-case scenario," I said, hoping to both reassure her and remain firm.

"Hmmm… I don't like these glass panels in your front door," I continued. "Too easy to break and reach right into the doorknob. Get someone to back them with wood."

"Okay," said Trina, taking notes.

"Now what furniture can you move by yourself if you do hear him?"

"Well, this easy chair for sure. Oh, the sofa rolls!"

"Good. Now for the dining room. Nothing much here, but the chairs that can be used to block the back door.

"You don't have any shades in your kitchen windows. Anyone can see right in at night from the street." *You're like a sitting duck,* I thought but didn't say. "Get some good thick wooden shutters and close them as soon as it's dark outside and you turn on the lights."

They won't stop a bullet, but at least the boyfriend won't know if she's in the kitchen or not.

"Now let's look at the bathroom. The shower is a good place to hide. Remember to turn off the lights and be very quiet."

This is getting kind of tedious and yet, it's important.

"You said you lie in bed and shake. Let's see your bedroom. Okay. Look. This dresser has wheels. It can be rolled against the door, and the closet next to the door would give you a good hiding place from which to crack him over the head as he enters. You could use this nice heavy vase that sits on top of the dresser. Shooters rarely expect resistance, so you have the advantage of surprise. From your bed, be ready to throw anything and everything nearby. Most people will get distracted by anything coming at them and start shooting at that."

"Gosh, Brooke. This all sounds both terrifying and empowering. I really hope I never have to do any of this!" Trina said.

"Me too. I think the most important thing to do is the first. Get Hope out of this house. And now, I really must go home and get some sleep!"

"Thanks so much, Brooke!"

She gave me a big hug and I drove home.

CHAPTER FIFTY-NINE

A few months after Marissa moved out, she called me in tears.

"Mama, it's not working out with Belinda," she said, crying. "She said she'd help keep the apartment clean, but it's always a mess! And I'm doing all the work."

"Well, Marissa, didn't you know this about Belinda from seeing her bedroom?" I tried to gently intervene.

"Well, yes, but she promised me she would change!" wailed Marissa.

"Change is hard. She probably thinks she is cleaning."

"I never thought of it like that. Maybe she is making more of an effort than I give her credit for. I wonder if we could find a different apartment that has two kitchens? That might solve it."

"What a good idea, Marissa. I'd be happy to help with the security deposit, if you can find a place like that. I always thought your dad and I would have gotten along a lot better if we had just lived next door to each other."

"Thanks, Mom."

"Let me know how it goes. Love you."

"Love you too."

Sigh. *It's so difficult to find the right balance in living with people. John and I seem to be doing okay. But I think that's because I've done a lot of work over the years to communicate clearly and learn how to negotiate. And he does more than his fair share of cleaning and cooking, since I'm now so limited. I try to balance things out in other ways, like helping him grade papers, plan lessons, and proofread his poetry manuscript.*

He did really like my idea of exposing his English students to the writings of Thomas Wolfe and O. Henry. Both are buried in the local Riverside Cemetery.

"I decided to use your idea and take my students to the cemetery on this beautiful spring day," he told me recently. "Here are some of their poems. Quite a range."

Haiku
Catbird is singing
Dogwoods and redbuds blooming
Spring arrives for the dead

Cemetery
A feeling of calm and days gone by
Are the dead soothed by the gentle beauty of spring
with its soft hues of pink and white
with the myriad shades of green?

The Baby's Grave
The tiny
baby grave
with its ribbon bracelet
and small stuffed elephant
broke my heart

ThomasWolf

Help! Help!

The worms are eating me.

I never expected I'd end up

like this

I was wrong

I have unfortunately

Come Home—

And those pennies you leave on my grave

Do not help me

at all

Maybe they help

O. Henry

—Thomas Wolf

"Quite a range is right. I think it's good you took them in the spring, although it would be interesting to see what they write in each season.

"I remember my first spring at Black Mountain Farm. It was amazing watching first the bright yellow-green leaves start at the bottom of the hill facing us and then ascend the mountain as the colors deepened lower down. And the white of the dogwoods, pink of the redbuds, light purple wisteria, and soft rust of maple was one of the prettiest things I have ever seen," I replied.

"Thanks for sharing these with me."

Brooke returned to her memoir. *Where was I? Oh yeah, the divorce.*

Well, Harold and I did work out a divorce agreement with the help of a friend. And then we paid lawyers to put it into legal language. That took forever and cost far more than it should have, but finally we were both free.

CHAPTER SIXTY

Easier said than done, though. This "both being free." I had already released a lot of anger by burning up a copy of our wedding program and scattering the ashes to the wind at an overlook in my beloved Blue Ridge Mountains. I had cried for hours in counseling sessions. I had removed my wedding ring as soon as Harold moved out. I had gone to court to affirm our separation agreement. But we both had a need for spiritual as well as legal closure.

We arranged a small divorce ceremony with our Unitarian Universalist minister. Some Unitarian Universalists call this a "Ceremony of Hope," but that seemed too Polyannaish for me. Every divorce holds enormous pain of the hopes that did not come to fruition. So we just called it a divorce ritual and each invited one friend to be a witness. We gathered in the minister's office one summer evening.

"I release you from your vows," I said, looking at Harold, my eyes tearing up but feeling steady.

"And I release you from yours," he answered.

"I forgive you for any pain you have caused me," he continued.

"And I also forgive you for any pain you have caused me," I answered.

Then together we read aloud, "We acknowledge that our marriage is over. We will continue to mutually support our children. We will remember the many good times we had together and the good we did in the world as a couple. We are both now free to pursue independent lives."

Our minister took out a thick "unity candle" and lit it. She said, "From this candle that symbolizes your partnership, draw strength to go back into the world as individuals."

She handed us each a thin taper, which we lit and placed in separate candleholders.

Then each friend spoke of what they had observed over the years of our marriage that had been good and wished us well in our new lives.

We ended by singing the Shaker hymn, "Tis the Gift to Be Simple." As I drove home, I felt a lightness and, surprisingly, even some hope.

CHAPTER SIXTY-ONE

I was still working my two part-time jobs, but I had grown wiser over the years. I didn't have so many "good ideas" that took hours more than I was paid. So, I began to want a social life again.

Friends who were also divorced told me about a group for separated and divorced people called "Step Up" that arranged group dinners and movie nights, plus seminars on dating and beginning over.

"You'll love being single again, Brooke! It's like getting to be a teenager again."

Oh, great. I hated that time in my life. One of my worst nightmares was dreaming I was sixteen again. But surely, this time around I know more?

I signed up for a few activities, grateful to meet other people who had never gone to a movie alone. And the discussion groups were also interesting. Most people were using online dating apps. I knew my kids used them and so I enlisted their help in setting up my profile.

It was weird going on dates and trying to see if there was mutual interest. I got awfully tired of men pontificating on whatever weighty book they had once read. I guess they felt threatened by a librarian. Nothing clicked for quite a while. Until I met Carlos.

AUTUMN: HARVEST

"The work of the mature person is to carry grief in one hand and gratitude in the other and to be stretched large by them."
—The Wild Edge of Sorrow: Rituals of Renewal and the Sacred Work of Grief, by Francis Weller

SEPTEMBER

"Let this radicalize you rather than lead you to despair."
—Mariame Kaba

CHAPTER SIXTY-TWO

Carlos and I were rated as a 96 percent match on the Cupid's Bow dating site.

Hmmm… that's pretty good. I think I'll check out his profile and his answers to some of the questions.

His profile picture was cute. He looked Latino; not surprising, since his full name was Carlos Cienfuegos. I learned that he taught in the Global Studies and Political Science departments of Warren Wilson, a nearby very progressive college. In fact, I had hoped to go there, but they didn't offer a library science degree.

His answers were in line with my own. "Which is worse: burning the flag or burning books?" Burning books, of course. A different answer on that would have been a deal-breaker.

And, I saw where we differed. *He drinks "moderately" and smokes a pipe. Ugh. I've never dated a smoker before. But maybe I should broaden my horizons?*

I went ahead and wrote him a short note: "I've read your profile and it sounds like we have quite a lot in common. Would you like to chat?"

Well, he got back right away and gave me his phone number. We set up a time to talk. I couldn't tell that much about him from the phone call. And, I'm sure that was true about me also, as I was so nervous.

"Would you like to meet me for dinner at a nice little taqueria downtown?" he asked toward the end of our conversation, sounding kind, and quizzical.

"Sure." Heart pounding. *I wonder if this will turn into something. I hope he's not arrogant or insecure like the other men I've met.*

Over dinner I asked him, "So, how did you come to live in Asheville?"

"Ah, that's quite a story," he answered, eyes twinkling. "My mother was born here in Asheville and was a student at Warren Wilson. She went on what was supposed to be a semester abroad to Cuba in 1950. But she fell in love with the Cuban people and apparently with my father, although I never knew him. When the revolution broke out, she decided to stay there. That is, until she heard that the civil rights movement had made it to Asheville around 1968. She felt called to return home and support the struggle here. She was one of the white allies who helped desegregate the restaurants. And I also got involved with the teen group."

"Was your father really the famous revolutionary Camilo Cienfuegos?" I asked. *Having done a bit of research on this name before we met.*

Carlos laughed. "Every kid born in those years whose father was absent was named Cienfuegos, or Guevara or Castro. But Cienfuegos was particularly popular because he disappeared and so no one could do paternity tests," he said, laughing uproariously.

"Well, why not name your child after a hero of the revolution?" I said.

"Why not, indeed? How about you? What brought you to Asheville?" Carlos was very attentive and listened well. He didn't try to impress me with some obscure book he had read. I thought things went pretty well.

A few days later I called him to see if he wanted to get together again. And then I was surprised.

"Well, I don't know. I didn't get any sexy vibes from you," he says.

"What!? We don't even know each other. And I'm not going to flirt," I said, somewhat taken aback.

"Well, frankly, I have enough friends. If that is all you're interested in, don't waste our time."

"I'm interested in more than that also, but I think it would be good to get to know each other better. I really like what I already know about you. And I had a good time the other day."

"Well, I think being intimate physically is a good way to get to know someone," he answered.

There was a pause in the conversation as I pondered this.

Hmmm… yes, that has been true for me too, I thought but didn't say.

"So, how about I cook you dinner Thursday night and we see where things go?" Carlos suggested.

"Okay. Should I bring anything?"

"Just yourself," he said with a smile I could hear through the phone lines.

CHAPTER SIXTY-THREE

Thursday came. *Well, if things go well and I still like him as much as I think I do, I'll probably stay over. Better pack my morning medications, a toothbrush, and a change of clothes.*

Carlos's house was in an older, and fancier, neighborhood than mine, Park Grove. Some of the houses were quite large, colonial revival or Tudor revival homes.

Ugh, I hate all this brick. Although it is the natural building material here, with all the red clay we have. Well, he is a university professor. But his house was certainly not the biggest nor fanciest. In fact, it was an older two-story brick house with a relatively unkempt yard. *Phew.*

Once inside, I noticed the deep red walls and the turquoise trim, similar to my own living room. There were many indigenous artifacts gracing the shelves of bookcases. And of course, many books ranging from Latin American history to poetry, drama, and music. It was a house that I felt at home in.

Things did go well. Carlos cooked a lovely dinner of roasted chicken with potatoes and salad. *It sure is easier to date now that I'm no longer a vegetarian,* I thought.

He didn't freak out when I declined wine and even had some Southern sweet tea on hand.

"So," he said, smiling and running a finger up my arm. "Would you like to go upstairs?"

"Sure," I said, picking up my backpack.

Carlos looked at it, looked at me, and said, "I convinced you?"

"Yup. I thought over what you said and realized it was my experience also. Physical intimacy can help with emotional intimacy. No need to be a slave to social conventions, especially at our age."

It was a memorable night. We did become more intimate both emotionally and physically. I learned that Carlos had several children scattered across the world. His youngest was Marissa's age and the only one nearby.

And then, at some point he said, "Why am I lying here talking about children when a beautiful woman is next to me?"

Then there was no more talking for a while.

CHAPTER SIXTY-FOUR

After that we tended to spend every Thursday night together. Sometimes he cooked. Sometimes I cooked, rediscovering how much pleasure that gave me. Sometimes we went out. I was still working my two jobs, so weekends were not readily available.

Once, though, on a Wednesday evening I had a near collision leaving work. I called Carlos up and asked if I could come over. I was pretty shook up.

"Sure. Come on over."

"Thanks. Ugh, feel how sweaty I am. It's so muggy out and I think I broke out in a sweat when that idiot almost backed into me."

Smiling, Carlos said, "If I put a hand on your beautiful sweaty body, we would have to go upstairs immediately."

"Ah, no thanks. I just came to calm down."

"You know, you *could* spend the night."

"No, I don't have my medications or a change of clothes and wouldn't have time to go home before going to work. But thanks for the offer."

So, it was a huge surprise when one day after Sunday school and church I phoned him to see if I could stop by and got a very brusque "No! I'm busy" for an answer.

Hmm... that's weird. Well, maybe he is in the midst of grading papers... I was so naive.

Another time, he mentioned that he had been dancing downtown to a great salsa band.

"Why didn't you ask me to go? I love to dance," I said somewhat miffed. *That was before the accident. Sigh. I do miss dancing.*

"I went alone. You could too. You don't need me to go dancing. Everyone just gets up and does their own thing."

Really? I hadn't seen anything like that since my days at Black Mountain. Maybe I'll check it out.

Once again I was so naive.

Carlos was unlike any other men I had been involved with. He drank, he smoked, he brawled, and he was obviously a "ladies man." Every story from his life involved adventure, sticking up for the underdog, and a different woman. He was not adverse to using violence.

"I got tired of being beat up in high school as one of the only Latinos in town. So I finally fought back. Once I put someone in the hospital; I was left alone after that," he said with great satisfaction. "I'll always go to the side of someone I see being picked on."

"When's the last time you did that?" I asked, hoping it was years ago and he had mended his ways.

"Oh, about three years ago. Some guy was being bullied in a bar, so I just started throwing punches," he said, laughing. "That put an end to it." He nodded in a pleased way.

He had even served some time in federal prison due to a similar instance. In that situation, it was actually a police sting operation with the purpose of luring him into violence in order to put him in prison. He was involved with documenting police brutality and they wanted to silence him. Luckily he knew to call the ACLU. The police in their arrogance had left a clear paper trail of their plan. The charges were dropped and he was released from prison.

When he got out of prison, he traveled all over Central America, joining in social justice movements. He had many tales of adventure there. Once he had to hide from right-wing vigilantes for three days in the tropical rainforest of Guatemala.

Eventually, he went on to get degrees in Latin American history at UC Berkeley. Then he was able to get hired back here, in his mother's hometown and at her alma mater. It's a school known for its dedication to social justice. Even as a teen, he had helped integrate the public library of Asheville.

"I never knew this history," I said. "Of course, it makes sense. We think of Asheville as a bastion of liberal values here in North Carolina, but I did know that things had been segregated. I think I'll do a display about it for Black History Month."

On Valentine's Day he called me and said, "Hey, I don't really go in for these capitalist plots to make people buy chocolate and flowers, but I happen to have a coupon for Hemingway's Café in the Cambria Hotel. They have pretty good Cuban food. Would you like to meet me there?"

"Sure. And I totally understand about Valentine's Day. My father made that same speech to my mother every year. But then he would surprise her with something. And Harold did the same thing. I wasn't expecting anything, so I'm already surprised."

"Good. How about seven o'clock?"

"Works for me. See you there."

Oy, what should I wear? This sounds like a date! I hate worrying about how I look. I hate that I'm still so tied up in wanting to please a man. It makes me feel like a very bad feminist. I guess I'll just wear something that I feel good in. I know Carlos doesn't care much about my clothes.

We ate a nice dinner, even though it was too cold to sit outside and take in the panoramic view of the Blue Ridge Mountains. The restaurant had a very active and noisy bar, lots of chrome and black decor. Not exactly my style.

But we found a small table next to a mural of Havana, featuring the '50s-style cars the Cubans maintain in excellent condition out of necessity due to the U.S. embargo. There was one other mural of a small fishing boat by the coast that helped set a bit of atmosphere.

"Entrees are half price, so get whatever you want," said Carlos.

"Hmm… the shrimp in coconut sauce sounds delicious," I said.

"Good. We'll have one order of camarones con coco, one order of ropa vieja, and one order of tostones to share," Carlos told the waiter.

The food was delicious, although it took forever to come out. Hmm…maybe part of an authentic experience?

"I didn't even know this place was here," I said. "What a nice treat."

"It's pretty new," Carlos said. "I'm glad you like it. It's a bit of a taste of home for me."

We shared a flan for dessert and then went back to his house.

When we were in bed, he handed me a piece of folded-up paper. His eyes were kind of shining as he said, "I wrote you a little poem."

I opened it up and read:

Your nipples like dusky velvet roses
Your skin the smoothest silk
Your hair lives wild and free
Like an overgrown bramble
Calling the wayward

How I long to take all of you
In my arms and entwining legs
My tongue caressing those roses, tasting their sweetness

As the sun slowly sets
soaking and bathing us
In golden light

"Oh!" was all I could say, as I turned to him and we consummated that most romantic poem.

OCTOBER

I want to build a home in a peaceful valley
Where the river of life flows by my door.
I want to plant an orchard of forgiveness
And share its fruit forevermore…

Where there's room to welcome every stranger
A store that leaves no one unfed
A balm to heal all the wounded
Where all the weary have a bed.
—Tom Davey

CHAPTER SIXTY-FIVE

In late July, I got an email from the Peace and Justice Center. A young African American high school student, supported by an African American college student, was calling for a "die-in" at City Hall to protest the acquittal of George Zimmerman in the killing of Trayvon Martin. I called up Carlos to see if he wanted to join me. He did, and so we met downtown.

The organizers had asked allies to "stand guard" on the outside of the circle of African Americans doing the actual die-in. But when Carlos and I arrived, we were directed to lie down with the others. I guess in this lily white town, having an olive complexion makes you a "person of color." It was a hot day and I was glad for the rest and the cold marble of the city hall floor.

I was lying between an elderly African American man and Carlos. I remarked to the African American that "I think this is the most relaxed I've been all week."

He laughed and said, "Yeah, it's a nice rest for me too. It's been hard to listen to the news and feel so helpless. God bless these young women for organizing this protest."

It was during the protests about this case that the phrase "Black Lives Matter" really took off. Our vigil was one of more than one hundred cities nationwide to protest racial profiling, demand the repeal of "stand your ground" laws, and call for a federal trial of Zimmerman for violations of civil rights laws.

The federal government did open a civil rights case, but did not end up charging George Zimmerman. "Stand your ground" laws still exist in about thirty to thirty-five states, depending on how you define it. Most upsetting is that some states expanded these kinds of laws after the murder of Trayvon Martin. And racial profiling is still a huge ongoing problem. I try to remember that change takes time.

After the die-in, Carlos told me more stories about his past, including staring down the barrel of a gun of a right-wing vigilante in the middle of a Guatemalan plaza. He had joined a left-wing group fighting for economic justice for the Mayan population against the corrupt, U.S.-backed government forces. There were enough indigenous Mayan people around that time that the death squad member backed down.

I was a bit in awe of him.

But I also was determined not to repeat my past mistakes. He had mentioned that it might be nice to go tubing down the French Broad River sometime, but had never followed up. I suggested several times that we go, but it was never a good time for him. In the past I would have yelled. But this time, I just persisted. Finally, I called him during the last week of the summer.

"Carlos, the weather looks good this weekend. This is the last time I will have a free weekend before Sunday school starts again that we could go tubing. Would you rather go on Saturday or Sunday?"

"Well, I could go on Saturday," he answered.

We met at Urban Outfitters to rent our inner tubes and eased ourselves down into the river. It was a lovely day and the water was very calm. The late-summer foliage along the banks of the river was a deep, deep green. We could smell the decomposing vegetation under the slow-moving water. The sunlight sparkled in places, and fish were jumping, like in the old-time song, "Summertime."

I had walked along the river path in the park many times, but I'd never been tubing. "Thank you so much for doing this with me," I said, truly grateful as there was no way I would have done this alone.

"It was my pleasure," he answered in his gallant way and seemed to really mean it. I thought we were getting along very well.

But when he didn't answer his phone for three days in a row, I was first angry and then got worried. I decided to call one more time and if I didn't get an answer I would go on over there, even though that is not how we operated.

On the sixth ring, his daughter picked up the phone.

"Oh, Brooke, I'm so sorry to have to tell you this. Carlos had a heart attack and died this morning. We haven't had a chance to tell anyone yet."

What a shock. I really didn't know what to do. I went over to his house with some food for his daughter. I had met her once or twice. She was a sweet young woman and grateful for the meal. Her mother,

Carlos's ex-wife, was there also. They seemed at a loss. He hadn't left a will and that was going to make everything very difficult. I gave them my phone number and told them to call me when they had made funeral arrangements.

I went home and cried. I also downloaded a standard will. *I'm not going to leave my children with such a mess! I should have done this years ago. I guess I'm coming to terms with my own mortality.*

Then I posted something about Carlos on FB and got yet another shock. An old friend texted me, wanting to know how I knew Carlos. "I've been dating him for the last nine months," I answered.

"Really? My Carlos? The professor at Warren Wilson? The person I've been in an exclusive relationship with for the past seven years? That Carlos Cienfuegos?"

"We need to talk! Call me."

Well, talk we did. At the time I thought if I ever write a novel, this will be the one thing people wouldn't believe. But I guess it's all too common. But what a risk he took. Of course, he had no way of knowing that Janice and I were friends. I didn't even know she had moved back to Asheville. But still... we could have run into each other at any point.

Why am I writing all this? I guess I want people to know to be more careful than I was. But I also don't want my older peers to give up on finding love and companionship in our later years. This whole situation was much more difficult for Janice, as Carlos and I did not have an exclusive relationship.

After his unavailability that Sunday, I had asked for an open arrangement. Boy, that would have been a great time for him to be honest! But what he said instead was, "Sure. I wouldn't want to prevent you from other opportunities."

I still don't know whether to laugh, cry, or be angry about that. But I guess I forgave him because our time together was so good. He never "mansplained" me, was attentive and giving both in bed and out, and was extremely respectful of my area of expertise. I still miss him.

I recently saw this quote from Dostoevsky that resonated with me: "If you truly love, either jealousy will kill your love, or your love will kill jealousy."

CHAPTER SIXTY-SIX

Well, Janice and I rekindled our relationship, so I lost a lover but gained a friend. Even though I had been deceived in my last foray, I wasn't ready to give up on the hope of an intimate relationship. I dated a couple more men, but nothing really clicked until I met John.

He was another 97 percent match. *Hmm, I wonder what our few differences will be this time. He doesn't drink or smoke. That's a relief.*

He looked kind of ugly in his picture on the website. *Brooke, surely you're not going to be prejudiced by looks*, I admonished myself. I went ahead and wrote him my typical little message.

"I've looked at your profile and it seems we have a lot in common. Would you like to chat?"

John answered right away and suggested that we meet. I agreed and suggested we meet downtown. We could get ice cream and then sit in Pack Park to talk. I knew enough by then to suggest a public space and an afternoon rather than an evening. It was early fall and the trees had begun to turn colors. It was a nice day to be outside. As I waited, I was pretty nervous.

But then up walked a tall, good-looking man with long hair pulled back into a ponytail that bore enough resemblance to his picture that I was pretty sure it was John.

I smiled (partly in relief), rose from my chair, and said, "John Williams?"

"Brooke? Glad to meet you."

We had a nice time. After picking out our cones, we strolled over to a park bench and talked for at least an hour. John asked if I'd like to get together again and we set a second date.

We settled into a routine of one lunch date and one night together for quite a while. John was semiretired from teaching English and creative writing at the local community college.

"Here's a pretty cool poem one of my students wrote, he said one day.

"The cars are killing

the roads today

they are tired

of being told what to do

and where to go

So they have escaped

over the guardrail

and are rolling over

dead corn fields

and green alfalfa plots."

"Oh, I like that. Did you give a particular prompt?" I asked.

"Yeah. We've been working on the themes of wishes, dreams, and lies. I'm not sure if this was a wish, a dream, a lie, or all three, but it kinda works, doesn't it?"

"Yes. It's creative and quite vivid imagery. I can picture it in my mind."

"Yup. That's one of the elements we've been working on."

John still worked a few days a week. He was trying to get a second book of poetry written and published. Our politics meshed, except he seemed to have given in to a fair amount of despair over the years.

I couldn't really blame him, given our acute climate crisis and the slow pace of progress, but I have to do whatever I can see to do to make things better.

CHAPTER SIXTY-SEVEN

Which is why when I began to hear about the protests happening at Standing Rock, I felt a huge call to do all I could to help. The Lakota people were protesting the Dakota Access Pipeline that had been rerouted to go through sacred unceded land and threatened the water of both the Missouri and Mississippi Rivers.

I first heard about it at services when our minister prayed for "the water protectors." Then Lucinda started sending me information, with links as to how to get involved. Finally, the Unitarian newsletter carried an article about the protests. The Unitarian Universalist congregation of North Dakota was the only church in all of North Dakota that supported the protests.

In October our Sunday school students and families gathered medical supplies and made cards to send to the encampment. In November, the Presbyterian minister on the reservation sent out a call to religious folks saying, "If you've been thinking of joining us, now is the time!" Protesters had been attacked by "security dogs" and sprayed with water in freezing weather, along with tear gas, rubber bullets, and concussion grenades, injuring hundreds.

But, I couldn't go then, as we had scheduled a big "coming-of-age" ceremony for our eighth graders.

A few weeks later, a young woman's arm was seriously injured by an explosive flash-bang grenade thrown by law enforcement. The victim's father stated in a press conference that his daughter had seen a police officer throw the explosive device directly at her as she was backing away.

At this point, Chief Arvol Lookinghorse called for all religious leaders to come support them. And this time I could go. Jewel, a young woman who taught in the Sunday school, asked to go with me. I was very happy to have a young companion.

John took me shopping to get enough warm clothes for North Dakota in the winter. We had to go to an outdoor camping store as our winters did not compare. But since John had grown up in Minnesota, he knew what I would need.

"This down coat with a hood looks good. Be sure to wear the hood if it's windy. It's the wind that will get you," he advised.

He picked out nice warm socks and gloves. The salesperson guided me to some warm, no-slip winter boots.

Lucinda had been working at a national hotel chain and got me a great price for a room in Bismarck. I knew I was too old to try and camp in the middle of winter in North Dakota!

Not to mention the difficulty of getting up and down from the ground.

Parallel to the religious folks arriving, a Native American man who was in the army had sent out a call to people in the military to come. We pledge to "support and defend the Constitution of the United States against all enemies, foreign and domestic," he wrote. "The Dakota Access Pipeline and Energy Partners are indeed a domestic enemy."

My minister had read that the military folk wanted donations of beef jerky, so she pressed fifty dollars into my hand to buy some when we got there.

Before Jewel and I left, we had both read through and signed the agreements for being there. These included a complete commitment to nonviolence, respect for the traditional dress, including women wearing skirts or dresses, and "being in ceremony at all time." This basically meant that everything was done in a prayerful manner.

CHAPTER SIXTY-EIGHT

We arrived in Bismarck late Friday night and checked into our hotel. The next morning after breakfast, we went to the local grocery store to buy food to bring to the camp. At this point it was housing over a thousand people.

Food was very cheap in North Dakota! We bought a sack of potatoes that was almost as tall as me. Well, it was at least three feet long. It only cost $3.47. "Idaho is right next door, where they grow all these potatoes," I said. "But still, what a bargain." We then got some giant cans of beans, the beef jerky, and a huge container of water, which we had heard they needed.

I wanted to bring a gift of tobacco to offer and got carded by a young man who looked about fourteen.

"You've made my day," I said, laughing and pulling at the white streak in my hair. "Do you really think I'm not over eighteen?"

"We have to card everyone," he answered, turning red and looking embarrassed.

"It's okay. I understand. Cover your bases."

We got everything packed and headed out for the reservation. We had heard that the state police often blocked the shorter route to the camp, but thought we would try our luck anyway. We passed a few unmanned barriers and were probably very close when we did get stopped by a young state trooper.

"Where are you going?" he asked.

"To the Standing Rock Reservation. We're here as religious supporters," I answered truthfully.

"I'm sorry, but you can't go this way," he said, actually looking pretty sorry for the role he was being made to play by the governor. "You'll have to turn around and follow this map. It will take you to the reservation."

So we turned around and followed the map he had given us. It took us through a desolate snow-covered landscape of low-lying hills, passing only a few scattered farmhouses along the way.

We had been in the car for several hours and had to pee so badly, we couldn't wait.

"I'm going to pull over to the side of the road. We can squat down between the two open doors on the passenger side. There's no one anywhere in sight," I said.

What a relief. Not too long after that, we found the first camp, the Sacred Stone Camp. But this was not the main site of the protesters. That was a bit down the road, the Očhéthi Šakówiŋ camp.

As we were continuing down the road, we saw a pickup truck with a local license plate drive up, bringing a load of wood. The driver looked like what some might call a "red neck." He flashed us a smile and waved and we waved back.

"It just goes to show you not to judge people by their appearances," I remarked to Jewel. "I had heard that the locals didn't support these protests."

"Yeah, I would not have guessed by looking at him that he was bringing wood to donate. I guess we all have our prejudices," she answered.

"And did you notice the worker in the hotel this morning in the breakfast area? She kept asking if we and everyone else had enough food. At first, I thought to myself, 'She probably doesn't know why we are here.' But then, that group of nurses with the T-shirts saying 'Water is life: nurses are first responders' got up to leave. She called out, 'You all be careful out there!'"

"Yes," I said. "I noticed that too."

*   *   *

At last we arrived at the Očhéthi Šakówiŋ camp. Our car was searched to make sure we were not bringing in any weapons. They had found one dude with a gun.

Big surprise; he was employed by Energy Partners. He was thankfully kicked out before he could do any harm. It would be especially damning for the protesters if they were accused of violence.

The day was unseasonably warm for North Dakota in December, a balmy thirty-three degrees. The ice and snow were thawing and the dirt road had turned into a river of mud. As we pulled up and got out, people saw the white streak in my hair and ran to help us unload the food and water.

All that day, I got to experience the way elders are honored in Native American culture; something I had read about but had no idea what it looked like. When we went to cross the muddy road, people again ran to help, to hold out a steadying hand. And as we backed out to leave the crowded parking area, the folks directing everyone said, "A little to the right, Grandmother. You've got this," using "Grandmother" as a title of great respect.

Jewel had hoped to camp with local Unitarian youth, who had built a yurt at the camp. But, when we got there, it was too full and she was suffering too much from the cold. She would come back to the hotel with me. I was glad to have her. Being completely on my own in the middle of nowhere North Dakota was a bit daunting.

Sunday was scheduled for an interfaith service and a possible walk to the "bridge." That had been the site of several confrontations between protesters and police. We were willing to do whatever we were asked.

We wrote the National Lawyers Guild phone number on our arms in Sharpie, just in case we got arrested. We weren't planning on it, as we heard horrible things about the way protesters were treated at the local jail, but we also knew that "plans" can go out the window in volatile situations.

It had gotten colder and I was glad for my warm clothes. The interfaith gathering proceeded. First came representatives from each of the Lakota tribes, in full ceremonial regalia, carrying their medicine wheels.

Chief Lookinghorse explained the meaning of these symbols, and then the allies were invited to speak. The allies had been asked to keep their remarks to ten minutes. Everyone complied, even Cornel West, who is not generally known for being succinct. He was, however, very eloquent and spoke of the "original sin" of the United States being the genocide of the Native Americans. When it was my turn, I shared a prayer my friend Trina had written and gave an offering of tobacco to Chief Lookinghorse.

I was offered a seat on the makeshift stage. After a few other speakers, a Native American man got up and started to speak. And he spoke for an hour. No one interrupted him. No one looked pointedly at their watch. We just listened and learned.

"You are on sacred ground. You are seeing the first time all the Lakota tribes are coming together since Wounded Knee. We are very close to Wounded Knee. We have suffered but we have survived."

This was another example of the respect given to elders. I thought of the times I had cut off some of the elders in my congregation when they took up more than their allotted time and I felt ashamed.

There was a Native American delegation of young women from Canada, who had traveled by water in dugout canoes to get here. One of them rose to chant prayers in her native language. She was dressed in beaded doeskin. Her face had symbolic tribal paint. Her long black hair was braided and entwined with feathers.

I couldn't help thinking that she looked exactly like a Native American doll I had as a child. We always put that doll, along with two Pilgrim dolls, on our table as part of a centerpiece for our Thanksgiving dinner. *We totally bought into the myth of the first Thanksgiving. Now that I know more, I am once again ashamed.*

Then Chief Arvol Lookinghorse spoke.

"I've changed my mind about going to the bridge. That young woman who got her arm blown off is weighing heavily on my mind. I'm asking you instead to spread out along the perimeter of our camp and hold the space in prayer."

So that is what we did. Jewel and I headed toward the right side of the entrance and sat down in the snow. People were passing out granola bars and apples, which we gratefully accepted. Then we began chanting.

The chant, "We Shall Be Known", by Karisha Longaker of the singing group MaMuse was a favorite of our choir back home and seemed especially appropriate here, where a sacred fire, augmented with sage, was kept burning at all times.

The aroma of sage permeated my scarf. I loved smelling it when I got home. It would bring the whole experience back to me. When it finally dissipated, I was so sad.

We continued chanting for at least an hour. And then we heard a great shout go up from the vicinity of the sacred fire. As we made our way toward the sounds, we saw people hugging and crying and jumping up and down. Finally we asked someone what had happened.

"Obama just canceled the pipeline!"

Oh my God. Have you ever been at a protest where you get a win right there?? I had never experienced anything close to that. And yes, we knew it could be reversed if Trump won. But for that moment it was a peak experience of solidarity, community, and the possibility that folks working together could win.

"Maybe this is how people felt when women finally won the right to vote," I said to Jewel.

"Or when the Supreme Court declared gay marriage to be legal," she answered.

In retrospect, we should have probably gone to help cook a meal for the people who lived at the camp, but instead we just wandered around in a daze, along with many others.

And then, it was already time to head back to Bismarck. The temperature kept dropping and a blizzard was on the way. We woke the next morning to a lot of snow.

"I really, really want to be there today when the veterans arrive!" Jewel begged.

"Look. I couldn't get a four-wheel-drive rental car and I'm not very experienced driving in snow," I answered. "I'm willing to try and see how it goes, but I will make the final decision."

I didn't care at that point about being democratic. I cared about our safety. I drove slowly out of the parking lot, which had been plowed, into the local street, which was also not too bad.

Okay, maybe we can do this, I thought to myself.

But then the road began to get mushy and then frozen and in the next town we were driving on ice.

"I'm sorry, Jewel. I can't do this. If it's this bad here, it will be impossible at the camp."

I turned around and got us safely back to our hotel, breathing a huge sigh of relief. The wind was picking up and the temperature kept dropping. I was glad to stay put. But Jewel was hungry and thought she could walk a few blocks to a nearby Chinese restaurant. I shook my head, made sure she had a charged cell phone on her, and wished her luck.

About a half an hour later, I got a call. "The wind and cold are ferocious! I couldn't make it. I'm going to buy some snacks from the hotel vending machine. Do you want anything?"

Smiling to myself, I said, "Sure. Can you bring me some chips?"

We listened to the news and heard that many veterans had arrived at Standing Rock. They were pitching tents, unloading firewood and lumber, and generally uplifting everyone's spirits.

By dinner we were both starving, so we decided to brave the weather to try and get some dinner. There was a Friendly's restaurant on the other side of the parking lot. The wind was incredibly strong and pushed us along. It was so cold, my eyes hurt. I had my hood pulled up over my head and held onto Jewel for dear life.

Luckily after dinner, the wind had died down, so we made it back to the hotel. By the next morning, the highways were shut down due to the weather. Once again, luck was with us, as the local roads were open and our flight was still on schedule.

"I guess they're used to weather like this," I said to Jewel. At this point we were both eager to get home to temperate North Carolina.

And we did make it home. I knew I was home when my Lyft

driver did not offer to help me with my small wheeled suitcase or backpack. *But I will never forget the way elders were treated at Standing Rock,* I vowed to myself.

I went directly to bed and slept for most of the day. In the afternoon, Rachel stopped by. "How was it?" She was eager to hear all about it.

"Rachel, it was one of the high points of my life! I feel so lucky to have been able to be there! And Cornel West hugged me after I presented our prayer," I said smiling. I knew Rachel would understand that.

"Oh, cool. I heard him speak a while ago. He's wonderful."

"Yes. I feel like I could die and go to heaven as a contented person right now."

"Well, don't die just yet. Eat some dinner first," she said, laughing. "I brought you some shepherd's pie made with ground turkey and a salad."

"Thanks so much, Rachel, that sounds delicious. And then I think I will go back to bed."

John came over later that evening, when I was already in bed but not yet asleep. He enveloped me in a big hug. "I'm glad you're back. I was worried about you. Were you warm enough? How did you manage in the blizzard?"

I snuggled down next to him. "You were right about the hood, it helped a lot. And I wore two pairs of socks, leggings under my corduroy pants, and a long winter skirt over that, so I was warm.

"And I got us all the way to the parking lot of the airport, but it wasn't plowed, so I did get the rental car stuck in the snow. Some very nice folks who had probably been at Standing Rock saw we were stuck and went in to get help. A local came out from the car rental place and started rocking the car back and forth, back and forth and got us out."

John nodded his head. "Yep, I've done that many a time in Minnesota. Kind of like how we old folks rock ourselves to get out of a chair."

I laughed. "Yeah, I never really understood that analogy before this. And I have to admit, I had my doubts if we would get out. I asked the ticket agent if our flight was still on. She was one of the grimmest people I have ever seen: right out of Norman Rockwell's 'American Gothic,' and she said, 'We never shut down,' without a hint of a smile.

"I'm so glad I went and so glad to be home."

The next day, I was still jet-lagged and knocked the side mirror off my car. I took it to the dealer. I was embarrassed by this and so I explained where I had been.

"You were at Standing Rock?" asked the young Latino man writing up the work order.

I nodded.

"I'm not going to charge you for the labor," he said.

I was very touched. It also led me to wonder about who knew what was going on there and who didn't. Years later in a discussion of activism with some visiting librarians when I mentioned how I had been at Standing Rock, one of them said, "What's that?"

Even when Trump reversed the permit, we knew what we had done was significant. Chief Lookinghorse was interviewed and he said, "Everywhere is Standing Rock now." And it's true. People woke up to the dangers of pipelines.

When I visited friends in Virginia, there were signs saying "Stop the Appalachian pipeline." And we won that battle in court. When

John and I visited his family in Minnesota, we saw signs to "Stop Line Three." That struggle continues. And Jewel joined a struggle in Florida against yet another pipeline.

CHAPTER SIXTY-NINE

That February when Valentine's Day rolled around, John said, looking down in his characteristic manner, "I know this doesn't match that amazing poem Carlos wrote you, but still…" and handed me a slightly crumpled piece of paper.

I read:

Like wisps of cloud
your hair
Escaping from your hat
Entices as if from
A castle window

Who are you?
An enchanted princess locked up
 in stacks of dusty books?
Long ago having given up
All hope of a prince

Perhaps you will accept
These gnarled hands
Of a lowly gardener
Who sees you clearly

"Oh, John. This is lovely. Thank you. And, I've been thinking… maybe we should change our status on Facebook as our Valentine's Day celebration?"

"Ha! That's just what my kid said. 'Dad, don't you think it's time to admit you're in a relationship?'" he answered.

"Okay. Let's do it simultaneously," I said, a bit nervous but also happy.

Sean had moved back to Asheville a few years before. He had met John and liked him. But then again, Sean likes almost everyone. If he doesn't, I would watch out for that person!

Lucinda saw the Facebook notification and took an almost parental role, saying, "As long as you're happy, I'm happy." She hadn't yet met John.

Marissa and John's kid, Halcyon, hit it off right away. They both seemed to approve. We got along with each other's friends also, although most of our time was spent just with each other.

So don't give up, my fellow humans. It's never too late to find love.

CHAPTER SEVENTY

About three years later I was driving back from Black Mountain Farm along Route 40 after a Halloween party. The road is twisty, but I had driven it many times before. I was driving very slowly, as the fog had come in. Suddenly, I saw a pair of headlights coming straight at me.

This can't be happening, I thought. And then, everything seemed to move in slow motion. I heard a terrifying crunching sound and slammed on my brakes. I felt a sharp pain in my left knee and multiple stabbing feelings in my right ankle.

I heard voices calling, "Are you alright? Are you alright?" but I couldn't seem to answer. I was vaguely aware of some bright lights and much later a siren. I must have passed out because the next thing I knew, I was in a hospital bed with a cast on my left leg and right ankle and an IV in my arm.

I looked around and John was sitting in a chair next to the bed.

"Oh, you're awake. I'm supposed to call the nurse."

He reached over and pushed the call button. A nurse came bustling in. "How are you feeling?" she asked, while simultaneously taking my temperature.

"Okay, I guess? What happened?"

"Let me measure your pulse first, and then we can talk," she said, expertly placing her finger on my wrist and silently counting. "Pulse is okay."

"A semi-trailer ran into you," said John. "You are lucky that you both were going slow. But your knee and ankle are broken. And you're pretty bruised up from the seatbelt."

"I don't remember much. Just seeing headlights coming at me," I said, shuddering.

"Yeah. Other truckers stopped and called 911. You were in shock and then passed out. When it got so late that I began to get worried and phoned you, one of the people on the scene picked up. They told me you were being taken here. So I was able to be here when you were admitted."

And this began a new phase of my life. Neither the knee nor the ankle healed completely. It was extremely painful to walk more than a few steps even after months of physical therapy.

We bought a wheelchair and put in a chair lift to my upstairs bedroom. Trina set up for folks at the Unitarian congregation to make me meals. First it was every day, but then I suggested that once a week was enough.

But I had to resign from my educator job. It was just too much. The library job was still doable once I bought myself an electric scooter. And yes, I had to buy it myself as Medicare would not pay for even the wheelchair much less a scooter. Only if one couldn't get from "bed to bathroom" would they pay for a wheelchair.

"It's ridiculous!" I fumed to John. "I already knew they didn't care if old people can see *(because they won't pay for glasses)*, or eat *(no dental care)*, or hear *(no hearing aids)*, but I guess they think it's just fine if we can't leave the house either!"

"Yeah. Our so-called health care system sucks," he answered. "And, I've been thinking," he said hesitantly, looking at me quizzically.

"Yes?" I said, looking back at him, wondering what he was going to say.

He took a big breath. "I think I should move in with you. You need more help and the congregation can't be making you meals forever. That is, if it's okay with you."

"You would do that?" I said, tearing up.

"Yes. I'm not necessarily the best person to live with, but I think I can be more help than hindrance."

"John, this is very generous of you. I'm not always the best person to live with either, but let's give it a try. You could have Sean's old bedroom to sleep in and use Lucinda's old bedroom for your office. I always thought I would do that, but never got around to organizing it. I'm so used to working at the kitchen table. Marissa's is still full of her stuff, so it's not really available. I'm kind of blown away with this offer." I leaned over to him and hugged him.

"Okay, then it's settled. I'll start moving my stuff in over the weekend."

"I'm sure Sean will help you."

CHAPTER SEVENTY-ONE

"Hi, Brooke. Can I come in?" Rachel called through the open screen door. It was a balmy spring day and I was enjoying the breeze.

"Sure. Come on in. Would you like some lemonade?"

"No. Just water with lemon for me. I'm not eating any sugar these days."

"Okay. Help yourself. The lemon is in the door of the fridge."

As Rachel sat down, I thought to myself, *I hate having to hear about everybody's more healthy lifestyle than mine. I once gave up sugar for about a month. It was a useful exercise. I learned that sometimes I eat sweets because I'm bored, or lonely, or tired. I try to pay more attention now, but other than that, I like to have a glass of lemonade on a warm day, my small daily chocolate quotient, and homemade desserts within reason.*

Rachel got right to the point. "Brooke, the Peace and Justice Center is joining the efforts calling for reparations. Will you join us? I know you have a lot of connections."

She doesn't want to mention the bad experience from years ago with the Peace and Justice Center. So I won't bring it up either.

"Of course. It's about time this city faced its history of racism, including slavery, and that horrible urban renewal that displaced a good chunk of our Black community."

"We're collecting signatures on these petitions that you can scan, and also individual letters. As you know, letters carry more weight, but many people just prefer to sign a petition," Rachael continued.

"Sure, I'll share the petitions on the UU listserv and announce it at our Zoom service. It's a bit hard to do in-person organizing during a pandemic, but I'm sure I can get one hundred signatures from our congregation and probably some letters as well," I said.

"In fact, although it's good to see you, why didn't you just email me or call? I hope you are being careful. The last thing I need is to get Covid," I said, getting a bit alarmed.

"Oh, I just miss you, Brooke! I'm careful. I wear a mask when I have to go out to the grocery store, but that's all that I do. I haven't seen anyone in ages. We do our Peace and Justice meetings over Zoom also."

"I've been ordering my groceries online," I said.

"Yeah. I would do that too, if I could, but we live too far out in the country. No one will deliver to us."

"Oh. I didn't think about that. ... I can also post the petition on the library website. We have a fair number of folks that we reach through the libraries. It's kind of amazing how quickly we have adapted to taking book orders online and setting them out for folks to pick up in the lobby. We take turns going to work in person. So far no one has gotten Covid-19 in our staff."

Just then John walked in.

"John, would you be willing to post this petition for reparations at the community college?" asked Rachel.

"Sure, I'd be happy to. We have an electronic bulletin board that is open to the community."

"And maybe you'd be willing to write a letter also? You know letters are more effective than petitions, but we really need both," continued Rachel.

"Nah, I think what I'd rather do is assign my writing students to write letters for or against this proposal. They need to learn persuasive writing. It's good to have a real-life application. And I won't tell them what to write, so they can't accuse me of anything," he said, laughing.

"That's fantastic. Thank you both. You can send everything to the city council."

"Well, that's a good initiative. It's good to see something concrete come out of the demonstrations around George Floyd," I said after Rachel left.

John sighed. "Well, we will see if anything substantial happens. Frankly, I'm doubtful, but I didn't want to get into it with Rachel."

Rachel called me in July. "Brooke, the city council passed a reparations resolution unanimously!"

"Wow. That's great. How are they going to implement it?" I asked.

Rachel sighed. "Well, that's the tricky part. They don't want to give people money directly, God forbid. So they are setting up a study commission to address barriers to home and business ownership, health care, educational inequality, and career development."

"Oh, boy. The old 'we'll study it' dodge," I said. "One of the oldest tricks in the book to pretend like something is going to happen, while not actually taking any action."

Goodness, I sound like John, I thought.

"Yes. I know what you mean, Brooke. But it's not as bad as it sounds. They are allocating money and have appointed really good people to the commission. And they are asking the county to join them. Of course, we will probably still have to put pressure on them, but it's a start, Brooke. It's a start."

Just then, my call waiting rang. It was Marissa. I hung up with Rachel and took her call. "Hi, Marissa. What's up?"

"I bought a blow-up swimming pool for Seth and I wanted to

know if I could set it up in your yard. We don't have room here at the apartment."

"Sure. That sounds like fun. I miss my sweet grandson, and you too," I hastily add.

It's *true that grandchildren hold a special place in our hearts. And, they are changing every week, while our adult or young adult children are growing at a slower rate. But it must be hard to not feel as appreciated.*

CHAPTER SEVENTY-TWO

I woke up on the late-summer day of my seventieth birthday to find a small bouquet of flowers on my nightstand and a notebook inscribed "To Brooke."

I opened up the notebook and read, "To Brooke, you flow through my heart like a clear stream. Happy 70th birthday, John." *Wow. He didn't forget.* I had been wondering, as he hadn't said anything about my birthday in the previous week.

About a month earlier I had confessed to him and Rachel that I couldn't figure out how I wanted to celebrate this year. I had said at the time, "I leave it in your hands." *This is lovely,* I thought as I began to read the short poems in the notebook.

Haiku

songbird calling

in the waning darkness

should I sleep or wake?

Before I had finished reading, John came into the bedroom. "Oh, you're up. Happy birthday," he said, kissing me on the forehead.

"John, this is lovely. Thank you so much!" I replied, smiling up at him.

"You are welcome. And would you like breakfast in bed or outside?"

"I'll get up and come outside. It looks like a nice day."

I got up and put on one of my favorite summer dresses. I've had it for years, but it was still so pretty: a salmon-colored batik with a pattern of blue and green leaves.

John had prepared a bowl of yogurt and peaches, plus whole wheat pancakes and decaf coffee just the way I like it.

He sat down next to me and we ate in contented silence.

I was scrolling through my phone and someone had posted this quote from Anne Lamott: "In my experience, most of us age away from brain and ambition toward heart and soul, and we bathe in relief that things are not worse."

I read it out loud to John. "I would agree," I said, "although I never had any ambition in the conventional sense of the word."

"Yes, that is true for me too," he replied. "I'm happy to teach my students, and this new book of poetry is all heart and soul. And every day I'm thankful things are not worse."

Around noon, Lucinda called to wish me a happy birthday. "Thank you, sweetie. So far it has been lovely and peaceful."

Then the phone rang and it was Rachel.

"Hi, I was wondering if you would like to come out to my place in about an hour for some tea? I also have a lot of extra vegetables from my garden that I want to give you."

"Sure. That sounds nice," I said, not being sure if this was because of my birthday or not.

As I drove out to Rachel's place I was, as always, amazed at the lush greenery of a North Carolina summer. With each rainfall, the colors deepen and deepen. Having grown up in Southern California, this never ceases to delight me.

When I got there, I saw that indeed, this was my birthday surprise from Rachel. She had a big bouquet of flowers for me, filled with sunflowers, zinnias, and cosmos. The bright yellows, oranges, and reds were a vibrant symphony of late-summer glory.

There was a homemade card attached. Inside was this note:

"I saw this on a meme somewhere and thought of you:

"*We're at that age where we see wrinkles, gray hair, and extra pounds. We see the cute 25-year-olds and reminisce. But we were also 25, just as they will one day be our age. We aren't the "girls in their summer clothes" anymore. What they bring to the table with their youth and zest, we bring our wisdom and experience. We have raised families, run households, paid the bills, and dealt with disease, sadness, and everything else life has assigned us. Some of us have lost those who were nearest and dearest to us. We are survivors. We are warriors in the quiet. We are women, like a classic car or a fine wine.*

"*Even if our bodies aren't what they once were, they carry our souls, our courage, and our strength. We shall all enter this chapter of our lives with humility, grace, and pride over everything we have been through, and we should never feel bad about getting older. It's a privilege that is denied to so many.*

"*Happy Birthday, Brooke!*"

"Thank you *so* much, Rachel! All this applies to you too," I said, hugging her.

Rachel also gave me a jar of her famous pickled "dilly beans," a jar of watermelon rinds pickled with cloves, and a small jar of homemade pesto.

"The pesto is not canned, Brooke, so you need to use it pretty soon," she said. "Would you like to ride your scooter out to the garden? I want to pick some fresh vegetables for you. The path is pretty smooth. I think you'll be able to get there."

"Well, let's try," I said, thinking, *This is a very "Rachel" kind of birthday present.* She gathered tomatoes, green beans, and cucumbers for me in a huge basket.

"You can keep the basket too. I made it for you in a class I took."

"Rachel, thank you so much! You really surprised me! I wasn't even sure you had remembered my birthday."

She just smiled and said, "Let me help you load all this into your van."

As I drove home, I thought what a thoughtful, low-key birthday this was. I was very content.

But then as I drove up to my house I saw a suspicious number of cars parked along my street.

As I got out of the car and rode in my scooter up the sidewalk toward my house, about twenty people jumped out and yelled, "Surprise! Happy birthday!"

Was I surprised! Oh my gosh. Trina and other friends from the Unitarian congregation were there, several coworkers from the library, all my children and their partners, and most surprising of all: Jake. *Jake.*

Rachel and John had really outdone themselves. Everyone brought my favorite foods. Trina had made deviled eggs, Becky brought pimento cheese spread, Amarah brought vegetable biryanis and samosas, and Sean was busy grilling salmon, tofu dogs, and corn on the cob.

Marissa and Belinda had made my mother's potato salad. *So, that's why she called for the recipe last week.* And Lucinda, who had flown in from Seattle with Jinny, made an amazing checkered chocolate and white birthday cake. Funny how she had called earlier that day, as she usually does, just to not give away the surprise.

John had hired The Looney Tunes, a local band that I loved. They began their set with the old Weaver's song, "Get Up and Go," to much laughter and singing along. They included Janis Ian's song, "I'm Still Standing Here."

Janis Ian wrote our youth and now she writes our aging process. What an amazing talent.

And then they ended with " Cut the Cake" by Tina Liza Jones. I have surely grown out of my baby ways, I thought, laughing along with the others.

Trina read a beautiful poem by Bernadette Noll. And then we ate and mingled. During this time, Jake made his way to my lawn chair.

"Hey," he said, kind of shyly.

"Hey. This is a real surprise."

"Yeah. I haven't really been in touch with practically anyone lately. But then I did a Native American meditation out in the desert where you envision your own death. And you invite the spirits of whoever needs to be there to come. And you came. So I knew I had to show up for you."

"Wow. That's amazing. What did I say?"

He looked down, took a big sigh, and said, "You wanted to know if you had meant anything to me," he said slowly. "I want you to know that you meant more than I can say."

"Thank you, Jake. You have always meant a lot to me too. We have both been committed to creating a better world through nonviolence all these years. I'm very glad you told me that."

And then, the mood changed drastically as Seth ran up to me excitedly showing me how he could make fart sounds with his armpit. I laughed and Jake wandered away.

That night, snuggling in bed with John, I said, "Thank you so much for a wonderful day. Aren't you grateful that we have managed to live this long and have such a good life?" But I was only answered by a gentle snore. John had fallen asleep.

So, I turned to my bedtime ritual. "Thank you, God, for this good life. Please protect all my children and children everywhere. Help us to open our hearts so that we can create a better world where no child goes hungry and we live in peace."

AUTUMN LOOKS TOWARD WINTER

May dawn find you awake and alert, approaching your new day with dreams,
Possibilities and promises.
May evening find you gracious and fulfilled.
May you go into the night blessed, sheltered and protected.
May your soul calm, console and renew you.
—From "May the Light of Your Soul Guide You"
by John O'Donohue

Rachel and Brooke were once again talking in Brooke's sunny kitchen. It was early fall.

"You know, Rachel, now that my memoir is done, I realize I didn't manage to write everything I wanted.

"Like, I wanted to show more of Marissa's development as a young adult. And how she found her calling to be a physical therapist.

"And I hoped to write more about the joys of being a grandmother.

"And of course I've kind of come out of retirement to take on the whole issue of book banning and censorship of books in libraries. Since I'm now retired, I can speak up without fear of losing my job.

"I also wanted to confront my own mortality more directly, but maybe I haven't really. Because although I have an advance directive and a will, I haven't made any real arrangements for my burial. Even though I keep getting those pesky messages for 'burial insurance.' I keep wondering, 'Do they know something I don't know?'" I laughed.

"And I often pray for an easy death at home in my sleep. But maybe that's partly based in denial."

"Well, once your memoir is published you could write a sequel. You could call it *SwanSong*," she joked.

I laughed. "But you know, Rachel, that's not a bad idea. Maybe I will write a sequel. I want to go a bit deeper into how we find our soul's purpose. I'd call it *ElderWisdom*. But for now, I'll be content with my memoir."

ACKNOWLEDGMENTS

As strange as it sounds, having long-haul Covid is definitely one of the contributing factors of me writing this book. If I had been able to get out in the world more after the lockdown ended, I may never have taken on this project.

In addition, I want to acknowledge my iPhone. Since I am mostly confined to bed and cannot sit upright, due to long Covid, this novel was written on my phone. And a special shoutout to "suggested text," which meant that I could use my one-finger typing method with great utility.

My in-home aides have made my whole life doable. I extend my unlimited thanks to Madely Perez Cruz, who in addition to being my hands and feet, also assisted with the manuscript, and to Avril Costa, who fills in when needed. My housemate Desiree Bolling checks in on me every evening and cooks a delicious breakfast every Sunday. My friend David Hersh graciously drove me to Asheville, North Carolina, to do research. This entailed schlepping my wheelchair in and out of his van numerous times each day for a week.

Shai Zohav and Vathany Say, son and beloved daughter-in-law, are always nearby to lend a hand and heart when needed. My daughter Laila Zohav calls every Sunday for a great chat. My daughter Mariyama Scott is a level head for consulting on dilemmas and a warm listener.

My former foster daughter Gabriella Lopez is perhaps the most affectionate of all my children and has also blessed me with my beloved grandson, Jacob. Former foster son Sam Dobson has recently converted my favorite CDs to MP3s. This is greatly appreciated, as music sustains me as much as my protagonist. Being surrounded by so many loving and helpful people was an incalculable asset in completing this novel.

The general theme of elder wisdom was informed by the work of Rabbi Abraham Joshua Heschel in several essays contained in his book, *The Insecurity of Freedom*.

This regard for elders was deepened by the teachings of Reb Zalman Schachter-Shalomi, author of *From Aging to Saging*. My spiritual director, Rabbi Shaya Isenberg, was the embodiment of this elder wisdom and taught me much by his example. I followed Reb Zalman's poetic schema of the life cycle as expressed by the four seasons in my chapter titles, using "Embracing Wisdom: Soaring in the Second Half of Life" by Rabbis Malka Drucker and Nadya Gross as my guide to this schema. However, I found that my protagonist's life was not as clear cut as this schema. Perhaps there is a senior thesis lurking there for a rabbinic student.

My very first reader and dear longtime friend, Robin Wilmer, was invaluable in encouraging me to keep going and had many helpful suggestions.

The first professional editor to give me some very useful feedback and ask important questions was Danielle Ofri, of *Bellevue Literary Review*.

I was fortunate to take a class titled "Social Justice Fiction Writing," sponsored by Hugo House and taught by Kate Raphael. From this class, our Activist Fiction Writers Circle was born.

The Activist Fiction Writers Circle has been and continues to be a major support. Many thanks to Juliana Barnet, author of *Rainwood House Sings*, for organizing us and keeping us on track; Maritza

Arrastia, author of the upcoming novel *Grito 2086*, a climate fiction novel, for her encouraging feedback; and Elena Schwolsky, author of the upcoming novel *Thursday's Child*, for much useful information on the processes of bringing a novel to publication.

Family and friends who have listened to parts of the novel read out loud include Desiree Bolling, Tom Davey, Vathany Say, and Shai Zohav.

Richard M. Heilberger is a colleague who served as a "test case" for a male demographic. He gave substantial feedback that is much appreciated.

Many thanks for the initial layout, invaluable questions, suggestions, and copy editing to Denise Casey.

Final copy editing and proofing was done by Katherine Pickett with precise attention to detail, much thought, wisdom, and understanding. I have found a kindred spirit and am so grateful for all her work.

It has been a pleasure to work with Nuno Moreira who formatted, typeset, and designed the interior and also designed the front and back covers.

This is a work of fiction. However, the characters are mostly composites drawn from my own life. So, friends and family, if you think a character might bear some resemblance to you, rest assured that the admirable qualities were inspired by you. But the less admirable qualities were probably someone else.

The environmental issues raised in this book are real issues, as are those of racism, war, and authoritarianism.

I hope that activists and parents will see themselves realistically portrayed in this novel. And that those new to activism or parenting will find useful models for both these essential tasks.

Lastly, it is a great privilege to enter elderhood. May we learn to appreciate and respect this generative time of life.

PLAYLIST IN ELDERSONG

In Order of Appearance

"California," Joni Mitchell

"The Trumpet Vine," Kate Wolf:

"Worried Man Blues," Woody Guthrie:

"Can't Help but Wonder Where I'm Bound," Tom Paxton:

"Tis a Gift to Be Simple," Shaker hymn:

"Ninna Nanna," traditional Italian lullaby:

"Ebony and Ivory," Stevie Wonder:

"Start Me Up," Rolling Stones

"Swing Low, Sweet Chariot," traditional

"You Can't Kill the Spirit," Naomi Littlebear Morenas

"Common Threads," Pat Humphries

"Give Yourself to Love," Kate Wolf

"Like an Ocean," Tom Davey

Laura Boosinger

"New Shoes," Timmy Abel

"I'll Fly Away," Albert E. Brumley

"Boots of Spanish Leather," Joan Baez

"Summertime," George Gershwin

"We Shall Be Known," MaMuse

"Build a Home," Tom Davey

"Get Up and Go," The Weavers

"I'm Still Standing Here," Janis Ian

"Cut the Cake," John McCutcheon

BIBLIOGRAPHY OF BOOKS MENTIONED

Alcott, Louisa May. *Little Women: Or, Meg, Jo, Beth, and Amy*. Peter Pauper Press, Inc, 2024.

Baldwin, James A. *The Fire Next Time*. Vintage Books, 1992.

Freeman, Don, and Viola Davis. *Corduroy*. Findaway World, 2019.

Gaskin, Ina May. *Spiritual Midwifery*. ReadHowYouWant, 2014.

Giovanni, Nikki, and Bryan Collier. *Rosa*. Scholastic, 2006.

Gordon, Thomas. *Parent Effectiveness Training: The Proven Program for Raising Responsible Children*. Harmony Books, 2019.

Hughes, Langston, et al. *The Collected Poems of Langston Hughes*. Vintage Books, 1995.

Hurston, Zora Neale, and Michele-Denise Woods. *Their Eyes Were Watching God*. 1937. Repr., Recorded Books, 1994.

Lazarre, Jane. *Beyond the Whiteness of Whiteness: Memoir of a White Mother of Black Sons*. Duke University Press, 2016.

Lazarre, Jane, and Reddy Maureen T. *The Mother Knot*. Duke University Press, 1997.

Memmi, Albert. *The Colonizer and the Colonized*. Beacon Press, 2007.

Miller, Sharee. *Don't Touch My Hair!* Little, Brown and Company, 2019.

Montgomery, L. M., and Barbara Caruso. *Anne of Avonlea*. Recorded Books, 1996.

Noble, Elizabeth. *Essential Exercises for the Childbearing Year: A Guide to Health and Comfort Before and After Your Baby Is Born*. New Life Images, 2003.

Paley, Grace. *The Little Disturbances of Man*. Penguin Books, 1985.

Rich, Adrienne, et al. *Of Woman Born: Motherhood as Experience and Institution*. W. W. Norton, 2021.

Walker, Alice. *In Search of Our Mothers' Gardens: Womanist Prose*. 1983. Repr., Amistad, 2023.

Walker, Alice. *The Color Purple*. Pocket Books, 1985.

Warner, Diane. *How to Have a Big Wedding on a Small Budget*. 4th ed. North Light Books, 2002.

Woolf, Virginia. *A Room of One's Own*. 1929. Repr., Mariner Books Classics, 1989.

Yashima, Tarō. *Crow Boy*. Viking Press, 1955.

ABOUT RAIN ZOHAV

Rain Zohav has been a lifelong activist and advocate for peace, justice, the environment, and dismantling racism. She has lived communally and raised both biological and foster children. She has worked as an educational director and rabbi. She now resides in Rockville, Maryland, with two housemates and a couple of hardy houseplants.

IF YOU LIKED ELDERSONG:

You might be interested in these other books written by members of
The Activist Fiction Writers' Circle and published by
Life in the Liberated Zone:

Grito 2086, a Climate Fiction Novel by Maritza Arrastía
In 2086, power in the world teeters precariously between the many
and the few, the rebels and the Empire of the Diez Familias. Elder
Marina flees the City to track her disappeared husband, Ori.
Emboldened by her son, Machi, Marina joins the winner-take-all
fight to take back Earth, but will she find the courage to get her son
and husband back? Coming soon!
Find other writings by Maritza here:
TheWritingRoom.org. (https://thewritingroom.org)

*Rainwood House Sings, a Movement Mystery, by Juliana Barnet w/Sophie
Barnet-Higgins*
Former union organizer Marlie wakes one November night in 2006 to
the roar of a helicopter, unaware that community activist Demetrius,
fleeing that same helicopter, has taken refuge in her basement. Under
the sharp-eyed gaze of Marlie's young granddaughter Samantha, the
characters confront past and present injustices in Rainwood House.
A taste of this book Rainwood House Sings is serialized in Juliana's
newsletter Activist Explorer (https:julianabarnet.substack.com).

Thursday's Child, a novel by Elena Schwolsky

In 1972, Ruthie, the young mother of a 4-yr-old daughter, Sasha, leaves her with her ex-husband at a commune north of San Francisco and travels to Cuba with other American activists to work in solidarity with the newly triumphant revolution. When she returns after three months, Ruthie learns that Sasha and her father have vanished. Her quest to find her daughter forces Ruthie to confront the complexities of being an activist mother. See Elena's Facebook Author Page at https://www.facebook.com/elenaschwolskywriter.

The Activist Fiction Writers' Circle is a collective whose work depicts activists' adventures, struggles, romances, conflicts, and humor working for a just and compassionate world. Find us on Facebook! (https://www.facebook.com/profile.php?id=61566536273350

www.ingramcontent.com/pod-product-compliance
Lightning Source LLC
Chambersburg PA
CBHW070746190726
48292CB00002B/431